PRAISE FOR
THE *NEW YORK TIMES* BESTSELLING
BIBLIOPHILE MYSTERIES

"Kate Carlisle never fails to make me laugh, even as she has me turning the pages to see what's going to happen next."
—Miranda James, *New York Times* bestselling author of the Cat in the Stacks Mysteries

"Saucy, sassy, and smart—a fun read with a great sense of humor and a soupçon of suspense. Enjoy!"
—Nancy Atherton, *New York Times* bestselling author of the Aunt Dimity Mysteries

"Fun and funny . . . delightful."
—Lorna Barrett, *New York Times* bestselling author of the Booktown Mysteries

"A delicious, twisty tale."
—Julie Hyzy, *New York Times* bestselling author of the White House Chef Mysteries and the Manor House Mysteries

"Carlisle's dialogue is natural, her prose has great flow, and her striking descriptions bring Brooklyn's world to life."
—*Crimespree Magazine*

"Captivating. . . . The action builds to a surprising final showdown."
—*Publishers Weekly*

"A terrific read . . . great fun all around!"
—*Library Journal* (starred review)

W9-AXF-534

ONCE UPON A SPINE

A Bibliophile Mystery

Kate Carlisle

BERKLEY PRIME CRIME
New York

BERKLEY PRIME CRIME
Published by Berkley
An imprint of Penguin Random House LLC
375 Hudson Street, New York, New York 10014

Copyright © 2017 by Kathleen Beaver
Excerpt from *Buried in Books* copyright © 2018 by Kathleen Beaver
Penguin Random House supports copyright. Copyright fuels creativity, encourages
diverse voices, promotes free speech, and creates a vibrant culture. Thank you for
buying an authorized edition of this book and for complying with copyright laws by not
reproducing, scanning, or distributing any part of it in any form without permission.
You are supporting writers and allowing Penguin Random House to continue to
publish books for every reader.

BERKLEY is a registered trademark and BERKLEY PRIME CRIME and
the B colophon are trademarks of Penguin Random House LLC.

ISBN 9780451477736

Berkley Prime Crime hardcover edition / June 2017
Berkley Prime Crime mass market edition / June 2018

Printed in the United States of America
3   5   7   9   10   8   6   4   2

Cover art by Dan Craig

This is a work of fiction. Names, characters, places, and incidents either are the
product of the author's imagination or are used fictitiously, and any resemblance to
actual persons, living or dead, business establishments,
events, or locales is entirely coincidental.

If you purchased this book without a cover, you should be aware that this book is stolen
property. It was reported as "unsold and destroyed" to the publisher, and neither the
author nor the publisher has received any payment for this "stripped book."

The recipes contained in this book are to be followed exactly as written.
The publisher is not responsible for your specific health or allergy needs
that may require medical supervision. The publisher is not responsible
for any adverse reactions to the recipes contained in this book.

*This book is dedicated with affection and gratitude
to the brilliant Christina Hogrebe,
literary agent extraordinaire,
who accomplishes the impossible on a daily basis
and always looks fabulous while doing so.*

Chapter 1

Lately, I have resorted to stalking. Not a person, but a book.

For weeks now I'd been visiting the book almost daily. It was a little embarrassing to continually beg the bookstore owner to let me hold it, page through it, study it. I just wanted to touch it, stroke it, and once, when he wasn't looking, sniff it. But he didn't seem to mind my fixation. He's as big a book nerd as I am.

The owner kept the book inside a clear, locked glass case displayed on the shop's front counter, so it was pretty obvious he didn't want people touching it. And who could blame him? The book was exquisitely bound in vibrant red morocco leather. Rich gilding swirled along the spine, spelling out the title, author's name, and year of publication in fancy gold script. More gilding outlined the thick raised cords that lent gravitas to the already weighty tome.

In the center of the front cover was a brightly gilded

rabbit wearing a topcoat. The well-dressed creature glanced down at a watch he held at the end of a chain, and he appeared nervous, as though he might be running late for some important event.

The fact that a gilded illustration could convey real emotion was pretty awesome, above and beyond the binding work. The first time I saw it, I checked the inside cover for the bookbinder and was thrilled to find the name George Bayntun of London. Favored by the late Queen Mary, Bayntun's bindery in Bath, England, was world renowned and was still operating to this day. I'd visited once and had come away starstruck.

On the back cover of the book was another elaborately raised figure in gold, an odd-looking woman wearing a crown and carrying a scepter. The red queen. She appeared headstrong and irate, as though she might order someone's head lopped off at any moment.

The book was *Alice's Adventures in Wonderland*, of course. This copy was a fairly hard-to-find version in excellent condition, with dark green-and-red-marbled endpapers and virtually no foxing on its clean white pages. It contained dozens of classic illustrations by the famous artist John Tenniel. The binding was tight and even. And I wanted it.

My name is Brooklyn Wainwright, and I'm a bookbinder specializing in rare-book restoration. I love books of all kinds, and I love my job. It was exciting to know that I could give tired, torn, droopy, bug-bitten books a brand-new life that would allow them to continue to bring enjoyment for hundreds of years to come. It might have sounded boring to some, but in my career so far I had saved dozens of treasured childhood favorites from being thrown away, rescued any number of priceless museum-quality books from being carted off to the used-book store, and even solved a murder or two—or ten—while I was at it. Just in case you thought bookbinding sounded like a yawn-fest, trust me, my life was rarely dull.

This particular copy of *Alice* didn't need restoring, though. It was pristine. I wanted it because I had a fascination—okay, call it an obsession—with the iconic *Alice* and her creator, Lewis Carroll.

I gazed longingly at the book on display near the front counter of Brothers Bookshop. The store was a book nerd's dream: a cozy, tome-filled haven for people like me who were content to while away an entire day browsing the shelves in hopes of discovering the perfect little gem of a book to sink into.

The shop carried both new and used books along with all sorts of charming gifts and cards and paper goods. There were comfy chairs in every corner of the store, and a small section along one side was devoted to antiquarian books.

A magazine section was located at the back of the shop. At the front, a wall of windows looked out onto the neighborhood, and from there I could see my vintage apartment building on the other side of the street.

Derek Stone and I had decided to walk over here to do a little book browsing on our way next door to shop for vegetables for dinner.

The bookshop was part of a group of small stores located in a charming three-story Victorian-era building across the street from us. The building, known as the Courtyard, formed a large square, with four shops on each side. Above each shop were two floors with one spacious apartment on each floor. In the interior of the square was a delightful little courtyard overflowing with flowers and trees and several groupings of chairs and small tables. It was the perfect place to enjoy a caffe latte and read a book.

"Hi, Eddie," I said to the bookshop owner as I inched closer to the display.

"Hey, Brooklyn," Eddie Cox said without glancing up from his perch at the front counter. He knew it was me. Probably had seen me hovering nearby for the last few minutes. "I suppose you want to get another look at the book."

"I do," I said. "How did you know?"

He chuckled. "Just a lucky guess. Might have something to do with the fact that you show up here every other day and beg to see it."

All too true. But at least so far I hadn't drooled on the glass case. "And here I thought I was being so subtle."

"Subtle. Right." Still chuckling, he opened the drawer beneath the cash register and pulled out a small set of keys. I had known Eddie Cox and his brother-in-law, Terrence Payton, for almost four years, ever since I'd moved in across the street from Brothers Bookshop. The two men owned the charming shop together, and yes, I was there almost every other day because, you know, books.

Eddie carefully handed me the *Alice*, and it was all I could do not to clutch it to my chest in excitement. Instead, I put it down on the counter and ran my finger across the smooth leather cover.

Eddie raised an eyebrow. "I don't do this for everyone, you know."

"I know you don't, and I really appreciate you doing it for me. I'll be careful."

"I know you will." He winked at me. "Otherwise, I wouldn't allow it anywhere near your greedy little hands."

With a quick laugh, I scanned the store and spied Derek at the end of the middle aisle, where the latest mysteries and thrillers were displayed. He appeared to be involved in one particular book, so I knew I had a few minutes to enjoy the *Alice*. I opened it slowly, turning as always to the title page, where the publication date was posted: 1866.

This copy was considered a first edition, but actually it wasn't. The original version of the book had been published the year before, in 1865, but those books had been taken off the market by Lewis Carroll when his illustrator, John Tenniel, stated that the quality of his drawings had been poorly reproduced.

That earlier, 1865 version was known as the "Suppressed *Alice*" or the "Sixty-five *Alice*." All of those books were returned to the publisher except for fifty author copies that Lewis Carroll had kept for himself.

Eventually, most of those author copies had ended up in others' hands. Very few remained on the market today, and any that did were considered beyond rare. One had been auctioned off recently for almost two million dollars.

I would probably never get my hands on such a rare treasure as that, but I was perfectly happy with the one I currently held in my hands. This book was as fine as any I'd ever seen.

"Hello, Brooklyn."

I turned and saw Eddie's brother-in-law standing nearby. "Terrence. Hello."

"Is he going to sell you the book this time?" Terrence asked with a twinkle in his eye.

"I don't know." Glancing at Eddie, I bit back a smile. I knew he wouldn't sell it to me, since I'd tried to buy it a few hundred times before. But no harm in trying again. "What about it, Eddie? Will you sell me this book?"

"Never," Eddie insisted, as always. Then he added, "It was a gift from a very special friend."

"Wow." He'd never mentioned that before. I gazed at the book in my hand. "Must be a nice friend."

"I had a book just like that," Terrence grumbled. "But someone stole it."

"Are you kidding?" Did I look as confused as I felt? "You had a copy of this same book?"

Eddie barely suppressed an eye roll. "Terrence always claims that, but where's the proof?"

"I said it was stolen." Terrence's eyes narrowed in on Eddie, and I suddenly wondered if he suspected his own brother-in-law had taken the book from him.

Eddie shrugged. "That's why I keep mine locked inside this shatterproof case, right here in plain sight where everyone can see it, which means no one can steal it. I'm no fool."

"I'm not a fool, either." Terrence huffed, clearly insulted. He turned to me. "I'll have you know, my copy was locked inside the safe in my closet upstairs. Fat lot of good that did me," he added, muttering.

"You're just not as lucky as I am," Eddie said with a crooked grin as he flexed his biceps. "Or as manly."

I laughed, but Terrence was not amused. He continued to glower, shaking his head. "You're the fool. I'm as lucky as anyone else. Except when it comes to in-laws."

They were both ignoring me now. Over the last few years, I'd realized that the two men butted heads more often than not. Family was never easy, but still . . . If you didn't get along with your brother-in-law, why go into business with him?

The two men were in their forties and fairly nice-looking in different ways. Eddie had a classic runner's physique, tall and slim, with silver hair and a rakish goatee, which suited him. Terrence was a few inches shorter and bulkier, but most of his girth was muscle. He looked as though he might've been a boxer in his youth.

The two men had married sisters who divorced them within weeks of each other and moved to Florida together. I got the feeling that Eddie and Terrence didn't miss their ex-wives too much. They were both book fanatics who spent all of their time in the bookshop. I'd never known them to take a day off.

Handing the book back to Eddie, I tried to veer our conversation around to the original subject. "Not that you both don't deserve the very finest things, but who in their right mind would give up such a beautiful book?"

Eddie wiggled his eyebrows and grinned slyly. "A generous person who recognizes greatness, I suppose."

It was Terrence's turn to roll his eyes. I started to grin, but something bumped into my ankle and I jolted. Glancing down, I saw Furbie, the bookshop cat, staring up at me with his teeth clenching a stuffed mouse. Stuffed with catnip was my guess, if Furbie's lazy gaze meant anything.

"Hello, Furbie," I murmured, and reached down to scratch the soft gray fur around his ears. "Aren't you a pretty kitty?"

In response to the flattery, he dropped the toy at my feet. I picked it up and tossed it a few yards down the nearest aisle, expecting the frisky cat to pounce after it. Instead, he gave me a censorious look, tossed his head imperiously, and sidled awkwardly after the mouse.

"I think Furbie's drunk," I said.

"It's Terrence's fault," Eddie claimed. "He's an enabler."

"You're just jealous," Terrence retorted, "because Furbie likes me best."

"Of course he does, because you feed him catnip and empower his bad behavior." Eddie turned to me. "I'm the disciplinarian."

"You're just a meanie," Terrence muttered, and they were off on another squabble-fest, this time over the cat. These two would tangle over anything!

After letting them go off for a few more seconds, I tried to steer them back to the topic of Terrence's missing book.

"When did you lose your copy of *Alice*?" I asked Terrence as Eddie unlocked the glass case and gingerly slipped his *Alice* back inside.

"I didn't lose it."

"Sorry. When was it stolen?"

Terrence thought for a moment. "I guess it's been about six months."

In the grand scheme of tragedies, I knew this would come in low on the list. But as a book person, I really felt bad for him. "I'm sorry, Terrence."

"Yes," he said pointedly, still glaring at Eddie, "so am I."

Eddie put the key to the case back in the drawer and turned to Terrence. "You should be more careful."

"Oh, shut up."

Eddie grinned at me, a silent acknowledgment that he had just won this little argument. Their bickering was usually more good-natured, but this time Terrence looked truly offended, which worried me a little. It seemed like they might have quarreled over the stolen book before.

Derek approached and placed a short stack of books on the front counter.

"What have you got there?" I asked.

"I found a few spy novels I thought my father might enjoy."

"Oh. That's nice." But my stomach gave a little twist at the mention of his father. Derek's parents were going to be visiting from England for the first time the following week, and I still wasn't ready to meet them.

Derek and I had been together three years, and the one time I'd traveled to England with him, his parents had been away on an anniversary cruise around the Mediterranean. Now that he and I were getting married, it seemed ridiculous that I'd never met them. But as Derek arranged for their whirlwind trip to San Francisco, I found myself growing more and more uneasy about our first encounter.

Would they like me? It sounded so neurotic to worry, but these were my future in-laws! Of course I was worried. But still, I was sure they were wonderful, and I knew we would all love one another. They had to be the nicest people in the world because Derek was simply a delightful man. But they were *English*. I had lived in London for a short while years ago, and I truly loved the people, but there was a reserve to some of them that I didn't always understand. I had been raised in a thoroughly American peace-and-love commune founded by fans of the Grateful Dead, and I still wore Birkenstocks to prove it. My family was boisterous and fun loving. I simply couldn't imagine what Derek's parents would think of me. And Derek, while awesome, could be intimidating to others when he wanted to be. At times it was one of his best attributes. But it made me wonder if his parents might be intimidating as well.

Not that I was one bit intimidated by Derek. Not at all. Well, not anymore, anyway. When we first met, there might have been a few moments of intimidation. But at the time he'd had a gun pointed at my head and was accusing me of murder. Who wouldn't have been apprehensive? But the moment passed, and we grew to be great friends. And more.

Derek glanced at the *Alice in Wonderland* safely locked up in its glass case and turned to me with a look of shock. "What? He put it away? He's not going to sell it to you?"

I grinned. Derek knew very well that Eddie would never sell the book, but it was fun to tease the man. "He said no, but maybe I should double-check." Glancing at Eddie, I asked, "Are you going to sell me the book?"

He snorted. "No, for the hundredth time. But nice try."

"Well, then . . ." I stepped closer to the glass display case, gazed again at the dapper gold rabbit on the front cover, and then sighed. "Thanks again for letting me look at it."

"For you, Brooklyn, anytime."

Knowing how much I coveted the book, Derek gave my shoulder a sympathetic squeeze. "Sorry, love. But keep trying. Eddie might change his mind."

Eddie's burst of laughter was interrupted by the sound of high heels tapping against the hardwood floor. We all turned to see Bonnie Carson walk into the store. She owned the Courtyard building and enjoyed keeping a close watch on everyone's business.

"Hi, Bonnie," Terrence said, his voice soft with emotion.

"Well, looks like the gang's all here," Bonnie said, her gaze wandering from Terrence to Eddie to Derek. She was an attractive, flirtatious woman in her forties who wore clothes designed to show off her voluptuous figure. Her stiletto heels looked high enough to cause nosebleeds, and her distinctive floral perfume surrounded her wherever she went. Despite her obvious ways, I liked her. Bonnie knew a lot about books, and I'd heard that at one time she was the owner of the bookshop. But when her husband died a few years ago and she inherited the entire building, she'd decided to become a lady of leisure rather than a shopkeeper and sold the store to Eddie and Terrence.

These days she seemed to enjoy going from shop to shop, kibitzing with the owners and customers. Occasionally I would see her sitting outside in the court-yard, relaxing in the sun.

I had never realized that Terrence had a crush on her, but it was pitifully obvious now, just by the way he spoke her name and stared at her.

Unlike Terrence, Derek was not attracted to Bonnie at all. Apparently that made him even more attractive to her, and she did her best to draw his attention. Derek, who wasn't afraid of anything or anyone, often walked in the opposite direction when Bonnie came around.

"We've got to get going, love," Derek said now, look-ing a bit desperate. I felt his pain as I watched Bonnie continue to eye all three men.

"Okay, let's go."

"Have a nice evening, you two," Terrence said.

I glanced back at the brothers-in-law. "Thanks. We're making soup tonight."

Eddie's eyes widened. "You're cooking soup, Brook-lyn?"

"I am," I said, beaming. "I've been practicing, and I'm getting a lot better."

He and Terrence exchanged looks of doubt, and they both gave Derek a sympathetic frown. It wasn't meant to be hurtful. My lack of cooking expertise was widely known. But I'd been experimenting with differ-ent techniques and utensils lately, and I really was get-ting better. Of course, a year ago I hadn't even known how to boil spaghetti, so the bar was pretty low to be-gin with.

We waved good-bye and walked out to the court-yard, where I glanced at Derek. "Do you still want me to make soup?"

"Absolutely. Your vegetable soup is delicious."

"Thank you." But I hesitated, glancing around at the options available to us. The Rabbit Hole was our local produce market and juice bar. It was a popular spot for athletes and other healthy types, which I was trying to be. Across the courtyard was Thai to Remember, our favorite Thai restaurant, and next door was a pretty good burger joint. And then there was Sweetie Pies, the pie shop. I was tempted to blow off our plans to make healthy veggie soup and pick up something fast and yummy. Maybe cheeseburgers or Thai food. With pie for dessert.

But I couldn't do it. Because the truth was, I was on a mission. Maybe it wasn't the most philanthropic mission I'd ever set out on, but I was determined to be in the best shape of my life for our upcoming—*gulp*—wedding. I wasn't out of shape, particularly. I'd been blessed with healthy genes, so it wasn't like I would have to go on a hunger strike to fit into my wedding dress. No, I just wanted to be . . . awesome. I wanted to have beautiful, perfectly toned arms like my friend Alex had. Of course, Alex was also a fifth-degree black belt in at least two, maybe three different martial arts disciplines and taught some heavy-duty workout classes, so I was light-years behind her when it came to achieving true buffness. But I could improve things a little. And I had three whole months to do it. Piece of cake, right? I winced. No. No more cake. No pizza or ice cream. And a double order of Thai ginger chicken soaking in spicy peanut sauce was simply out of the question.

"What will it be, darling?" Derek prompted, some-how in tune with my thought process.

I took a deep breath. "Soup." Determined to keep to my goal, I steered us toward the Rabbit Hole. And once I was safely inside the happy walls of the healthy little shop, I began to breathe easier. First of all, the place was pristine. The vegetables in the produce section were fresh and beautiful and all stacked up in orderly rows. Even the green beans were laid out in neat lines, and that was no easy trick. The popular juice bar at the far end was painted bright yellow and pink. It was impossible not to smile when you walked into the Rabbit Hole. The stainless steel shelves that formed the aisles were modern and bright and held hundreds of canned goods and bottles of juice and vitamins and skin care products.

Just being in there made it easier to think about good health and clean living.

Unlike some health food stores I'd been in, the Rabbit Hole didn't smell like castor oil or rotting produce. There were no scary posters diagramming body parts or shelves filled with strange medicinal remedies that smelled like dead fish. If you'd ever met my mother, you would recognize me as someone who was all too familiar with places like that. I couldn't count the times she had dragged me and my siblings into those creepy shops in the past.

And besides all that good stuff, the Rabbit Hole was owned by a guy named Rabbit! Will Rabbit was the nicest fellow in the world, cute and funny and smart and kind, and so helpful it was a pleasure to shop there, even if the prices were slightly higher than in the supermarket six blocks away.

"Hello, Will," Derek said as we walked inside.

"Derek. Brooklyn. Hello," Rabbit said, smiling at us. He was tall and lanky, and he had a habit of wearing vintage vests of all kinds. He probably thought it made him look older than his thirty years, and more distinguished. It didn't. He remained a sweet, appealing guy with a slightly jittery manner that made me think his last name fit him well.

I waved. "Hi, Rabbit."

"If I can help you with anything, please let me know."

"We're picking up veggies for soup."

"You might want to add some of our frozen corn," he said, pointing to the wall where the frozen vegetables were located. "It's still on the cob and was flash frozen in the field. We just got a shipment from Mexico yesterday, and believe it or not, it's the sweetest I've ever tasted."

We took his advice and grabbed one package containing two ears of corn, along with a half head of cabbage, a bunch of carrots, onions, potatoes, green beans, and celery.

As we were bagging up our groceries, Bonnie walked into Rabbit's store. I watched Derek's jaw tighten, and I wondered if Bonnie might have been following us—well, Derek—from store to store. Not that my suspicions mattered. She had every right to go wherever she wanted to. And it made sense that she would visit Rabbit since he was, in fact, her nephew. She had given him the health food store ten years ago, when he'd turned twenty-one. *Pretty swell birthday present,* I thought.

"Hi, Auntie," Rabbit said. "You ready for a little afternoon delight?"

Derek and I turned and gaped at him. Rabbit grinned.

"It's a drink. Raspberry green tea mixed with lemonade and a sprig of mint."

"Ah," Derek murmured.

I gulped. "Sounds . . . delightful."

And on that note, we took off with our veggies and headed for home.

Out on the sidewalk, waiting for the traffic to clear, I turned to Derek. "Did you hear any of my conversation with Terrence and Eddie?"

"You know I did," he said with a smirk.

I smiled. "I was hoping. What did you think?"

"I was particularly interested in Terrence's claim that his book was stolen."

"That bothered me, too."

Derek's lips twisted in thought. "Their exchange was more bitter than usual. It made me wonder if perhaps Terrence blames Eddie for his book going missing."

"That's what it sounded like to me," I said. And the fact that Derek had picked up on the same thing I had made me love him even more. Surely his parents would see how perfect we were for each other. Right? Not to change the subject or anything.

"Is Eddie's book terribly valuable?" Derek asked.

I nodded. "He could probably sell it for twenty-five thousand dollars."

One eyebrow quirked up. "I see."

We crossed the busy street, and Derek unlocked the front door to our building. As we waited for the elevator, he asked, "Is there a way to find out if a similar book was sold in the last year or two?"

"I was curious enough to look up the comps a few months ago, but I was only looking at books that were still for sale. I never thought to research books that might've been sold around the same time his was stolen."

The elevator arrived and we stepped inside. Derek said, "I wonder if Terrence ever reported the loss."

"I could find out."

"Twenty-five thousand dollars is a lot to lose."

"The price for that book has probably gone up by now," I said. "We recently celebrated the one hundred and fiftieth anniversary of the publication of *Alice's Adventures in Wonderland*. There were a number of book festivals hyping the book and a lot of articles being written about it, so I wouldn't be surprised to find out that the price has climbed to thirty thousand or possibly higher."

Derek whistled softly. "Thirty thousand dollars for a book. So if Terrence's copy truly was stolen, that was no minor theft."

Chapter 2

Once we had greeted and played with our adorable cat, Charlie, for a few minutes, Derek went to work chopping vegetables while I sat at the dining room table with my computer. Charlie curled herself around my feet as I searched for any news of a finely bound *Alice in Wonderland* being sold around the same time Terrence told us his book had been stolen.

I tried to ignore the sight of Derek with his sleeves rolled up peeling carrots, but it wasn't easy. The man was just too attractive for his own good. And mine, too, obviously. But if you could see his arms, tanned and sinewy, working that peeler on those carrots . . . Well, I digressed.

I dragged my gaze back to the computer screen to see a list of similar *Alice in Wonderland* copies bought and sold in the last year. It mentioned that a copy of the 1865 Suppressed *Alice* was about to be auctioned off the following week. The auction house's book expert was quoted saying that they expected to sell the rare version for between two and three million dollars.

That was exciting news, of course, but it had nothing to do with the fate of Terrence's book. So I continued down the list, looking for any sales of the 1866 version in the past six months. I did find one for sale for seventy-four thousand dollars and another for fifty-one thousand dollars. Clearly, some of the finer copies of the book had become even more valuable than my original estimation. Those two had sold in the last two weeks. Terrence said he'd discovered his book missing about six months ago. Had the thief held on to the book for months before deciding to sell it?

There was no definitive way to determine whether either of the two recently sold books—or the other six that were listed for sale on the Web site—was actually Terrence's book. I would have to either contact the bookseller for the date they'd first acquired the book or simply give up. Did I want to devote more effort to this search? I didn't have a lot of time, but I was always intrigued by odd stories about rare books. But at the moment, I was even more intrigued by Derek peeling carrots in all his gorgeousness.

Choosing between the Internet and Derek was no contest. I shut down the computer, knowing I would return to do more searching the next day.

My vegetable soup was a major success. I would even go so far as to call it a cooking miracle, given my lack of almost any skill in the kitchen, but really, I was getting a lot better. This time the year before, it was all I could do to make a decent cup of coffee.

So I'm not sure how I did it, but everything in the

soup came together just right. The veggies didn't turn gray, which meant that I hadn't overcooked them. The broth was clear and pretty and a perfect blend of flavors and seasonings. The crusty bread—just one piece for me—and a crisp sauvignon blanc rounded out the meal.

As we enjoyed the meal, I realized it had been several long weeks since a gun had gone off in our apartment and a bullet had hit the ceiling above our heads. The vicious murderer who'd intended to kill a person I loved was wrestled to the floor and later arrested. I must've buried the memory because today was the first time I looked up and noticed that the bullet hole was gone. No trace remained. When had Derek arranged that? I wondered as I gazed at him sitting across the table from me, sipping his soup. I would ask him about it eventually, but for now I was amazed and happy to realize he'd done it without fanfare as a gift to me.

Derek and I spent two hours enjoying our dinner while wondering and theorizing about who might have stolen Terrence's copy of *Alice in Wonderland*. Eddie had implied that the book was a figment of Terrence's imagination, but Terrence had been adamant that it did exist. So if the book really had been missing for six months, where was it now?

The next morning, after Derek left for work, I had a long telephone conversation with my parents, who were planning to come into the city to meet Derek's parents later in the week. Along with my anxiety over meeting his folks, I was starting to flip out at the prospect of introducing my free-spirited New Age mom to Derek's proper English mum. Don't get me wrong—I love my mother, but it wouldn't have surprised me to see Derek's mother gasp in shock at some of Mom's aerie-fairy statements. I could feel my blood pressure spiking as I imagined the poor woman being totally appalled by Mom's witchy Wiccan-Pagan-Astral-Travel personality. Derek's parents' visit would turn into a complete disaster.

What if Mom started talking about her astral-traveling spirit guide, Ramlar X? What if she wanted to cast a spell in the middle of dinner? Or give Derek's mother a lecture on panchakarma and hand her a cup of sweat-inducing tea to eliminate her toxins? I let a quiet moan escape before gently mentioning my fears to my mother. She just chuckled, causing my stomach to churn painfully.

"Mom, I'm begging you. Please be normal."

"Sweetie," she said kindly, "I wouldn't be normal if you paid me a million dollars." There was silence for a moment; then she added, "You know, I'm not even sure I could pretend at this late date."

"Dad, help me out here."

They both laughed, and my father said, "Brooklyn, your mother is a unique, wonderful person and everyone loves her."

"I love her, too," I hastened to say. "You know I love you, Mom."

"Of course I do," she said. "And I know you're worried about meeting Derek's parents, but please don't be concerned. We'll all get along just fine."

"That's right, honey," Dad said. "Try not to freak out, okay?"

A minute later I hung up the phone, feeling as if I'd

fallen into the pit of doom. It wasn't my parents' fault. Dad was right: The imminent arrival of Derek's parents was freaking me out.

But why? My parents were pillars of society in our small town of Dharma up in the Sonoma wine country. Dad was on the board of directors of our commune's winery. He was also on the town council. Mom had raised six kids and was a vital part of the fabric of our town. That didn't mean they were straitlaced and dignified, of course. On the contrary, they were still two wild and crazy kids who had always loved a party as much as the next guy did.

They had met at the tie-dyed T-shirt booth during a Grateful Dead weekend at the Ventura Fairgrounds in 1972. It was love at first sight for both of them, and they were just as much in love today as they had been on that first day.

Somehow those thoughts didn't soothe me as much as they usually did. I was still clutching my hands together in worry and wondering how I would make it through the next week.

To change my vibe and calm myself down, I decided to run over to the Rabbit Hole and treat myself to a fruit smoothie.

Ordinarily, when I found myself all discombobulated like this—which was rare, really!—I would jog across the street to the coffee shop for a grande triple-shot caramel mochaccino deluxe and a small box of donuts. But I was on a mission now, so with a smoothie I figured I was being virtuous while still indulging myself a little.

I grabbed my purse and carefully locked up before leaving the apartment. Waiting for the elevator, I flinched when I heard some commotion behind me. I was still a little jumpy from the last time our apartment had been broken into.

"Yoo-hoo, Brooklyn!"

I sighed with relief as my neighbors Vinnie and Suzie headed toward me with their darling baby, Lily. Vinnie was pushing the baby stroller while Suzie balanced a four-foot-tall wood carving of a woman's head, her hair appearing to stream wildly in the wind. The art piece was almost as wide as our hallway, which made it bigger than Suzie and Vinnie put together. The two of them were talented sculptors who specialized in burl wood.

"Wow, that's gorgeous," I said, staring at the statue. "You guys have done it again."

"Thank you, Brooklyn," Vinnie said, bowing her head slightly. "We are entering it in the Golden Gate Art Show."

"You're sure to win."

"If I don't fall over and break it," Suzie muttered.

"Poor Suzie," Vinnie said. "We need one stroller for Lily and a second one for the sculpture."

Suzie grunted. "There's a good idea."

I couldn't look away from the sculpture, and moved in closer to examine it. "Those individual strands of hair are almost as thin as real hair. And they look like they're floating in the air. How do you do that with a chain saw?"

Vinnie's laugh was musical. "We don't always use the chain saws, Brooklyn. For this work, I used a small serrated spatula, about the size of a surgeon's scalpel."

"Amazing."

"And Suzie carved the eyes. Aren't they mesmerizing?"

I gazed into the eyes of the sculpted woman and shivered. "I feel like she's staring back at me."

"I know." Suzie grinned. "Like she's alive."

"Yeah. Wow."

Our massive ancient elevator arrived and we all piled inside. As the elevator traveled down, I stooped to be at eye level with Lily. I murmured some nonsense baby phrases to make her smile, then glanced up at my friends. "She gets more beautiful every day."

"Lily is captivated by you, Brooklyn," Vinnie said.

"And I'm captivated by her." I took the baby's tiny hand in mine. "She's getting so big."

"She is almost fifteen months old now and is talking a mile a minute."

"She'll be off to college any day now," I said.

Vinnie chuckled, but sobered as I stood up. "I am glad we ran into you today, Brooklyn. Have you heard anything about the latest attack of vandalism?"

"What?" I glanced at Suzie, whose lips tightened in a scowl. "No. What happened?"

Suzie rested the sculpture on the elevator railing. "I ran across the street earlier to get Lily some juice and had a minute to talk to Rabbit. He said the creeps hit the Courtyard again late last night. Apparently it's not the first time it's happened."

"I can't believe it. Derek and I were just there last night."

"There's graffiti covering the entire south side of the building."

We lived on the north side of the street. I scowled. "So we wouldn't even see them if we looked out the window. The parking lot butts up against that old warehouse that's being redeveloped. Nobody lives there yet."

"Right. So nobody saw anything."

"Cowards," Suzie muttered.

"And that is not the worst of it," Vinnie said, her Indian accent growing thicker as her anxiety seemed to rise. "Last night we stopped at Pietro's for pizza, and Pete told us he's been hearing more talk about developers taking over the neighborhood."

Pete, the owner of our favorite local pizza place, was a font of neighborhood information and gossip.

"Why haven't I heard anything about this?" I said. "We were just over at the bookshop last night. And we stopped in at the Rabbit Hole, too. Nobody said anything."

"They might be trying to keep it on the down low," Suzie said. "Don't want to start a mass exodus out of the area."

"According to Pete, it's inevitable," Vinnie said. "But I don't believe that. Something has got to be done to stop it. I don't want them to sell the Courtyard. You know a greedy developer would tear it down without a second thought and build cold, soulless condos."

"No way can we let that happen," I said. "I'm on my way over to the Rabbit Hole right now. I'll see if he knows anything more."

"Better yet, talk to Kitty," Vinnie suggested as the old elevator shuddered to a stop. "She knows everything."

Kitty owned the hat shop at the west side of the Courtyard.

"I'm not sure that's a good idea," I said, stepping out

at the ground floor. "I'll be stuck talking to her for an hour, and then I'll end up buying a hat."

True to my word, I pestered Rabbit to tell me more about the vandalism, but he refused to add anything other than what he'd already told Vinnie and Suzie.

"Did you call the police?" I asked.

"Sure did," he assured me. "And Bonnie's arranged to have the city come by and paint that side of the building for free."

"They'll do that?"

He turned to the cart behind him, effortlessly lifted a crate filled with bottles of flavored tea, and walked down the aisle to stock the shelves. "Yeah, they've got a team that goes around cleaning up graffiti at no cost to the victims."

"That's really good to know." Especially since it was a known fact that once a building or wall had been tagged with some particular form of graffiti, other taggers would be drawn to do the same. I asked the disturbing question that was foremost in my mind. "Do you think we're starting to get gang activity in this neighborhood?"

"No." Rabbit frowned. "At least not according to the police. I'm in charge of the neighborhood watch for our building. I talked to the cops just the other day and they didn't say anything about it."

"I hope they're right."

"Me, too. This neighborhood has been so nice for the past couple of years, I would hate to think it was changing. The shopkeepers around here are like family to me. I cover Kitty's shop every afternoon so she can take a lunch break, and Terrence does the same thing for Joey."

"That's really nice."

"Yeah. When I reorganized my store, Terrence and Joey and Eddie helped me after work every night for a week. And Colin at the pie shop is always bringing around leftovers."

"Now, that's my kind of neighbor."

He laughed. "I know, right? And remember three months ago, when Pietro's had to shut down because of smoke damage? I remember Eddie was sick, but everyone else showed up on a Sunday to help Pete scrub down the place so he could reopen as soon as possible. Makes me sad that a vandal is messing with our vibe."

The subject of graffiti and gangs seemed like something I should've known about, given my strange interest in crimes of all sorts. But I'd never had to deal with either before. Murder, yes. Graffiti, no.

I followed Rabbit around the shop, sipping my blueberry smoothie. "Would Bonnie ever sell this building?"

"Never," he said firmly. "Aunt Bonnie loves this place. She'll live here till she dies."

It had to be nice for Rabbit to have an aunt who owned such a valuable piece of real estate. The Courtyard was a beautiful old building that had been part of the view from my workshop windows since I'd moved there five years ago. It added so much charm to the street with its Victorian roofline, wide bay windows, and beveled glass panels in each of the shop doors. Handsome forest green awnings shaded the shops' windows from the glare of the afternoon sun. The building had been painted recently and each morning I watched the shopkeepers sweeping the sidewalks outside their doors. In recent years, the Courtyard shops had become a cool destination spot and the individual shop owners showed a lot of pride in being part of it all.

I hated the thought of looking out my window one day and seeing yet another high-rise apartment building directly across the street. Not only because the view would be so mundane, but also because the Courtyard was so important to our neighborhood. There was Brothers Bookshop, of course, and the Rabbit Hole, plus all those restaurants. There was Kitty's hat shop and a lingerie boutique and Joey's shoe repair and the yoga studio, and more. I found myself crossing the street to look for something or other at least three or four times a week.

Every time I met a new neighbor, they would talk about the Courtyard shops. And besides being the heart and soul of the neighborhood, the building also provided homes for the shopkeepers. Most of them lived in the apartments above their stores. If the building were sold, besides losing their livelihoods, the shop owners would also lose their homes.

I stayed and pretended to shop for almost an hour, trying to wheedle as much information out of Rabbit as I could—being a good neighbor and all—but finally I had to go home. I paid for my bags full of healthy goodies, left the store, and crossed the street to my apartment. It was time to get to work and start my next project.

Charlie greeted me at the door.

"Hello, cutie," I murmured, picking her up to snuggle for a minute as I walked into the kitchen to freshen her water. Then she followed me into my workshop and jumped onto my desk chair to watch from a safe spot as I gathered my supplies and equipment. While moving from one end of the room to the other, I realized that hanging around with Rabbit had caused my worries over Derek's and my parents getting together to vanish. Now that I was back home, however, the doubts returned and I had to spend a few minutes focusing my energy in order to just let the uncertainties go. Derek was right. Mom and Dad were right. Everyone would get along famously, and someday I would look back on my parental qualms and have a good laugh.

Besides, I was ready to start a challenging new project, and I needed all my creative juices flowing in the right direction in order to concentrate on the job ahead.

I was really psyched about this one. I had been asked to create something new for the spring festival at Bay Area Book Arts, or BABA, as we called it.

I had decided to do another tribute to *Alice's Adventures in Wonderland*. There were many books that had woven themselves into and out of my life over the years, and *Alice* was one of those books. I had read it countless times when I was younger and had even begun collecting it, starting with a wonderful 1927 illustrated version I had picked up in Edinburgh a few years back. And last year I had created a really cool pop-up cutout scene from the book, featuring Alice on trial in the courtroom with the entire population of Wonderland flying up to attack her. "You're nothing but a pack of cards," she'd shouted, and indeed, the people in her dreams had turned into playing cards.

It had been a feat of sheer willpower on my part—

and maybe a bit of skill—to arrange the cards so that they appeared to be floating in the air a foot off the page. To be honest, getting those cards to fly off that page was a technological and architectural victory I never thought I'd achieve, but it turned out pretty awesome, if I did say so myself.

In the story of *Alice in Wonderland*, the attack of the cards happens right before Alice wakes up from her dream. And it was a dream of mine and an honor to have my *Pop-Up Alice* chosen to be part of the permanent collection of the Covington Library's children's museum.

There was another reason for me to celebrate the *Alice* connection. Last year I had attended the BABA festival celebrating the 150th anniversary of the publication of *Alice in Wonderland*. That had led me to create the pop-up book. So now I would bring it full circle by creating handmade playing cards, à la the cards in *Alice*. I would be incorporating the arts of papermaking, letterpress, and calligraphy, as well as my bookbinding skills. It was a little bonus that all of these arts were offered as part of the curriculum at BABA, so that was a nice tie-in. I was excited to get started.

I had originally planned to design a clamshell box and fill it with the handmade cards, but I was thinking of making a matchbox-style box instead. The playing cards would be set into a main container that would slide in and out of a protective outer case. This outer case would be larger, with a narrow, hollowed-out space on top that would hold a small accordion-style book that would extend out to fifty-two pages with a playing card on each page. It would be tricky, but my hope was that it would turn out to be whimsical and fun.

There were at least two ways of making paper: the *hard* professional way, which involved batting the pulp with a mallet and stirring it in a water bath for hours; and the *easy* professional way, where your essential tools were a blender and a wooden frame and the timing was more along the lines of a few minutes rather than a few hours.

I used the term *professional* for both techniques, because whatever route you chose to take, you would end up with a beautiful piece of handmade paper at the end of it. And since I was making a deck of playing cards and would have to repeat the process fifty-two times—or fifty-three if I included the joker—you could bet I was going to take the easy way this time.

I went through my workshop cupboards and drawers and pulled out all the supplies and equipment I would need. One old blender; a stack of white junk mail envelopes to use for my paper base; the bag of various twigs, leaves, flower petals, and grass blades I'd been collecting over the previous week; a pitcher for adding water to the blender; my homemade double-inset wood frame complete with Velcro straps, screens, and a bottom grid that I'd made myself for this project; a small tub halfway filled with water, in which the frame would be set; a cookie sheet; dried sprigs of parsley, rosemary, lavender, and dill; and a jar of silver glitter.

A few years ago, when I first got into papermaking, I'd built a wood frame to make standard-sized paper, eight and a half by eleven inches. But for this project I'd added a wooden template to the interior of the frame so that I would be able to make two smaller pieces of paper at the same time. The size of my paper cards would end up being about five and a half inches high by almost four and a quarter inches wide. That was bigger than your usual playing card, of course, but this was an art piece after all, so I decided it would be nice to see the cards and easier to enjoy them if they were slightly larger than life. I figured a little artistic license was allowed in this case.

I filled the tub halfway with water and lined all of my equipment along the counter. I took one of the envelopes and began tearing it up and tossing the pieces into the blender. I covered the bits of paper with water and pulverized the contents for about five seconds. Stopping the blender, I opened the top to add a few snippets of flowers and leaves and grass, tossed in a pinch of silver glitter, and then blended it for another few seconds until everything was nicely mixed up.

I placed my wood frame into the tub of water and poured the contents of the blender into the frame. I mixed the pulpy substance around with my fingers, then lifted the frame straight up from the tub and held it there while the water drained out.

Inside the double frame I could see two newly formed pieces of paper, still very soggy, but looking pretty with the little bits of twigs and grass and glitter. I unlatched the Velcro straps, pulled out the bottom screen, and set the newly created pieces of paper down on the cookie sheet. Then I went to work arranging my sprigs and pressed petals and seeds on each card to spell out my first playing card, the ace of spades. I spent another two minutes tweaking the design to make sure I could actually read the numbers and the suit. I did the same for the next card, the two of spades.

I placed a thin mesh screen on top of the two newly made cards and, using a soft, dry sponge, pressed down on the screen to draw up more moisture. Then I peeled the still-damp paper cards off the bottom screen and slipped them both between two blotter papers and pressed down with my fingers, once again squeezing out every last bit of water I could. When this was done, I laid them out on my worktable to dry.

And then I started the whole process over again with the next two playing cards.

It may have been repetitive, but it was fun. I was always happy when I was making paper. It satisfied something in me that straightforward bookbinding didn't—probably the way it reminded me of those mud pies I used to make when I was a little kid. This wasn't quite as messy, but it was just as pleasing to me.

A few hours later, I was finished for the day and took a moment to admire the twenty cards I'd made. I loved the feathery edges of the cards, a distinctive feature of handmade paper. This was because the wooden frame, which was once called a *deckle*, invariably allowed a bit of the liquid pulp to slip under the frame, creating that slightly uneven edge, which was one of the prettiest aspects of handmade paper, in my opinion.

This was also where the term *deckled edge* had originated.

I left the cards spread out on my worktable and went to the sink to clean my tools and thoroughly wash my hands.

I changed from my old jeans and Birkenstocks to a nice pair of slacks and my favorite burgundy heels.

Perfect timing, I thought, when Derek walked in a few minutes later.

"You look lovely," he said, earning a kiss from me. "All set to go?"

"I am." And I silently gave thanks that Derek truly, really, actually thought my sedate slacks and comfy shoes were lovely.

We had an appointment that afternoon with my lawyer, Carl Brundidge. I wasn't looking forward to the meeting, even though I'd known Carl forever and liked him very much. He was the lawyer for my parents and many of their friends who lived in Dharma. He had an office in San Francisco, where he worked a few days a week, and he had been bugging me and Derek to write up a prenuptial agreement before we got married the following month.

His motivation for having me sign a prenuptial agreement had originated almost three years ago, when my longtime mentor, Abraham Karastovsky, was murdered at the Covington Library. In the midst of all that pain and confusion, Carl had informed me that Abraham had left his entire estate to me. In his will, he had called me "the daughter of his heart."

Mine had nearly broken when I heard his words.

But the most astounding news was that Abraham's estate was worth six million dollars. It blew my mind. At the time I had wondered what in the world he'd been thinking, leaving all his money and books and properties and portfolios to me. But I knew the answer. He had loved me as much as I had loved him. As a teacher and a dear, dear friend.

There was so much more to the story, including the startling revelation that Abraham had had a daughter he had never met. She quickly became a friend and moved to Dharma, where my mother treated her like another daughter. I asked the lawyers to restructure things so that she could live in Abraham's house in Dharma and also draw from a trust fund we set up.

The meeting with Carl that afternoon went well, after I assured him that I was absolutely not going to sign some endless agreement filled with lawyer-speak gibberish. Carl must have anticipated my determination because, in the end, Derek and I signed a two-page agreement that stated, essentially, that what was mine was mine and what was his was his. And what we shared would always be ours together.

Carl was just doing that thing that lawyers do: protecting his client's best interests. I understood that and so did Derek. What Carl didn't understand was that Derek and I were never going to part ways. So that made it simple.

As we walked to the elevator after the meeting, I turned and gazed up at Derek. "All that talk of portfolios and investments is making me hungry."

"I anticipated as much," he said, his lips curving in a shrewd smile. "I've already made reservations at Alexander's for dinner."

I grabbed him in a tight hug. "You know me so well."

To tell the truth, the meeting had depressed me a little. It was the thought of all that money just sitting in a bank somewhere when I could be using it to help people. I said as much to Derek, who reached over and squeezed my hand. "Let's give it some thought. Together we can come up with a way to put some of it to good use."

At the restaurant, we ordered a nice bottle of wine to start. After a few sips, we placed our order. But just as I was about to mention my favorite twice-baked potato, I remembered my mission. I sighed and switched to a side of grilled asparagus. Derek promised to give up a few bites of his potato, so I figured I would survive the meal without too much of a problem.

We talked about his parents and some of the things we had planned for them.

"Afternoon tea at the Garden Court is a must," he said. "And we should find my father a good piece of pie."

"I've already made reservations for tea," I said between bites of steak. "But what's this about pie? Is that a requirement?"

"My father loves pie. All sorts of pie, but especially chocolate cream pie. It's a quirk of his."

I nodded. "We all have our quirks."

"Yes, we do." He grinned. "I thought we could search for the best places in town for pie and surprise him."

"I'll get right on it."

It was nice to relax and chat while dining in a dark, quiet restaurant. Derek told me stories about his parents and I grew happier with the idea of meeting them.

But on the way back to the car, I stumbled on a crack and started to fall forward. Derek grabbed me just as I was about to tumble face-first into the blacktop.

"Are you all right?" he asked, gripping my arm.

"I'm okay," I said, but I was breathing heavily. "Thanks for saving me from a face-plant." I had to wait a moment before trying to walk again, then took one step and faltered. "I'm afraid my shoe is ruined."

"Let's get to the car and we'll inspect the damage."

With that, he lifted me into his arms and carried me the remaining fifty feet to his car. I'm relatively tall and not exactly waiflike, so I considered this a major feat. And sure—hooray for feminism! But come on, what woman wouldn't enjoy being swept off her feet by a gorgeous man who looked down at her with love shining in his eyes. My little heart was pitter-pattering like a drum line.

"You are truly my hero," I said, resting my head on his shoulder.

"And you are mine," he said, and kissed me before setting me down on the ground so I could climb into the car.

Was it any wonder I was marrying the guy?

Once we were in the car, Derek examined my shoe in the overhead car light. "It's only the heel that was damaged. See how it popped right off? The rest of the shoe is perfectly fine."

"I'm so bummed. I was going to wear those shoes when we take your parents to dinner on Saturday."

"Surely you have another pair, darling."

"Of course I do," I said with a laugh. "But these are my favorites." And the thought of breaking in a new pair in less than a week was discouraging. These shoes were the perfect heel height and they looked good and felt wonderful, especially to someone who spent most of her day wearing Birkenstocks.

I didn't want to mention it out loud, but I had already made a list of all the outfits I planned to wear for every activity we'd scheduled for the week with the parents. My burgundy heels were featured in at least three of them.

"It serves me right for trying to wear high heels when

I walk around all day in sandals. But heck, I haven't seen Carl in a long time, so I wanted to dress up for our meeting."

Derek reached over and squeezed my hand. "You'll take them to Joey the Cobbler tomorrow. Perhaps he can have them ready before my parents arrive."

"I'm sure he can fix it in a few days." *And if not,* I thought as my stomach began to churn with anxiety, *I'll be going shoe shopping tomorrow.*

The next morning, feeling some residual panic at the thought of having to shop for new shoes in a hurry, I jogged across the street to the Courtyard, where Joey the Cobbler had his shop. If he could fix my heels in time, I would be saved.

Joey had inherited the shop from his father, the original Joe the Cobbler, and he was standing at the front counter, examining a pair of men's oxfords.

Joey was in his mid-thirties and genuinely hunky with dark hair, strapping arms, and a sexy smile. His shop was reasonably clean and tidy, which was sort of unusual in a shoe repair shop.

Joey also had a good heart and took pity on me, promising he'd have my heel fixed in two days.

"Thank you, Joey," I said, my relief obvious.

"No worries, Brooklyn," he said. "I'll have them ready for you by Friday afternoon."

"I really appreciate it."

"And I really appreciate your business," he said in a wolfish whisper that let me know he *really* appreciated my business.

I smiled and walked out of the shop, wondering if I had any other shoes that needed mending.

*   *   *

Early the following morning at breakfast, Derek reminded me of my pledge to find a good piece of pie.

"That's my main goal for the day," I said, then took a sip of coffee. "But you know, it might entail some taste testing."

"Poor baby." He sighed theatrically. "We do what we must."

I laughed and he joined in.

But slowly his eyes glazed over and he stared off at nothing in particular. "My mother bakes the best pies."

"My mother is a pretty good baker, too." A talent I had *not* inherited. Derek's mood was so odd, I blew out a breath and made an offer. "Derek, did you want me to bake a pie for your father?"

That brought him right back to earth. "Good Lord, no."

I blinked. "You don't have to be so quick to answer."

He laughed. "I'm sorry, love. I only meant that I don't want you to go to the trouble. Look, you'll go across the street to the pie shop. They have perfectly decent pies, as I recall."

I thought for a moment. "I'm willing to taste a few of them, because I'm a giver. And if one of them is fantastic, I'll buy it. Otherwise, we can wait until your father arrives and go around town tasting together. We'll make an afternoon of it."

"That's an excellent idea. I'm glad you thought of it."

I smiled fondly. "What made you think of pie?"

"I'm feeling nostalgic, I suppose. What with the parents arriving and all." He reached across the table for my hand. "How are you feeling about the visit?"

I'm terrified, I thought, but couldn't say it. Instead I kept smiling and nodding. "I'm excited."

Derek chuckled. "No, you're not—you're worried. I'm not quite sure why you don't want to admit it, but, darling, you have no reason to be dreading this meeting."

So he could read my mind. I should've known; he'd done it before. "You're right. I'm not fine at all. 'Scared stiff' would be more accurate."

He stood and circled the table, knelt down, and rubbed my knee affectionatcly. "Why, love?"

I looked him in the eyes. "I want them to like me, of course. But what I'm really panicking about is the thought of introducing your parents to mine."

His eyes widened briefly and then he nodded slowly. "I wish I could convince you that everyone will get along, darling. My parents are lovely people, but . . . oh, why sugarcoat it? You *should* be terrified. You should run for your life. My parents are brain-sucking zombies. Don't laugh now. I'm serious."

But I was already laughing. Somehow the words "brain-sucking zombies" sounded even more absurd when uttered by someone as cultured and serious and *English* as Derek Stone.

"All right," I said finally, after another good laugh. "Thank you. I feel like an idiot, but I'll snap out of it any minute now."

"I'm here to help." He chuckled, but his smile faded. "Darling, honestly, you mustn't worry. My parents are going to love you. They're cheerful and easygoing and they can't wait to meet you. And as for your parents, I adore your family. My parents will, too."

"I'm sure you're right. I don't know where all this

anxiety is coming from. In my more rational moments, I absolutely know we're all going to have a great time."

"Yes, we are." He stood and gathered our dishes and walked them into the kitchen. After coming back to the table, he squeezed my shoulder. "Are you sure you're all right?"

"I'm fine, and I really mean it this time."

"Okay, good. I've got to get going." He walked into his office, formerly my second bedroom, before our big remodeling job a few months earlier. He came out carrying his briefcase, and I stood and kissed him and gave him a warm hug.

"How do you feel about having a party at the office for my parents?" He paused for a quick moment. "Probably next Saturday would be the best evening."

"That's a great idea," I said. "I'm sure they would love to see your offices and meet all your people."

"I'll get Corinne working on it," he said. His assistant was brilliant at organizing such things.

"If she needs anything from me, just have her call."

"Thanks, love." And after another quick kiss for me and an affectionate scratching behind the ears for Charlie, he left for the day.

After cleaning up from breakfast, I went to pour myself another cup of coffee and found the pot was empty.

"Bummer," I muttered. Derek must've grabbed an extra cup earlier, before I was awake. I washed out the pot and then headed for my workshop to continue working on my deck of playing cards. But as soon as I walked into my workshop, I realized I wouldn't be able to function without another cup of coffee. I wasn't addicted, I told myself. I just wanted a little more.

I gazed out the window at the beautiful cold morning and decided to jog over to the Beanery to get a caffe latte.

Maybe I was just trying to avoid work, but I didn't think so. I loved my work. I just wanted a latte. I shrugged as I grabbed my warmest vest and slipped it on. If caffeine was an addiction, there were worse ones out there. Right?

It was barely six thirty in the morning, but happily, the Beanery opened early.

Crossing the street, I noticed that Sweetie Pies was open, too, for those who craved an early-morning breakfast pie. And who didn't? I wondered, smiling. Maybe after I bought my latte, I would pop in to check out the pie selection for Derek's dad's visit.

I passed through the center archway and strolled into the inner courtyard. The tables and chairs were deserted this early on such a cold day. Following the winding path to the Beanery, I glanced through the window of the Rabbit Hole—and noticed a strange sight. Something was definitely out of place.

Rabbit didn't usually open this early, but I tried the door anyway—and walked in on complete chaos.

One of the massive stainless steel grocery shelves was toppled over and hundreds of cans and bottles were scattered across the floor. I heard moaning and almost tripped over Rabbit, who was sprawled on the floor.

"Rabbit!" I shouted, and knelt down to find his pulse. It was weak, but he was still alive. The pressure of my fingers against his neck caused him to moan again. Thank God. Usually when I stumble upon people sprawled across the floor, they're dead.

I pulled my phone from my purse to call 911 and that

was when I saw a pair of feet sticking out from under the heavy shelf. Someone was trapped beneath it!

"Hold on!" I yelled. After kicking several cans out of the way, I grabbed the edge of the shelving unit and tried to lift it. It wouldn't budge. It didn't look that heavy at first, but now I realized it had to weigh hundreds of pounds. It was double sided and weighted at the bottom. It couldn't have fallen over on its own, could it?

Had there been an earthquake? I hadn't felt anything—certainly not one strong enough to dislodge a huge grocery shelf in the last twenty minutes or so.

Maybe a rod or something in the shelf itself had broken off, causing it to collapse.

I was thinking all those thoughts as I gingerly crept to the other side to get another angle on the situation. There were cans of vegetable juice and jars of tomato sauce and veggies everywhere, so I had to walk gingerly, because one wrong step would send me flying. As I knelt down to see what I could see under the shelves, I caught the distinct scent of perfume.

Perfume?

I sniffed again. It was Bonnie's scent. Oh no! Was she the one trapped beneath this crushing weight?

"Bonnie!"

But after shouting her name, I stared back at those feet again. They definitely belonged to a man, based on their size and shape and the black hairs showing around the ankles. I had to wonder why he wasn't wearing shoes on this cold spring morning, but that was a question I would save for later.

I shifted my body to get a better hold on the shelving and tried to lift it again, using every ounce of strength

I could muster. After a moment, I had to quit. It was just too heavy. I exhaled from the exertion and flexed my fingers to shake away the soreness.

"I can't lift it," I said loudly, hoping the guy under there could hear my voice. "I'm going to get help."

I stood up, and that was when I saw the trail of blood wending its way out from the vicinity of the man's head.

Feeling sick to my stomach, I staggered over to the door and called the police.

Chapter 3

As soon as the 911 operator assured me an ambulance was on its way, I called Inspector Janice Lee, the SFPD homicide detective I'd worked with so many times in the past. We were actually starting to be pretty good friends, despite the sad fact that our interactions always revolved around murder. And I was sort of worried that this phone call to her might slow down the whole blossoming friendship thing.

Not that this was a murder. How could it have been? But there was a body. And it was weird, for sure. Yes, the shelving could have toppled on its own. Stranger things had happened—usually to me. But no matter how the shelf fell, I had a sick feeling that the man buried underneath was dead. Which meant that the circumstances of his death were suspicious. I mean, how did a massive double-sided shelving unit just fall over and kill a guy? It couldn't hurt to have a San Francisco police detective here to check things out.

Janice—er, Inspector Lee—assured me that she would be here soon. After we ended the call, I telephoned Derek and gave him a quick rundown of the situation.

"I'll be right there," he said. "Are you still inside the store?"

I glanced around, growing more uneasy by the second. "Yes."

"Would you be more comfortable waiting outside?"

"Probably, but I'd like to stay inside in case Rabbit wakes up."

"That makes sense. As long as you don't have to look at any blood."

It came across as an offhand comment, but when I didn't immediately answer, he got a clue. "So there's blood."

"Yes." I took a deep breath, relieved that he knew me so well, knew all about my little blood phobia and often did what he could to help. Really, though, with all the dead bodies I'd come across in the last few years or so, you'd think I'd have gotten past that woozy "otherwhere" feeling I felt whenever I saw the darn stuff. Not so far, unfortunately.

"There's a lot of blood," I confessed, "and I'm pretty certain it's coming from the guy's head." I gritted my teeth and stared down at the rivulets of blood that had pooled on the hardwood floor.

"Step away from the blood, darling," Derek advised. "And focus on something else, just for good measure. I'm in my car and on my way."

"Okay," I said, absurdly grateful for his concern. "And don't worry. I'm fine, really." I would be eventually, anyway. Meanwhile I was sucking in deep breaths as we spoke. Derek was sympathetic, knowing that I'd actually fainted from the sight of blood more than once. That wasn't something I was proud of; it was just the way things were. Still, couldn't you train yourself to get used to things that upset you? Maybe I'd try hypnosis. The positive news was that I hadn't fainted this time, so good for me.

"Take your time, really. I'm fine." I gazed at the chaotic scene before me. "Besides, I'm in a lot better shape than these two."

"Point taken. I'll be there in fifteen minutes or less."

"Good." I heard the dim sound of a siren in the distance. "I think I hear the ambulance coming. And the police should be here any minute, too."

"All right, love."

"Thank you," I murmured. "Be careful."

But Derek had already hung up the phone and I suddenly felt very much alone. There had to be customers in some of the other shops around the Courtyard. Had anyone else heard the crash of the shelf falling over and the smashing of dozens of cans and bottles and jars as they hit the hard surface of the floor? We were talking about several hundred pounds falling over. There must've been a lot of noise. How long ago had it happened?

And why hadn't I gone straight to the Beanery? I lamented. Why was I always the one to come across dead bodies?

That last question was strictly rhetorical. I really wasn't feeling sorry for myself. But I was sad and completely stunned by the horrible scene I'd found inside the Rabbit Hole.

It occurred to me to check on Rabbit again, so I

dashed around the collapsed pile of stainless steel to find him still motionless, except for the faint rise and fall of his chest. I knelt down and pressed my fingers against his wrist to feel his pulse, just to be sure. I called out his name, but there was no reaction.

So at least he was alive and breathing, although obviously still unconscious. I frankly wasn't sure what else I could do, but it occurred to me that I could take some photographs of the damage before anyone else came in and moved things around. I grabbed my phone and took a few quick photos of the mess of steel shelving and cans everywhere. I took a few shots of poor Rabbit and several of the victim's feet, plus a photo of his blood seeping onto the floor. I'd experienced enough crime scenes to know that pictures like this could be invaluable. And even if this wasn't a crime scene—and I prayed that it wasn't—some photos would be helpful anyway. And taking them gave me something to do because I was truly at a loss.

I could hear the sirens growing louder, so I finally stepped outside to the courtyard to wait.

Within seconds the wailing grew loud enough that I had to cover my ears, until it finally came to an abrupt stop as the vehicle pulled into the parking lot behind the building.

Doors slammed and then three EMTs, two men and a woman, came running into the courtyard carrying medical equipment bags.

"Over here," I called, directing them over to the Rabbit Hole. I pushed the door open as they approached. "Be careful. There are cans and jars all over the floor."

They moved inside and I followed, of course. I

pointed to Rabbit. "I think he got conked on the head because he's been out cold since I got here. And there's someone buried underneath that shelving unit. It's too heavy for me to lift. I found blood on the other side. It's coming from . . ." I was blathering and knew it wasn't helping, so I stopped talking and watched the professionals take over.

The woman knelt next to Rabbit and began checking his vital signs. She looked up at me. "What's your name?"

"Brooklyn."

"Okay, Brooklyn. Do you know this guy's name?"

"It's Will Rabbit."

"Thanks." She went back to work, speaking calmly to Will, using his name as she examined him.

"Step out of the way, please, ma'am," the dark-haired man said. I scurried backward, and he squatted down, grabbed the shelf, and tried to lift it. It didn't budge, so he signaled to his red-haired, muscle-bound partner. "Take the other end."

The redhead did just that and together they managed to lift it a few inches, enough to shove it far enough back that I could finally see who was trapped beneath it.

"Joey! Oh my God."

"You know him?" the red-haired paramedic asked.

"Yes. He owns the shoe repair shop across the courtyard."

"You know his last name?"

I thought for a moment. "I don't, but someone around here will know it."

"Okay, thanks."

The other guy was already checking Joey's vital signs,

and at his signal the redhead began giving him CPR. I was almost certain there weren't any vital signs to be found, plus there was all that blood, but I wasn't about to say anything. I clung to every last bit of hope that the paramedics could save his life.

Without warning, an earth-shattering scream filled the air, and I jumped about a foot. After I whipped around, I saw Bonnie standing in the doorway, staring at the bodies on the floor. She kept screeching in a constant repetition of *"Noooooo!"*

Her face was so red, I thought she might explode. Then suddenly she bolted forward.

It happened so fast, I didn't think, just propelled myself into her path and grabbed hold of her shoulders. "Bonnie, stop."

The female paramedic held her hand up in warning. "Ma'am, don't come any closer."

Bonnie paid no attention as she struggled to get past me, her silky flowered bathrobe drooping off her shoulders and down her arms. "Get out of my way!" she shouted. "I have to help him."

Luckily, I was stronger and managed to keep her from getting any closer. "Bonnie, stay right here. You've got to let the paramedics do their jobs."

She began screaming again and I shook her hard. "Calm down."

Abruptly she ran out of energy and seemed to deflate. She stopped fighting me, but her sobs continued and grew even louder than the screams, if that was possible. I had seen people react badly to violent death, including myself, but her ear-shattering reaction was bringing it to a whole new level. I thought I might have to smack her across the face, but I knew she was in shock, so I finally just pulled her into my arms and squeezed. I mumbled nonsense words and swayed with her in my arms. "Shhh. I know, I know. It's bad. But I think he'll be okay."

I felt like I was soothing a big screaming baby. I understood her feelings, of course, since she and Rabbit were really close.

"Noooooo," she moaned. "Joey."

I paused midsway. While grateful that the high-pitched wailing had stopped, I was flummoxed. *Joey?* Her nephew Will Rabbit lay unconscious on the floor, but her tears and screams were for Joey? Not that he didn't deserve to be screamed over, but I guess I'd never realized that he and Bonnie were so close.

"It should've been me," she mumbled through her sobs.

"No," I insisted. "Don't ever say that. Nobody deserves to be hurt like this."

I didn't have time to say more because at that very moment I spied Inspector Janice Lee entering the courtyard and glancing around, looking for the Rabbit Hole.

Keeping one arm around Bonnie's shoulder, I led her over to the juice counter, where several high stools stood. "Why don't you sit here for a minute? I've got to go talk to the police, but I'll be back soon."

She was still sobbing, but managed to nod her acquiescence.

Inspector Lee strode into the Rabbit Hole and I rushed across the store to meet her. But just inside the entry she stopped abruptly, glanced around, and stared at me in shock. "What the heck? This isn't a bookstore."

I frowned, not understanding at first, then gave her a withering look. "Very funny."

"Yep, I still got it," she said, grinning.

Call it cop humor, or gallows humor, or just plain sarcasm, but she did have a point. Every time I'd ever been involved in a murder investigation with her, there had always been a book at the heart of the matter. Which made sense, given my chosen profession. But this time around there was hardly a book in sight. I was oddly relieved about that.

"Nope, no books," I allowed. "I was on my way to get coffee at the Beanery and happened to glance inside this place as I passed by."

"Lucky you." Inspector Lee shook her head as if trying to figure out why I seemed to attract death wherever I went. Well, she could join the club.

"Yeah, lucky," I muttered.

She glanced around, her gaze homing in on the two victims sprawled on the floor.

The redheaded paramedic continued to perform CPR on Joey, pumping his chest at regular intervals and then leaning over and checking for a sign of breathing. Inspector Lee walked over, flashed her badge, and asked about Joey's chance of recovery. The redhead looked up. "Not so good, but we'll keep pushing."

A few minutes before, the dark-haired EMT had jogged out of the shop and came back wheeling a gurney. He angled as close to Joey as he could get and then ran out again. Now he was back with another gurney for Rabbit. I was heartened to see that they weren't giving up on Joey. Not yet, anyway.

Two uniformed police officers walked into the store right after the paramedic and Inspector Lee waved them over. I couldn't hear what she was telling them, but she pointed toward the door. After a moment, the two cops left, probably going off to check the other shops to see if anyone in the area had seen or heard anything.

Lee walked back to me and pulled a notepad and pen from her jacket. "I take it you know these two victims?"

"I do." I had to swallow around the lump in my throat. And braced to look at the injured men again. "That one is Joey," I said, pointing toward him. "He's a cobbler who owns the shoe repair shop on the other side of the courtyard."

As she wrote rapidly in her compact notebook, I thought about the last time I'd seen Joey. It was just a day before and he was very much alive, flirting and grinning while promising to fix my shoes in record time.

How in the world did he wind up crushed and buried under that massive thing? What really happened in here earlier this morning? I refused to believe that Joey and Rabbit had been fighting. They were both too nice, too even tempered. Maybe the two of them had surprised a couple of burglars and been attacked. That was one good possibility. I couldn't think of another one.

Jerking her head toward Rabbit, still comatose on the floor, Inspector Lee asked, "What about that guy?"

"He owns this shop."

She glanced around. "The Rabbit Hole. Interesting name. So they sell healthy stuff."

"Right. Fruits and vegetables, and lots of juices and vitamins and protein powders and supplements. You know. And the juice bar does smoothies and all kinds of super-protein drinks. It's very popular." I glanced over as Rabbit was being lifted onto the gurney. "That's also his name, by the way."

"What do you mean?"

"His name is Rabbit."

She frowned. "His real name?"

"Yes. It's actually Will Rabbit. He's the nephew of the owner of the building." I glanced over my shoulder toward the juice bar. "That's her, sobbing over there."

Lee observed Bonnie for a full thirty seconds. "She's been like that since I walked in here. Doesn't look like she'll let up anytime soon. Do you know her well?"

I shrugged as guilt seeped in and took over. It felt terrible to admit that I hardly knew her at all. "As well as anyone knows their neighbors, I guess."

She nodded. "So not very well."

"No. Sorry."

"Hey, I get it. Most of us know our neighbors only well enough to wave to. But do you know anything about her? What's her story?"

I moved closer and lowered my voice. "When she first came in, I thought she was sobbing over her nephew. But then she cried out Joey's name. So who knows?"

"Ah. Curious." She scribbled a lengthy note and then slipped the pad and pen into her jacket pocket. "Thanks, Brooklyn."

"Oh, wait." I pulled out my phone. "Not sure if it matters, but I took pictures of everything before the paramedics moved the shelves. Just in case, you know."

"Yeah?" She looked surprised. "That was fast thinking."

"Thanks. I'll send them to you."

"That'd be great." She grinned. "Just in case."

The dark-haired EMT began to wheel Joey out of the shop while the other marched alongside, still giving him CPR. I admired their persistence, but I didn't hold out much hope for Joey. My eyes began to burn and I said a quick prayer before swiping away a couple of tears that had escaped.

The female paramedic stood next to Rabbit on his gurney. He now wore an oxygen mask over his nose and mouth and was bundled up under a thick blanket.

"Will he come through?" Lee asked her.

She gave Lee a tight smile. "He's got a lump on his head that's pretty serious and he's still unconscious, but he's responding to stimuli."

"Well, that's something. Maybe he'll surprise you."

"I hope so."

"What hospital are you taking him to?"

"SF General. Their trauma unit's pretty awesome."

"Good. Thanks."

The dark-haired paramedic returned to collect all of their bags of equipment and supplies, and then he accompanied the woman paramedic, who wheeled Rabbit out to the ambulance.

The silence was unnerving. Not even Bonnie made a sound, though her gaze was fixed on the door where the paramedics had just exited with Rabbit and Joey. Seconds later, we heard the siren kick into high gear, screaming its warning as they drove off to the hospital.

"Now what?" I wondered aloud when the sound faded.

Inspector Lee scowled. "Now we figure out what happened."

I glanced over at Bonnie, who had finally turned from the doorway to rest her head on the counter of the juice bar.

Inspector Lee followed my gaze and frowned. "Guess I'll start with her." But before she could walk away, she noticed something over my shoulder, and I saw her lips quirk up. "Well, look who's here."

Turning, I saw Derek push the door open and walk toward me. I rushed to meet him halfway and threw my arms around him. It wasn't until he pulled me close that I realized how shaken I really was.

I snuggled in to bury my head against his strong chest. And felt completely safe.

"Darling," he murmured.

"I'm so glad you're here."

"So am I."

The man epitomized pure power and rugged masculinity. As I breathed in his scent, I wondered how I'd ever lived without him. Don't get me wrong. Aside from a silly obsession over blood, I was perfectly fine on my own. But now with Derek in my life, it was a joy to know I didn't always have to be. We made a great team.

Sure, I could have handled today's situation all by myself if I'd had to. And I certainly wasn't intimidated by the police. Not much anymore, anyway. When I'd first met Inspector Lee, I admit, she scared me a little. But not now. And the Rabbit Hole was one of my local comfort zones, so I was certainly able to fend for myself there. The fact that I'd walked in and found two unconscious people—one almost certainly dead—was something I should've been used to by now. But I wasn't, and I was pretty sure I never would be.

Still, I could've taken care of things on my own. But with Derek here, we would be able to be more involved in whatever sort of investigation might take place and not just stand on the periphery, wondering what was going on. Derek's prestigious background in British intelligence had given him instant cachet with the San Francisco homicide detectives from the very first time we'd met. And his international security business allowed him instant access to worldwide sources that the local police couldn't always obtain as quickly.

With a sigh, I reluctantly broke away from Derek, who nevertheless kept his arm slung casually around my shoulders.

He smiled and nodded at Inspector Lee. "Hello, Inspector."

"Commander," she said, with a note of respect in her voice. "Good to see you."

The police always showed respect for Derek, addressing him as "Commander," since that had been his rank in the British military.

"They just took Rabbit to the hospital," I explained. "He's still unconscious, but they think he'll recover."

"Good." Derek glanced down at the heavy shelving that lay on the floor at an awkward angle. "And the other person?"

I grimaced. "I'm pretty sure Joey is dead."

Derek turned back sharply. "Joey? The cobbler?"

I winced. "I'm sorry I sprang it on you just now, but yes. After we talked on the phone, the paramedics arrived and were able to lift the shelf. That's when I saw him."

He squeezed my shoulder. "I'm sorry, love. That must've been tough."

"It was awful." I forced away the memory of seeing Joey crushed beneath the shelves. And all that blood. "Poor Joey."

He turned to Inspector Lee. "Are you here to investigate a homicide?"

She stared down at the ten-foot-long, double-sided, heavy-duty steel shelving unit and shook her head. "I have no idea. I suppose it's possible that it fell over accidentally. Or someone might've helped it along. There's simply no way to be sure at the moment. But I plan to find out."

"It's definitely suspicious," I said. "I'm pretty strong, and I tried lifting it. It's got to weigh close to half a ton. It's not something that would just tip over. And it's not as if there was an earthquake this morning."

Derek's eyes narrowed in on the woman at the juice bar counter. "Is that Bonnie sitting over there?"

"Yes." I lowered my voice. "She was screaming for Joey a little while ago. Looks like she's worn herself out."

Derek glanced back at me, questions in his eyes. "Joey?"

I nodded. I could see he was curious, and I was right there with him. Bonnie hadn't reacted at all to her nephew's injuries, but she'd been hysterical over Joey. I definitely wanted to explore that little love connection.

"I think it's time I had a word with her," Inspector Lee said, and walked back to where Bonnie was still seated.

I glanced up at Derek. "Come on. I want to hear this."

"Naturally." He winked at me. "Let's try to be subtle, though."

I gave him a sideways look. "I'm always subtle."

"Of course you are, darling."

Narrowing my eyes at him, I tried to figure out if that was sarcasm or pure truth. But the love of my life could be pretty enigmatic when he wanted to be. He took my hand and we crossed over to the last aisle, then moved quietly toward the juice bar. I stopped about three feet from the end of the aisle, where neither Bonnie nor Inspector Lee could see us. From there, we could hear the two women conversing.

It wasn't like we were hiding. We were just being subtle, right?

For the next ten minutes, we listened as Inspector Lee quietly questioned Bonnie. She asked about the other residents in the building, and Bonnie sniffled a lot but answered every question. Then Lee posed the big one. "What's your relationship with this man, Joey?"

"I was his landlady and his friend," Bonnie said, sniffling a little harder.

"You're talking about him in the past tense."

"He's dead, isn't he?" She moaned loudly. "Oh God. He's dead."

Oh boy. Sounded like the hysteria was making a comeback.

"We don't know that yet." Inspector Lee waited a moment, then asked, "Did you two have a personal relationship?"

Another moan, then Bonnie wailed, "Yes! I loved him. He was the most talented, wonderful man I've ever been with."

"Talented?" Inspector Lee repeated. "You mean, as a shoe repairman?"

"Oh, he was that, yes." Bonnie took in a gulping sob,

then spoke again on a pain-filled wail that should have been able to peel paint. "But he was also the most glorious lover I've ever known. The man was *magic*. There's no one like him. And I've known my share, believe me."

"Oh, ick," I muttered, and tiptoed away. *Too much information,* I thought, trying not to cringe as I walked out of earshot. Derek followed, and at the far end of the aisle we stopped and stared at each other.

"So Bonnie was having an affair with Joey," I murmured.

"Apparently so." One corner of his mouth quirked. "Who knew?"

"Clearly not us," he said with a shrug of dissatisfaction—as though we should've been informed of every single thing that had ever occurred in our neighborhood.

I frowned. "Remember Terrence's reaction when Bonnie walked into the bookshop the other night?"

He pursed his lips in thought. "Yes. He seemed quite smitten with her."

"Exactly. I wonder if he knew about her affair with Joey."

Derek nodded, considering. "Jealousy is a lovely motive for murder."

"One of the classics." I sighed and shook my head. "I don't know why I'm suddenly questioning Terrence's motives. Sure, he might've had a crush on Bonnie. And yes, he does have a bit of a temper when it comes to arguing with Eddie. But other than that, he's pretty mild mannered, don't you think?"

"I do." Derek swept the edges of his suit jacket back and stuffed his hands into the pockets of his slacks. "The only thing he's ever seemed truly passionate about is his books."

The door to the shop opened and we both turned at the sound.

"Good God in heaven!" a man cried. "What in the world is going on in here?"

I blinked at the sound of that voice. "It's Terrence."

"Speak of the devil," Derek whispered, and grabbed my hand again. "Let's go."

We skirted around the end of the aisle and found Terrence gaping at one of the police officers who'd apparently circled around to the other Courtyard shops and was now back inside the Rabbit Hole. He stood with his arm extended to stop Terrence from advancing any farther into the store.

"Terrence," I said.

"Brooklyn! What are you doing here?"

"How about if we talk outside?" I said, not wanting to annoy this cop or Inspector Lee with too much chatting.

"But . . . but . . . what happened? What's this all about?" He craned his neck to see around the uniformed cop. "That isn't Bonnie, is it? Oh my God—it's her!" He surged forward, but the cop moved to stop him again, and Terrence staggered backward. Derek reached out to steady him.

"Easy there," I said, taking hold of his other arm.

Derek nudged Terrence toward the door. "Stepping outside is a good idea. Shall we?"

Terrence was so dazed that it was easy to lead him out to the courtyard. But once there, he protested. "I should go back inside. Bonnie might need me."

"She's fine," I assured him, pulling out a chair for him. "She's upset, of course, but she wasn't hurt. The police are interviewing her right now."

"Yes, the police." He slid down into the chair. "What are they doing here?"

I sat down next to him, zipping up my hoodie to guard against the chill. The morning sun hadn't made it over the walls and into the courtyard yet, so it was still cold. I checked my watch and saw that it was only eight o'clock. I felt as if I'd been in the middle of all this for hours.

After exchanging a quick glance with Derek, I folded my arms on the small bistro table and leaned in close. "There's been a terrible accident, Terrence. Joey was injured very badly and Rabbit was knocked unconscious. They've both been taken to the hospital."

"Hold on." He seemed confused. "Joey? Our Joey? Shoe repair Joey?"

"Yes."

Terrence looked from me to Derek and back again. "And—and Rabbit? He was hurt?"

"Yes. Rabbit is expected to recover."

"I saw the shelf toppled over," Terrence said, shaking his head as if he still couldn't believe it. "What happened? Was there an earthquake? I didn't feel it. Did you?"

"There was no earthquake that I know of."

He sat back in his chair, his face pale as he breathed in and out slowly and deeply, trying to come to grips with everything we'd just told him. But suddenly he sat up straight. "Wait. You said Rabbit is going to recover. What about Joey?"

Derek, still standing, put his hand on Terrence's shoulder in a consoling gesture. "We're not sure about Joey."

"Oh God." I watched Terrence's face crumple like the mask of tragedy as tears sprang to his eyes. "You're not sure, though, right?"

Derek glanced at me before looking back at Terrence in sympathy. "I am sorry, but I'm afraid it doesn't look good for Joey at all."

Instantly Terrence buried his head in his hands and his shoulders shook as he sobbed at the loss of his friend.

I felt my own eyes tear up as I watched him suffer. It was a fact that nobody cried alone when I was around, and this proved it once again. Derek knew it and came around the table to sit down and pat my knee.

I had to smile as I snuffled and dabbed at my eyes. "Thanks, love."

Before we could say another word, someone came sprinting through the courtyard, screaming, "Where is she?"

"Kitty?" Terrence said, scrambling to stand up. He blinked like a blind man, tears still coursing down his cheeks.

I turned and saw Kitty Barnes, the owner of the cute hat shop on the corner, her face red with rage. As she came closer, she teetered on her shiny black high heels and almost tripped on the flagstone pavers.

I jumped up from the table to help her. "Are you okay?"

"No, I'm not okay!" She whipped her arm away from my reach and managed to straighten herself up.

Shimmying a little, she yanked the hem of her tight red sheath back into place and fluffed her curly brunette hair until it surrounded her head like a dark, bouncy halo. She wore a thick fake-fur stole that wrapped around her shoulders but barely covered her arms. It looked like something out of a Doris Day movie from 1960, but it worked for Kitty. Despite being absurdly overdressed for any early-morning occasion I could imagine, Kitty was a pretty woman in her forties. Her adorable hat shop catered to some of the wealthiest, most refined women in town. I had no doubt that her original wardrobe was part of the draw.

But right now she looked a little demented. She swallowed a few times, clearly anxious, and possibly in need of a big glass of water. Her eyes were wide but unfocused. "Get out of my way, Brooklyn."

"But where are you going?"

"None of your business." She continued to fume like a petite angry bull as she glared about in all directions. "Where is she?"

Derek and I exchanged another quick frown, then looked back at Kitty. "Where is who?"

"Don't pretend you don't know."

"But I don't," I told her. "I just came over here for a cup of coffee. And then I found—"

"Fine," she retorted. "I'm looking for Bonnie. She's not in her apartment. Have you seen her?"

I really didn't like the look in Kitty's eyes, but my inherent honesty and natural urge to help had me blurting, "Yes, I have. She's in the Rabbit Hole. But she's busy right now."

"Busy?" she said, sneering. "Give me a break."

"No, really. She—"

"Just get out of my way," Kitty snapped. And with that, she pushed me hard.

Derek was out of his chair in an instant and grabbing her arm. "That's enough, Kitty."

Her eyes panned up at Derek towering over her and they widened even more. She took a meek half step backward and fluttered her eyelashes in his direction. "I didn't mean it."

So now she was flirting? From rage to flirtation in under ten seconds? The woman was a basket case. It was temporary, I hoped.

"Why don't you explain what's wrong?" Derek said. "Maybe we can help you."

Derek's calm, masculine presence seemed to mollify her, though not by much.

"How can you ask me what's wrong?" she wailed, and burst into tears, her snorts and sniffles effectively dampening her wrath. It seemed that this was my morning for hysterical women.

Finally, though, Kitty managed a deep breath and, with all the soggy fury she could muster, cried out, "That lying, murdering cow killed my boyfriend!"

Chapter 4

It took me a few seconds to mentally sort through the tears and the wrath to figure out what Kitty had just said.

"Wait," I said, still confused. "Who's your *boyfriend*?"

"Murdering cow?" Terrence whispered, moving his head back and forth in denial. "What kind of talk is that?"

"You heard me," Kitty muttered through gritted teeth.

"Do you mean Bonnie?" he said, still befuddled. "But she wouldn't hurt a fly."

"Oh, get a life, Terrence." Kitty gave her hair an imperious shake. "You're so flippin' naive."

I took a step back. I'd never seen her like this, so harsh and out of control. The look in her eyes had me wondering if this was the *real* Kitty who'd been hiding beneath the surface of the woman I thought I knew. Maybe it was a common occurrence for Kitty to rant, but I wouldn't have thought so. Of course, I'd never been an insider at the Courtyard. Just a frequent visitor. Still, this was downright bizarre. And Terrence seemed to agree with me. And he was definitely an insider.

So now I had to wonder if Joey had been having affairs with both Bonnie and Kitty behind their backs. Was that how he'd gotten himself buried under a thousand pounds of stainless steel? But that would mean that either Bonnie or Kitty would have had to push the massive thing over by herself. And that was highly unlikely. So if somehow one of them had managed to do so, she would've needed some seriously heavy-duty equipment or the help of some really strong friends. Or maybe the two of them had worked together to take out the man neither of them could trust. Either way, that would have meant that Joey's death was premeditated murder.

And that possibility almost knocked the breath out of me. Could I be staring at a murderer? Kitty? But would she be shouting out accusations if she was the actual killer? I would think she'd be keeping quiet as a mouse, not wanting to bring attention to herself. So why was Kitty loudly hurling accusations of murder in Bonnie's direction?

Kitty's hat shop had been a delightful mainstay of the Courtyard for as long as I'd been living in the neighborhood. So that meant that Kitty and Bonnie had to have known each other for at least five years, probably longer. I imagined the two women had been friends once upon a time. They were similar types—flamboyant, flirtatious, attractive—and were both around the same age. On the other hand, maybe all of that similarity had bred contempt, to paraphrase the old saying. Judging from

Kitty's attitude at the moment, they were definitely not friends anymore. More like jealous rivals.

But that didn't mean that either of the women had done anything to hurt or kill Joey.

"Look, Kitty," I began, anxious to get the full story. "Why don't you—"

"Why don't you *buzz off*, Brooklyn?" she shot back, glaring at me so hotly it should have set my hair on fire. "Why don't you all buzz off?"

"Okay, then." I retreated a few steps and had a sudden wish for a rope of garlic and a cross to hold up in front of me for protection.

Terrence looked affronted, but Kitty didn't seem to care. Without warning, she whirled around and made a run for the Rabbit Hole door twenty feet away, yanking open the door before anyone could stop her.

Taking one step inside, she came to an immediate halt. "What in the heck happened here?"

I was watching and saw the annoyance on Inspector Lee's face. "Claymore," she called to the policeman guarding the entry to the store. "Why isn't that door locked? I don't want any civilians in here contaminating the scene."

"No, let me stay!" Kitty cried. Her fury faded away, turning to distress as she pointed at Bonnie. "Arrest her. She's a murderer."

From my spot at the doorway, I could see Bonnie finally focusing on the hubbub going on across the store. "Kitty, what're you doing here? What are you talking about?"

"Admit it, Bonnie," Kitty shouted. "You murdered Joey."

Bonnie's face turned red, but her voice was remarkably calm. "Be quiet, Kitty. You don't know what you're talking about. The shelves fell down on top of him. It was a tragic accident."

Inspector Lee turned and pointed at Bonnie. "You. Be quiet. Stay here. I'll be back." Lee slid off the stool and jogged around the periphery of the shop over to the front door, where Kitty stood waiting. With a tight smile, Inspector Lee held up her badge and introduced herself, then said, "What's your name and why are you here?"

Once again, Kitty backed down in the face of authority. "I—I'm Kitty Barnes. I own the hat shop a few doors over. I was looking for Bonnie."

Inspector Lee gave her a long, considering look. "I'm just finishing up with Ms. Carson, but then I'd like to talk to you, Ms. Barnes. Please wait outside until I call you."

Kitty wouldn't give up that easily, though. "But . . . did she already confess?"

Lee tilted her head, studying Kitty. "That's not a question I'm going to answer. But let me ask you, are you here to confess to something?"

Her eyes widened. "Me? N-no!"

"Okay, then," Lee said reasonably. "Wait outside until I'm ready for you."

Kitty's shoulders slumped as she turned and headed back outside to join Terrence at the table, despite the fact that Terrence didn't look too happy to have her back. Derek and I slipped past Kitty and moved into the shop while the inspector wasn't looking. I closed the door behind us. I thought it was a pretty bold move, what with the police watching, but Derek acted as if we were completely entitled to hang around. I guess that was what happened when you were a tall, dark, and dangerous former British secret agent. No one had ever asked him to leave anywhere. If they had, he wouldn't have gone anyway.

But since I'd been first on the scene that morning, and since Inspector Lee hadn't said anything specific like *"Get out of here!"* I figured I would stick around, too, until they kicked me out.

Inspector Lee hustled back to the juice bar and continued questioning Bonnie.

I turned to speak to Derek and realized he wasn't there. "Derek?"

I knew he hadn't left the shop, so I walked to the short aisle at the end of the store and peered down the other two aisles. I found him along the far wall, studying the shelving units that were still standing.

"What are you looking for?" I asked.

"I'm curious," he murmured, then knelt down and hunched over to take a good look at the bottom of the shelf where it met the floor. He got up and walked farther down the aisle, again kneeling down and checking along the bottom of the shelving unit. Standing, he glanced around. Walking over to the far corner, he reached into his pocket and pulled out his white linen handkerchief. Then he extended his arm into the narrow space between the two shelving units and pulled out something that resembled an extra-long pry bar or tire iron. He held on to it, using the handkerchief. Was he concerned that it was dirty, or was he worried about getting his fingerprints on it? I couldn't say, but the tool he was holding looked hefty, made from either steel or cast iron. It was about three feet long, with one end bent and flattened slightly to form a small square.

"What is that?" I said it softly, not wanting to alert Inspector Lee.

"Watch."

He took the tool and inserted the flat square end into a small square hole he'd found at the bottom of the steel shelving unit. It fit perfectly. Then, using the tool as a lever, he pushed down on the longer end and was able to lift the entire shelving unit.

I actually felt my eyes widen and my jaw drop. Derek had just discovered exactly how the shelf had been tipped over. And if it was that easy, Kitty or Bonnie *could* have done it on her own.

"Oh my God," I whispered, amazed that he'd figured it out.

"Exactly," he said. "It's a fulcrum." He eased the shelving unit down until it was flush with the floor again and walked back to the cubbyhole where he'd found the pry bar. Reaching into the space again, he pulled out a thin metal rack with casters attached to it.

"You see, love?" he said. "You lift the shelf with the fulcrum and slide these rollers underneath. Then you can move the entire unit anywhere you want."

I grinned in amazement. "You could reconfigure the entire store if you wanted to."

"Yes, or you could simply lift the one unit high enough with the fulcrum until you're able to push the shelves over quite easily." He simulated the movement. "And hundreds of pounds of metal shelving, along with the weight of whatever they contain, can be made to fall over."

I reached out and, using Derek's handkerchief, took

hold of the pry bar, feeling its heft and testing its strength. "I can't see Rabbit doing something like this to Joey, so it had to be someone else. Someone other than Rabbit who knew the way to move the shelves around."

"Indeed. I think it's safe to say that the shelves did not fall by accident."

Even though I'd been edging closer and closer to that possibility all morning, I was still troubled by the realization. Gazing up at Derek, I nodded glumly. "Joey was murdered."

A few minutes later, Inspector Lee escorted Bonnie outside to the courtyard. Derek and I watched from the doorway as Lee walked with the woman over to the staircase that led to her top-floor apartment. I couldn't hear the inspector's exact words, but she was pointing upstairs, and it was clear to me that she was advising Bonnie to stay home for a while and avoid speaking about the incident to anyone else.

On her way back to the Rabbit Hole, she stopped at the table where Kitty was sitting with Terrence. Thankfully for my nosy nature, we were close enough to overhear.

"Ready to talk to me?" Lee asked.

Kitty looked terrified. "I guess so."

Terrence took a hint and stood. "I've got to get back to my store."

"Which one is yours?" Lee asked.

"The bookshop."

"Ah." At the mention of books, Lee glanced my way. "I might stop by later and look around."

"You're welcome anytime."

Derek and I stepped out of the way and Lee ushered Kitty into the Rabbit Hole. Apparently the juice bar functioned as an effective interrogation space.

"Why don't you wait for me over by the juice bar counter?" Lee said. "I'll just be a minute."

Kitty complied, and when she was out of earshot, Lee turned and looked at me. "I can tell by the way you're hopping around that you've got something to tell me. What is it?"

"I don't hop." I turned to Derek. "Am I hopping?"

Derek bit back a smile. "I believe Inspector Lee is teasing you."

"Sure, yeah," Lee said, smirking. "Just teasing."

I sighed. "Go ahead and mock me. I can take it."

"I wouldn't do it if you couldn't," she said, giving my arm a friendly elbow nudge.

I leaned in close and said, "You'll be the one hopping when you see what Derek discovered."

She glanced at Derek. "Yeah?" He nodded, and she said, "Let's see it."

We led the way over to the last aisle and Derek demonstrated what he'd found.

"Are you kidding me?" She shook her head in dismay. "I've got to try that."

Still using the handkerchief to avoid adding our own fingerprints to whatever the police might find on the pry bar, Derek handed it to her. She tried it herself, fitting the square end into the hole, then pressing down on the longer end and managing to lift the entire shelving unit several inches off the floor.

So a woman could've done it after all, I thought again, as Lee set the unit down gently.

She stared at the pry bar for a long moment. "I wonder how many people know how these things work."

"Not that many, I'd guess," Derek said.

She sighed and shook her head. "I don't like this one bit."

Derek folded his arms across his chest. "Nor do I."

She turned to me, her frown marring the smooth skin of her forehead. "I can hardly believe I'm saying this, but, Brooklyn, it looks like you've walked into another murder."

I was no happier about it than she was. "I'm afraid that's what it looks like."

She shook her head, muttering, "You're a magnet, I swear."

"I'm really not," I insisted.

"Could've fooled me." Inspector Lee sighed a little. "Before I met you, my life was far less interesting."

"Yay me?" I tried a half smile, which she returned . . . eventually.

"You're hard work, Brooklyn."

I knew she was kidding, sort of, but I didn't need it right now. I already felt completely guilty just for walking in and finding Joey and Rabbit in the first place. Which was ridiculous when you thought about it. It wasn't as if my mere presence had caused the shelving unit to fall and crash onto Joey. And I certainly hadn't bashed Rabbit in the head. But still, here I was—and here was another murder.

Derek draped his arm over my shoulders and squeezed lightly. "We're just lucky she uses her power for good, Inspector."

Lee snorted. "You're right. Make sure it stays that way."

I shrugged helplessly. "You know, it's not like I wander around town *looking* for dead people. In fact, if I could change one thing about myself, it would be this death-magnet thing."

"I know, kiddo," Lee said, reaching out to squeeze my arm in understanding, surprising the heck out of me. After a silent moment of commiseration, she pulled back and flexed her arm muscles as a way of shaking off whatever mood she seemed to be edging toward. "Better get things rolling."

We followed her to the end of the aisle and back over to the mass of twisted steel and metal still piled in a heap in the middle of the shop.

Lee spied the two cops who were standing at attention by the door, awaiting further instructions.

"Officers," she said, holding up the pry bar like a championship trophy, "we've got ourselves a crime scene."

The cops immediately went to work, effectively scaling off the shop with yellow crime scene tape outside and photographing and marking spots inside wherever there was any sort of evidence or a trace of blood. The long pry bar tool was carefully wrapped in plastic and tucked inside the officers' police car trunk for safety's sake, in the slim hope that they might find fingerprints that didn't belong there.

As Inspector Lee joined Kitty over at the juice bar, Derek walked me out to the courtyard. "I should get back, but I hate to leave you here alone."

"I'll be fine," I said. "The police are going to kick me out any minute anyway."

"Call me when you get home."

"I will."

His eyes narrowed on me. "You aren't going to sneak upstairs and search Joey's apartment, are you?"

I smiled. Was there anything better than having the man you loved know you so well? "Not without you."

"That's my girl," he said with a half grin as he wrapped me in a tight hug. "Call me if anything exciting happens."

"Absolutely." I watched him walk away. Then I glanced around, wondering if I should just go home and forget everything that had happened that morning. But I wasn't quite ready to leave. Or forget. Instead, I wandered over to the Beanery to finally get my caffe latte. While I was waiting in the short line, my mind wandered back to the Rabbit Hole and Inspector Lee. I wondered what stories Kitty was spinning for her. If her earlier rant was any indication, the hat shop owner was probably filling Lee's ears with sordid tales of Bonnie's murderous inclinations. Which seemed ridiculous, but who knew? I thought the two women were friends, but Kitty had surprised the heck out of me. So maybe Bonnie was a killer. Inspector Lee had proven that a woman could lift one of those massive shelves. And Bonnie had admitted to being in love with Joey. So had Kitty, for that matter.

Again, I wondered if maybe Joey had done something to drive one of them insane. But then, they had both been screaming in pain at the realization that he might be dead. I couldn't believe one of them was faking their emotions. So who was the villain in this picture? Maybe no one. No, scratch that. There was a bad guy, and that person—whoever it was—had killed Joey. I just had no clue who that might have been.

My head was spinning in six different directions.

I stood in the courtyard sipping my latte, deciding whether to go home or back inside the Rabbit Hole to see if I could get some info on Kitty. At that moment, one of the cops walked across the courtyard and stopped in front of Joey's shoe repair shop. He turned and stood guard, and I realized that it made perfect sense. The police would want to do a complete search of Joey's place of business and his home to see if they could find any evidence that might indicate why he had been killed. It was absolutely reasonable of them to do so.

Except that my shoes were inside that shop!

Inside, I was screaming, *Noooooo!* I needed to get my shoes before they sealed the place off completely!

As I was pacing and watching and wondering what to do, Inspector Lee walked out of the Rabbit Hole with Kitty, who looked a little pale around the edges but still alive.

"Please be sure to call me if you remember anything else," Lee said, handing Kitty her business card.

"I will," Kitty assured her, and teetered off to her hat shop. I would have to remember to stop by later to commiserate with her—if she didn't close down the shop and hide out in her room the rest of the day. And if she wasn't on another one of her weird, scary rants.

"Brooklyn," Lee said. "What are you still doing here?"

I took a few deep breaths to calm myself as I approached her. "I went to get myself a latte and then remembered something. I really need your help." It wasn't easy to admit it, but I was desperate.

She grinned. "It'll cost you."

"Very funny." I tried to smile. "No, really, I need a favor."

"Did you think I was being funny?"

Even though she was smiling, I started to glare at her. That probably wasn't a good idea, even though we were friends. She did carry a gun, after all. But like I said, I was desperate.

She seemed to catch my vibe and shrugged. "Okay, okay. Chill out. What can I do for you?"

"I need my shoes," I said in a nervous rush. "I left them with Joey yesterday. He said he'd fix the heel right away and I'd be able to pick them up today."

"Seriously?" She barked out a laugh. "You're wasting my time over a shoe?"

"I'm not. Well." I chuckled ruefully. "Okay, maybe I am, but I can't help it. I'm freaking out a little."

"What's the big deal? You've got plenty of shoes."

I glanced down at my one good pair of sneakers. "Yeah, not really. The thing is, Derek's parents are coming to town this weekend and those shoes go with every outfit I own. I love them. They feel good and look good."

"Okay, but still . . . This is a crime scene."

"I know. But my shoes didn't kill Joey."

She frowned.

"Look, you might not understand my plight, because you obviously know how to shop for clothes and you always look fantastic. I'll bet you have shoes to match every outfit. Don't you?" I shook my head. It was a mystery how some women just knew how to do this stuff. I should've learned. I even had sisters who were really good at it, but I'd never bothered to watch how they did it. "Never mind. Look, shopping is a scary, depressing experience for me. I can't do it. And shoe shopping?

Forget it." I waved my hands in surrender. "I'm begging you. I'll do anything you say. Just please, *please* let me get my shoes out of there."

She folded her arms across her chest and breathed expansively. "I feel so powerful right now."

I rolled my eyes. "You're such a pain."

She stared hard at me. "Hey, you're not going to cry, are you?"

I began to laugh. "No, I'm not going to cry! Unless I can't get my shoes. Then watch me."

"Okay, calm down."

"I'm perfectly calm. Just . . . let's do this."

She smirked. "You can get awfully pushy when you're desperate."

I smiled. "You ain't seen nothing yet."

"Now I'm scared. Okay, let's go check this place out." She strolled across the courtyard, with me following close behind.

The cop standing in front of the door to Joey's shop handed her a key. I figured he must have gotten the key from Bonnie.

"Thanks, Peterson."

She unlocked the door and pushed it open, then stood before the threshold staring into the shop. There were no lights on inside, and I couldn't see past her.

She turned to look at me. "When were you last here?"

"Yesterday."

"So you might recognize if something's out of place?"

"Maybe. Joey was pretty organized for a shoe repair guy." I'd been inside some scary shoe repair places, with all their funky smells and shoe polish stains in odd spots, so when I moved here I was glad to find Joey's shop, which was always relatively neat and clean compared with those others.

"Okay, here's what we're going to do," she said. "I'm going to move out of the way, and I want you to stand right here where I'm standing and tell me if anything looks wrong to you."

The careful tone of her voice was a warning that something might not be quite right, so I kept that in mind as she moved aside to give me room to survey Joey's store.

"He kept it really clean," I muttered, shoving my hands into the pockets of my vest. "I'm not sure what you want me to see." But I stepped up to the doorway and glanced around the dark shop, just as she'd asked.

Everyone knew that shoe repair could be a messy, downright dirty business, but Joey had always been meticulous with his products, organizing them on the Peg-Board on the wall to the left of the cash register so his customers could take their time browsing through them. Shoelaces, leather conditioner and all shades of shoe polish, various types of arch supports and heel cushions, hardware-replacement pieces for belts and suitcases.

These were scattered all over the floor.

Joey had always lined his shoes up neatly on the front counter for customers to pick up. Now they were tossed everywhere. It couldn't have been an accident, any more than Rabbit's fallen shelving unit had been an accident.

"Well?" Inspector Lee asked. "What is it, Brooklyn? Anything look wrong to you?"

I felt sick to my stomach. "Of course it looks wrong. Somebody's been in here and they've torn the place apart."

Chapter 5

"Sorry I put you through that," Inspector Lee said quietly, taking my arm and leading me a few feet away from the view of the mess. "It was obvious the place had been tossed, but I needed to see your reaction when you saw it. And you told me exactly what I wanted to hear. That this is definitely not a normal situation."

"Definitely not normal," I muttered, clutching my vest closer.

"Good to know."

"I guess I could've been one of the last people to see him in his shop yesterday." Oh, I didn't like that thought. What had happened after I'd left Joey? Who had been here? Destroyed the shop? Why?

"That's entirely possible." Inspector Lee looked me in the eye. "So I'm glad you were willing to take a look and corroborate what I was thinking."

"I'm always happy to help." But I felt myself starting to shake, and I rubbed my arms in a futile attempt to warm up. One thing was clear to me. I would never be able to handle being a police detective. Inspector Lee was calm and cool, and I was a mess just being a bystander. Seeing Joey's shop torn apart like that was breaking my heart.

Inspector Lee called Officer Peterson over. "Do me a favor and call SF General. Ask about the patient that was just brought in. His name is . . . Wait." She pulled out her notepad and flipped the pages. "Joseph Falco."

"Yes, ma'am."

"And while you've got them on the phone, ask about the status of the other guy they took out of here. Will Rabbit. Thanks."

"Yes, ma'am."

The officer jogged off to make the phone call, and I stood there for a moment, wallowing in the misery of knowing I had never heard Joey's last name before. Falco. Joey Falco. I should have known that much. Sure, it wasn't as if we were close personal friends, but I saw him around regularly and I liked him. It would've been nice to know that one small detail about his life. And I suddenly thought of all the other people in my daily life who were a part of my world and yet strangers, too. Grocers, waiters, the mailman . . .

The sun had made it over the eastern edge of the building and rays of light caused the leaves of the aspen and olive trees to shimmer in the soft breeze. Grateful, I turned my face up to feel the radiant warmth. After a moment, I glanced around at all the police activity and felt out of place for the first time. There was nothing for me to do here and no doubt soon Inspector Lee would tell me I was in the way. And I was ready to go home and get to work.

I glanced at my watch. "I'd better get going."

"What about your shoes?" Lee asked.

I gasped in shock. "Oh, wow."

"You forgot all about them, didn't you?"

"Completely." But who could blame me? First, there was Joey and Rabbit, and then the shoe repair shop looking like rage-filled elves had run amok. It's a wonder I could remember anything. "Thanks for reminding me. I think seeing Joey's shop all messed up must've caused my brain to short-circuit."

"Yup," she said, nodding. "Happens all the time. You get wrapped up in something bigger than yourself and you forget about your own troubles. It shows that you're a good person."

I stared at her in surprise. "Thank you. That is really sweet."

"Yeah, well." She chuckled. "Let's not get too sloppy here."

"Too late," I told her. "Now I know you like me."

"Okay." The inspector rolled her eyes for dramatic effect. "What do your shoes look like?"

How embarrassing. My heels weren't exactly Jimmy Choos, but they were mine and they went with everything. With a sheepish laugh, I said, "Burgundy pumps, two-inch heels. Not exactly high fashion, but I think they're pretty."

"Come on. Let's see if we can find them."

We walked back to the edge of the door and gazed inside. Lee asked, "Do you see them?"

It was clear that Inspector Lee was trying to avoid having either of us step inside the shop. That was fine with me since I didn't want my footprints all over the crime scene. Looking for my particular shoes in the pandemonium of upended footwear and other items shouldn't have been easy. Luckily, though, I caught a break. I scanned the surface of the floor, spied my burgundy shoes, and pointed them out to Inspector Lee.

"Okay, I see them," she said, stepping back and closing the door. "Now here's the deal. I can't just walk in and pick up your shoes. I've got to let the crime scene guys get in there first."

She must have noted my disappointment because she quickly added, "But don't worry. I'll talk to them and work it out. Once they give the okay, I'll bring your shoes over. Hopefully it'll be this afternoon, but tomorrow at the latest. And I'll warn you: Don't be too shocked if they're covered in fingerprint dust."

"I don't mind cleaning them at all. I'm sorry you're going to so much trouble for a pair of shoes—but I'm pitifully grateful you're doing it."

Shrugging, she said, "I'm a sucker for a sad shoe story."

I laughed and she smiled back.

"Okay, truth be told, I'm simply a wonderful person."

"Yes, you are." I reached out and gave her a hug. "Thank you."

"No problem." She laughed shortly. "Besides, now you owe me."

Back home after spending all morning at the crime scene, I felt my emotions still churning. I knew from experience that the best way to calm down was to get right to work. I quickly prepped for more papermaking by first filling the plastic tub with water and carefully carrying it over to my workshop counter.

Next, I checked that the twenty playing cards I'd

made the day before were completely dry. I stacked them all and placed them between two felt squares. Then I slipped the stack between two smooth pieces of wood and slid the entire bundle into the book press.

Ordinarily, I wouldn't have used the book press to straighten out a piece of handmade paper, because I loved all the uneven ripples and waves that happened during the drying process. But since I was making a full set of playing cards, I wanted them to fit together relatively smoothly inside the matchbox cover. So a light pressing would help. They would still retain that deckle-edged, slightly uneven look of handmade paper, and I hoped the people at BABA would love that offbeat, artsy feeling as much as I did.

I spent the rest of the day with my playing cards, having fun tearing up white envelopes into bits and tossing them into the blender, filling it with water, and adding snippets of flowers and leaves and grass, along with a quick shake of glitter, and then blending it all together until it was nice and creamy.

It was five o'clock and I had almost completed all the cards in the suit of hearts when the security phone rang, indicating there was someone downstairs at the door to the building. I realized I'd been completely wrapped up in my own little papermaking world, but after the traumatic morning I'd gone through, it had felt good to zone out all day. But now I raced to the kitchen to answer the phone, hoping it would be Inspector Lee with more news from the Courtyard—and my shoes.

In the kitchen, I stared at the newly installed computer screen and picked up the phone.

"Hi, Janice," I said, smiling. It still felt a little odd to call her that, especially since I'd spent all morning at a crime scene where she was in full "Inspector Lee" mode. But I figured since she was bringing me my beloved shoes, we could transition over to friendship territory.

"Hey, Brooklyn. I've got your shoes," Lee said.

"That's great. I'll buzz you in." I pressed the pound key to allow her into the building and watched her disappear from the screen. As soon as I saw the green light on the edge of the screen indicating that she was inside the building and the door was safely locked behind her, I returned to my workshop to finish up for the day.

We had recently gone through another upgrade in our security measures after a group of horrible people was able to get into our apartment. They'd killed a guest of ours and threatened Derek and me and some of our friends. It was one of the worst experiences of my life, and I never wanted to go through that again. So far, this sophisticated new system was working well. And on the off chance that I noticed someone trying to sneak into the building behind Inspector Lee, I would simply press the asterisk key and an earsplitting alarm would go off by the front door. It also transmitted a signal to the local police department.

I knew it would take a few minutes for the elevator to climb to the sixth floor, so I had time to pour out the tub of water, clean the blender, and wash my hands.

As I walked into the living room, the front door opened and Inspector Lee walked in with Derek trailing right behind her. They both carried briefcases, although Inspector Lee's was more along the lines of a smart leather tote bag. The woman had the best taste in everything.

"Darling," Derek said, "look who I found in our elevator."

"Excellent timing," Lee said with a smile.

I chuckled as I walked over and gave Derek a kiss. "I didn't know you were coming home so early."

"I was at a meeting downtown and decided to come home instead of going back to the office."

"I'm so glad."

"Me, too," he said, and kissed me back. Then he turned to our guest. "Inspector, are you off duty? Would you care for a glass of wine?"

"I am, and I would, thanks." She looked from Derek to me and back again. "I'm glad you're here, Commander. I wanted to talk to both of you, and the news would probably be better told over a glass of wine."

I exchanged a glance with Derek. What was this all about?

"I'll put my things down and join you in a moment."

"I'll pour the wine," I said, walking into the kitchen. "Let's sit here at the bar."

The kitchen and dining rooms were separated by a wide counter with stools on either side. Inspector Lee— Janice—sat on the dining room side while I went to the kitchen cabinet to find wineglasses.

She set her tote bag on the floor and pulled out a smaller plastic bag and held it up for me to see. "I've got your shoes. I'll leave them right here." She set the bag down on the floor by her tote bag.

"Thank you so much. You have no idea how grateful I am."

"I'm getting the picture."

"Seriously, you're a lifesaver."

"I appreciate your gratitude, but, all joking aside, we need to have a long talk."

I was instantly on guard. "What?"

"Come on, Brooklyn." She snorted and shook her head sadly. "Having only one pair of shoes for every occasion is ludicrous. As a woman I'm offended by the very idea."

"I know." I uncorked a bottle of pinot noir and poured the first glass. "Robin and my sisters have said the same thing to me. But I'm not completely hopeless. I mean, I have other shoes—really pretty ones—but these are so comfortable. And besides, I might've mentioned that I suck at shopping."

"You just need a few lessons from an expert."

"Believe me, Robin's tried. But if you're willing to give it a shot, I would love it." I grinned. "I should warn you, though—I've gone shopping with Robin and Alex and all of my sisters, and the lessons just don't stick. Apparently I'm unteachable."

Robin was my oldest friend, who had recently married my brother Austin. She had a great sense of style that somehow had never been transferred over to me. And Alex was my neighbor who always looked fabulous. Whenever I needed wardrobe help, I ran down the hall for guidance from her.

Janice's eyes narrowed with intent. "I'll make it stick."

Only slightly alarmed, I nodded. If anyone could, it would be Janice Lee. "I believe you."

Derek walked in just then, pulled a box of crackers from the pantry, and filled a small bowl. Then he took a wedge of Brie from the refrigerator, set it on a plate, and placed cheese and crackers on the counter.

"Hey, thanks," Janice said with a surprised smile. "This is nice."

He sat down next to me and held up his glass. "Cheers." We all clinked our glasses and took sips.

"Janice was able to bring my shoes back," I said, making small talk before we got down to the real conversation I wanted to have.

"He had already fixed them?" he asked.

"Oh." I frowned at Janice. "I didn't think to look at them."

"They looked fixed to me," she said. "And all polished up, too. See for yourself." She reached for the bag and handed it to me.

I pulled the shoes from the bag and was thrilled to see that they were free of fingerprint powder. I took a moment to admire them, pressing on the heel to make sure it was firmly back in place. "Wow, he did a great job."

"Speaking of our cobbler," Derek murmured, "how is he doing?"

I gasped. "I'm so sorry I didn't ask sooner. Is Joey going to be all right?" I couldn't believe I hadn't thought to ask about Joey first thing. It really had been a long day for me.

"Yeah, about that," Janice muttered.

I could tell from her expression that the news wasn't good. I shouldn't have been surprised. Joey had looked near death when I first saw him after the paramedics had pulled the shelf off of him. And hadn't we all been wondering who had "murdered" Joey earlier?

Janice stroked her fingertips against the wineglass. "We did hear from the hospital."

I braced myself. "And?"

"Your friend died on the way there."

I took a deep breath. "That's just so awful." Even though I'd suspected it all along, it was difficult to hear it confirmed beyond a doubt. "I'm sorry. He was a sweet guy."

"That's what everybody said," Janice said.

We sat silently for a few seconds. Then Derek asked, "What about Will?"

"The news is better for Will Rabbit," she said, and took another sip of her wine. "He's still unconscious, but they expect him to come out of it in the next day or two. They don't think there will be any lasting damage, but time will tell."

Derek took my hand in his and squeezed in sympathy. "Thank you for letting us know, Inspector."

"You're welcome." She shook her head. "Worst part of my job is informing people of a death."

"I'm sorry you had to deliver the bad news," I said. "Have you been at the Courtyard all day?"

"Mostly, yeah." She blew out a breath as if relieved to have the hard part of the conversation finished. "It took a while to interview all the shopkeepers. I ran over to the hospital to check on our unconscious victim on the off chance that he'd be able to make a statement. No such luck, but maybe tomorrow. Anyway, then I hustled myself back to the Courtyard to keep tabs on the crime scene guys."

"You've been busy," I said.

"It's been a full day," she agreed.

"That brings up a question I meant to ask earlier," Derek said. "Are you still working with Inspector Jaglom?"

"Absolutely. Nate took a few days off to visit his son

at college." She shook her head as she sipped her wine. "That kid grew up too fast. Last thing I remember, he was playing Little League baseball."

I nodded. "That's how it is with my nieces and nephews."

"I'm glad to hear you're still a team," Derek said. "Do send him our best."

"He gets back tonight, so you might see him lurking around in the next day or so."

"Hope so," I said. Nathan Jaglom had been Inspector Lee's partner since the very first time we met them. He was a decade older than Janice, but a lovely man in a rumpled, comfortable sort of way. Quite the contrast to his fashionable partner, but they made it work.

After another sip of wine, Janice said, "Hey, that Courtyard is a really nice place. I never knew all those shops were in there."

"It's great, isn't it?" I said. "I just hate that it's now the scene of an awful tragedy. It's always been a wonderful place to hang out."

"It will be again," she assured me, sounding like the voice of experience. "I figured you haunt that bookstore pretty regularly."

"Like every day," I said, pleased that she'd gone into the bookstore. "They've got a great mix of old and new books, plus a lot of unique gifts and cards."

"I know." She suppressed a smile. "I might've picked up a few things while I was between interviews."

"Ah, I'm impressed." I really was enjoying getting to know Janice Lee in her off-duty persona. "So you truly are a good shopper."

"Told you." She shrugged as she took a bite of a cracker. "I'm not ashamed to admit it."

"Oh, no—you should be proud," I said, laughing. "It's a gift—believe me."

Derek coughed politely, clearly ready to change the subject. "I was wondering, Inspector—and I don't mean to suggest that we insinuate ourselves into your case. But the fact is, we live right across the street from your crime scene. Is there anything we can do for you from this vantage point? We're happy to offer our services."

I knew that if I'd been the one suggesting something like that, Janice Lee would have laughed me out of my own house. But coming from Derek, with his impressive background and lovely British accent, the offer had some gravitas. She considered for a long moment as she spread cheese onto her cracker.

"Let me think about it."

"Of course."

"I will say," she said, "that based on what I was told in several interviews today, I've arranged to have a patrol car drive by every two hours for the next few days. And of course I'll be coming back in the next day or so to check up on a few details. But other than that, I'm not sure what else the police can do to keep a closer eye on the place. I did suggest to the owner of the building that she hire a private security company."

And coincidentally, Derek owns an internationally renowned private security agency, I thought, but didn't say aloud.

We waited while she bit into the cracker and chewed. A few seconds later she continued. "I'm not about to advocate your involvement, but naturally, if you were to glance out the window and see something odd or questionable, I would appreciate a phone call."

"Naturally," Derek said. "And we do shop at the Courtyard several times a week, so we'll be happy to report anything out of the ordinary that we see or hear."

She nodded. "The SFPD appreciates your cooperation."

My gaze darted back and forth from Janice to Derek. They were clearly talking in code and I wouldn't have been surprised to hear later that she had just hired Derek to run interference for her on this case. It had happened before. But it made me smile to see them talking normally on one level while the subtext of their conversation was happening on a whole other level. It was nice that they spoke the same subliminal language—most of which I rarely understood—and I knew I'd get a full report from Derek as soon as Janice left.

I asked, "Did you talk to anyone who mentioned the graffiti attack and the spate of minor vandalism that's been going on around here lately?"

Janice looked frustrated. "I finally got wind of it, and that's when I called for the patrol. But it took a while. Those first two women I interviewed—after I got them to stop ranting and howling—just wanted to blame each other for what had happened. And a few of the other shopkeepers had similar opinions, frankly. But I finally talked to some folks who gave me the bigger picture of what's been going on. I may have to go outside the Courtyard to get to the truth."

"So today's crimes might actually center on something bigger in scope than mere jealousy or rivalry," Derek murmured.

She took a slow sip of wine. "It's too early to know anything for sure yet, but it's possible."

"At least it can't be blamed on a book this time," I muttered.

Janice laughed. "Not likely."

I stared into my wineglass. "When I first saw the damage this morning, I thought maybe Joey and Rabbit had walked in on a burglary. I couldn't think of any other reason they would both be out cold on the floor. They're both so nice. They couldn't have been fighting each other. Nothing made sense."

"A burglar would've had to have an intimate knowledge of how to move grocery shelving around," Derek said.

"That's the part that smells fishy," I said, wrinkling my nose. "I mean, how many people know that kind of stuff?"

Janice's gaze moved from Derek to me. "So you're thinking it has to be someone from the Courtyard."

"Well, yes," Derek said. "It's reasonable to assume that it would be someone with a good grasp of Will Rabbit's store layout and the means by which to move the shelves around. The person would also need to know Will's work hours, as well as Joey's schedule." Derek was talking to Janice, but he was frowning at me. "Brooklyn, what are you thinking?"

My "smelling fishy" line had jogged something in my memory and I had to speak up. "With everything that was going on, I forgot to mention this earlier."

Janice set down her wineglass. "Okay, something tells me I won't like what you're about to say."

"It might be important, and I really did plan to tell you earlier, but I sort of forgot until this very minute."

She sighed in resignation. "Go ahead."

I could feel my cheeks heating up, but I continued on. "When I first arrived at the shop and I was standing there, looking at that pile of steel shelving, I smelled perfume. It was Bonnie's scent. It's easily recognizable."

"Yes, it is," Derek muttered.

I nodded. "Right. And the first thing that occurred to me was that Bonnie was the person lying under the wreckage. But then I saw that the feet definitely belonged to a man, so I knew it couldn't have been her."

Janice's eyes narrowed as she thought it through. "So, if I'm hearing you correctly, you're saying that either Joey was wearing women's perfume or he had been with Bonnie just prior to walking into the Rabbit Hole."

"I'm inclined to go with the second option," Derek said.

"Me, too," I said, nodding. "Trust me, Joey is not the type to wear ladies' perfume."

Derek smiled wryly. "No, he isn't."

"And then, when Bonnie walked in wearing her sexy bathrobe and started screaming and wailing over Joey, I smelled the perfume again, and it suddenly made sense."

"She does wear quite a lot, and it's a heavy, unmistakable scent," Derek said, again corroborating my point.

I blinked and sat up straight. "Oh."

"What?" Janice said. "Is there something else?"

My brain was racing. I knew Derek and Janice were both watching me, waiting, but with the thoughts rushing through my mind, I had to take a second or two just so I could get them in order.

"Yes. It's all starting to make sense," I said finally. "Bonnie said something while she was sobbing and crying, and I paid no attention to it at the time. But now I wonder. She said, 'It should've been me.' I thought she was being dramatic and trying to be noble, you know? Like, she should've been the one to die instead of Joey. But now I wonder if it really *was* supposed to be her."

"Are you saying you think Bonnie was the intended victim?"

"I don't know." I shrugged, not quite sure of myself. "But maybe she had planned to go down to the Rabbit Hole, and Joey had offered to go instead. I mean, they were obviously together earlier in the morning."

Janice's eyes narrowed in on me. "Do you happen to know if Bonnie makes a habit of going to the Rabbit Hole every morning?"

"I don't know. but I could find out."

Janice scowled. "No, Brooklyn. Don't even think about snooping around. You don't get involved. I'll find out."

"Yes, ma'am."

"So all this was going through your mind and you forgot to tell me about it?"

"Yeah. Sorry." I grimaced. "But look, there was a lot going on at the time. I mean, the paramedics were scrambling around and then you showed up and then Derek arrived. And Bonnie was screaming, and then Derek discovered that fulcrum thingy that proved how easy it would be to topple a whole shelf over. And then Terrence showed up in a panic and then Kitty started screaming, and then, well, you get it."

"Yeah, I get it."

"And then again," I said, "it might not have anything to do with Bonnie's perfume."

"True." She pursed her lips in thought for a moment. "But if so, we seem to be circling back to the jealous-lover theory."

"Just for the moment," Derek said thoughtfully. "It's not a bad theory, but I'm still clinging to the notion that the two men accidentally interrupted a burglar."

"Or maybe they opened up the shop and surprised an unscrupulous property developer," I said, remembering my conversation with Vinnie and Suzie the other morning.

"And now we circle back around to the bigger picture," Janice murmured.

I sighed. "Frankly, I'd rather blame some unknown property developer or graffiti artist than the people I've gotten to know and like over the last five years."

"I don't blame you," Janice said. "There was a burglar breaking into apartments in my building a few years ago. Turns out, it was the quiet stay-at-home mom living on the second floor. And for some reason, that really bothered me. I would have much rather it had been a stranger, because I'd always liked that woman."

"That's terrible."

"Yeah. My point is that I don't want you going off investigating every property developer in town just to prove it's not one of your Courtyard friends. Understand?"

I tapped my chin, thinking. "Now, that's not a bad idea."

"Very funny," Janice said, shaking her head.

Derek gave me a pointed look. "She's kidding."

"She'd better be."

"I am—I swear." I reached for a cracker. "Besides, I don't see how a property developer would know how to topple a grocery shelf. But that's for the police to figure out."

"Exactly," Janice said meaningfully.

"Meanwhile, I've been trying to figure out the sequence of events." I took a quick sip of wine. "I think someone must've been lying in wait and pushed the grocery shelf over onto Joey. Or Bonnie, or whoever they were expecting. And then Rabbit must have walked in on the crime, and the guy panicked. He had to attack Rabbit as quickly as possible and get out of there. So Joey's death was premeditated, but Rabbit's assault was a spur-of-the-moment decision."

"Good theory," Janice said.

"And you've probably already considered it."

She smiled. "Among others."

"Of course you have," I said, just a little deflated at that news. "It's okay. We're still here to help if you need us."

"Yes, indeed," Derek said. "We're always available to assist the local constabulary."

She chuckled wryly. "I'm thrilled about that. Although I'll admit that an offer of interference coming in that British accent is much easier to take."

I laughed. "I know, right?"

Derek grinned and reached for the bottle. "Would you like another glass of wine?"

"No, thanks. This has been fun." She stood and reached down for her tote bag. "But I'd better get going before you two spring any new theories on me."

We laughed and chatted as we accompanied her

down the elevator and out to the street to make sure she got to her car safely. She seemed to find it amusing. "You know I carry a gun, right?"

"I know," I said, although I hadn't really thought about it for the past hour. And sure, Janice Lee was perfectly capable of taking care of herself. But it didn't hurt to have people looking out for you, either.

"We don't take chances anymore after the last security breach," Derek explained.

"Can't say I blame you," she said. With a wave, she closed her car door and started the engine.

Derek and I waited until she drove away, then walked two blocks down to Pietro's to pick up a pizza and salad for dinner. While we waited for our pizza, I asked Pete if he'd heard anything more on the neighborhood-vandalism situation.

"Pretty sure the Courtyard was the last place that got tagged," he said. "But they had some other kind of trouble there today. Cop cars were driving around here all day. You know anything?"

"Unfortunately, yes." I gave him the bad news about Rabbit and Joey, but avoided saying anything too specific about how it had happened.

"Ah, that just about breaks my heart." Pete picked up a clean white dish towel and mopped his brow with it. "Boy, poor Bonnie must be beside herself."

"You mean because of Joey?" I said. Had everyone known about Bonnie and Joey but me?

"Joey?" he said, confused. "Sure. Yeah, but . . ."

Oops. Clearly Pete had had no idea about Bonnie and Joey. Me and my big mouth. Although I had to admit I felt a little better knowing I wasn't the only one who hadn't noticed an affair. "I mean, because they were such good friends. But, wow, she was really worried about Rabbit."

"That nephew of hers is her pride and joy." He frowned, shook his head, and let out a low whistle. "Hoo-boy. I know this is going to sound bad, but once people start hearing about a death at the Courtyard, it could affect business around here for a while."

I didn't respond to that. My experience had been that death, and especially murder, was actually pretty darn good for business. People were essentially ghoulish when it came to such things. They wanted a front-row seat to the scene of the crime.

We walked home holding hands, with Derek carrying our pizza box and me clutching the bag of salad.

"It was good of Janice to stay for a glass of wine," he said.

"It was fun," I agreed, then winced. "Even though we were talking about murder."

Derek gave a shrug. "We might have to get used to that sort of thing being a normal aspect of our friendship with her."

I smiled up at him. "She really is getting to be a good friend, isn't she?"

"She is." He smiled and nodded. "It hasn't been an easy road to friendship, but it's getting there. I'm glad."

"Me, too." I had liked Inspector Lee from the first time I'd met her, even though she'd given me plenty of grief and even put me on her suspect list once or twice. I didn't hold that against her, though, since I figured she'd just been doing her job. I loved that she wanted to go shopping with me. The possibility was both wonderful and terrifying. I had to admit, the woman was intense.

As we came up to our apartment building, we both slowed down and stared across the street at the Court-yard for a moment. Although it wasn't late, all of the shops were dark, including the restaurants. I assumed it was in deference to Joey and Rabbit.

I wasn't sure what I would see if I kept staring, but for some reason I couldn't look away. I shook my head at my foolishness. I mean, it wasn't as if Joey's killer would start tap-dancing on the sidewalk, announcing what he'd done.

Finally, Derek said, "There's simply nothing for us to do right now, Brooklyn. We've no information and no road to explore. Come, love. Let's go up and have dinner."

"Yes, let's." Derek was right, of course. But my gaze continued to linger on the building across the street.

Derek nudged me. "You can let it go for now. I assume you'll be back there tomorrow morning to scope out the scene?"

He really did know me well. "What makes you so sure?" I challenged.

"Because, my darling," he said with a wink and a smile, "I wouldn't have you any other way."

How can you *not* love a man like that?

Chapter 6

The next morning, Derek left early for a conference call at the office, and I lingered at the dining room table, drinking coffee and planning my day.

Ever since our apartment had been invaded by murdering thugs two months earlier, Derek and I had been sticking pretty close to home. It wasn't something we had discussed at length, but rather the idea had evolved during one of those mind-melding moments that sometimes happened between two people who just loved being with each other and seemed to hold the same values and feelings about life and such. Or whatever. I had no real idea.

Whatever the reason, for a while now we had deliberately been spending much of our free time together exploring our eclectic *way* South of Market Street San Francisco neighborhood, rather than venturing too far away from home base.

That was why, at least three or four nights a week,

we would invariably find ourselves walking across the street to pick up dinner at one of the Courtyard restaurants. Naturally, we always took a few minutes to browse through the bookshop, visit with Terrence and Eddie, and pick up the latest fiction from a favorite author. Occasionally we would run into other friends from the neighborhood and wind up sitting in the inner courtyard to chat and maybe sip a beer from the Thai restaurant.

If I was out by myself, I would find a small table in the shade-filled courtyard and read a book while enjoying a smoothie or latte. And sometimes, on the weekend, Derek would join me to while away a few hours in the pretty surroundings.

We felt at home in all the shops—okay, Derek wasn't a huge fan of the hat shop; it was a little too pink and girlie for him. Even so, we both were enjoying getting to know the owners and other customers better. This section of the city had become like an oasis for both of us. Sure, one of these days we might start heading farther afield, so to speak. But for the moment, being here was what we both wanted.

But now our beloved neighborhood destination point had been touched by tragedy. The loss was personal and maybe it was selfish of me to feel this way, but I was furious. I hated that someone had destroyed the good vibes we'd always enjoyed in our quiet, cozy Courtyard shops. I especially hated that Joey, who wouldn't have ever hurt a fly, had been the target of some horrible person's violent actions. And Will Rabbit, who was as kind and friendly as anyone I'd ever met, was fighting for his life in the hospital. It wasn't fair. All of us who had known Will and Joey

were suffering, too, while some killer was walking
around the city as free as could be.

And again, maybe it was me being completely self-
absorbed, but I was sick of feeling this distinctive kind
of pain and anger. I'd been through it all before too
many times, and it made me want to lash out at something, anything. Of course, that wouldn't solve the
problem. Others who'd known the victim better than I
had suffered much more. Knowing that their lives
would never be the same again was a realization that
hurt me on a visceral level. I wondered how many times
a person could survive a blow to the psyche like this
before she simply crawled off into a corner and gave up
on the world.

I knew I was feeling sorry for myself, just as I knew
it wouldn't do any good to keep wallowing like this.
But darn it, why me? Why had I been the one to find
the body? Was there some cosmic thing going on? Was
I working off karma from a past life? And if so, who
had I been, Jack the Ripper?

And why was I already plotting my next move to
find out more about the victims and more about the
suspects, and trying to get answers to solve the puzzle?
If past history was any gauge, I would end up being the
one most determined to find justice for the deceased.
Oh, sure, the police would do what they could, but I
always seemed to be the one who took it as a personal
affront to the universe that someone was getting away
with murder. Maybe it was because I'd been the one to
stumble over the body in the first place. It stood to
reason that I would be unwavering in my quest to find
answers. In my mind, those two roles of *finder* and
avenger went hand in hand. I'd found the body; now it

was mine to avenge. That awareness hadn't come easily, but I was now at a place where, after some mental struggling, I could accept it. And I took my responsibility very seriously.

That didn't make me special, believe me. As I'd told Inspector Lee the day before, I would have done anything to change this weird proclivity for finding dead bodies. For now, though, this just seemed to be the way things rolled for me. And I had to say, I was getting pretty good at finding the answers to the mysteries that kept getting dumped on me.

As if she could feel my angst, Charlie wrapped her warm, fuzzy body around my ankles and made herself comfortable. I had to smile. How odd that, in an instant, a small cat could transform my mood from grumpy and suspicious to happy and grateful. It was a minor miracle.

"Time to get to work," I murmured a few moments later, and Charlie untangled herself from my feet. After pushing my chair away from the dining room table, I stood and shook away any remaining self-pity I was feeling. It was time to stop whining and take action. I began to walk and made it as far as the coffeepot, where I filled up my cup. I couldn't very well take action without a little more caffeine, right?

After placing the breakfast dishes in the dishwasher, I grabbed a pad of paper and a pen and sat down at the kitchen counter. My version of taking action always started with making a list.

First, I listed all the shops at the Courtyard, along with the names of their proprietors. From talking to them, I hoped to get an idea of whether Joey's friends or family members visited him much. Was there a jealous ex-wife in the background? Maybe he had an envious brother who had always coveted the shoe repair business but their dad had chosen Joey as his successor instead.

It could happen.

While I was at the Courtyard, I would have to remember to check out the pie shop, because, lest I forgot, Derek's parents would be here in two days. I wrote it down on the list, even though it had nothing to do with Joey, because I didn't want to forget the pie!

Next on the list were the property developers. I had no intention of going around investigating every property developer in town, mainly because I'd promised Inspector Lee I wouldn't. But I wanted to remember to bring up that possibility with my Courtyard friends.

I decided to stop at Kitty's hat shop first thing. She always seemed to know what was going on with everyone else in the neighborhood. I just hoped she had calmed down from her crazed rant the day before, because when Kitty was in a good mood, there was no one better to share gossip with. Even sticky subjects like a recent murder or assault, or the possibility that the building might be sold, would ordinarily be subjects Kitty would happily dive right into. But now, with her being so overwrought over Joey's death, all bets were off. I would have to proceed with great caution, especially since Kitty was just as likely to be Joey's killer as any other shop owner in the Courtyard.

I made a few notes on possible ways to bring up the topic without setting her off on a rant. I thought the best way to approach the subject might be to ask her what she thought of Bonnie being involved with Joey. The topic could very well send her into another tailspin, but on the other hand she might take it as an opportunity to commiserate and complain about her landlady. Who didn't love to do that? As long as she didn't start screaming and moaning, I figured I could put up with a few minutes of her raving.

I wondered if Bonnie would be out and about today. I wondered if the Rabbit Hole would be closed until Will Rabbit returned from the hospital. Would Bonnie try to keep it open in the meantime? I hoped so. It was a popular neighborhood spot for smoothies and for fresh fruits and vegetables. And I had a feeling that Will Rabbit would want it to stay open.

I didn't know the pie shop people very well. Sadly, it wasn't a place where Derek and I hung out on a regular basis, for our own health and welfare. But now I wanted to get their take on what had happened to Joey, and buying a chocolate cream pie seemed like the perfect excuse to make conversation.

With the bare bones of a plan of action sketched out, I grabbed my jacket, slung my purse across my torso, locked up the house, and took off across the street.

My first stop, as planned, was the hat shop. It was located at the southwestern corner of the Courtyard, and the window display had recently been changed to feature the latest spring hat fashions. Among the many delights were a number of lovely Easter bonnets and several insanely large flowery organza confections suitable for the Kentucky Derby.

Kitty was with a well-dressed woman who was determined to find the perfect fascinator for a spring wedding. Having stayed up all night to watch the royal wedding several years ago, I was familiar with the fascinator sensation. I just couldn't figure out how you could get that tiny excuse for a hat to stay on your head. I considered myself lucky that that would never be one of my personal problems.

I slowly browsed around the adorable shop with its clever displays of designer hats on mannequin heads and hanging on hooks along the walls. There were rows of scarves draped gracefully around a brass bar, and lots of jewelry in glass display cases on every table in the store. Each of those tables was covered in layers of flowery cloths with vases of beautifully dried roses.

I surreptitiously glanced over to observe Kitty working with her customer.

"Oh, honey," Kitty gushed. "You look absolutely Gaga-licious. Do you love it or do you *love it*?"

The woman stared at herself in the full-length mirror, turning her head this way and that. "It's cute, isn't it?"

"Cute?" Kitty practically snarled the word. "There is nothing *cute* about it. I'll have you know that this hat is a one-of-a-kind actual piece of art. It's structurally spectacular. But I understand if you can't handle something so extravagantly irresistible. Not everyone can. Let me show you something over here that I think—"

"No!" the customer cried. "I can handle it. Absolutely. I'll take it. I love it."

Kitty rewarded her with a gentle smile. "Of course you can handle it. You're marvelous. You look like a queen." She walked with her over to the counter and rang up the sale, cooing and calming her down and honestly making her feel like she was the smartest woman in the universe. Finally, the woman strolled out of the shop, carrying a large, flashy leopard-skin hatbox with her new veiled buttercream pillbox hat packed securely inside.

"Well, that took forever," Kitty said, tucking the paperwork from the purchase into a drawer in the counter. She suddenly shook her shoulders and arms with giddy excitement. "Finally, we can talk."

I grinned, wholly encouraged by her snarky eagerness. "That hat she bought was gorgeous."

"It was cute, wasn't it?"

I gaped at her. "Cute?"

"Oh, you heard that." Kitty laughed gleefully. "Well, you could see for yourself that she wasn't going to be convinced to buy something she thought was merely *cute*. She wanted unique, out-of-this-world, fabulous."

"I think she got it."

She wore a Cheshire cat grin. "I think so, too."

I smiled as I tried on a variegated blue silk scarf hanging along the wall. "I just thought I'd stop by and make sure you were feeling okay. After yesterday, I was so worried about you."

"That's really sweet of you," she said, replacing the blue scarf with a gold one. "I suppose I'd better get my apology out of the way. I'm sorry for going off on you yesterday. But I was in a panic. One of the cooks from the Thai restaurant ran over to tell me he'd seen the paramedics wheeling Joey out to the ambulance and I just lost it."

"That must've been awful for you." Yes, I was laying it on a little thick, but I wanted to hear her story and this seemed the best way to get it.

"Unfortunately, I didn't realize the police were already there. I thought I'd be able to go full bore on

Bonnie, but I hadn't planned on putting on a show in front of San Francisco's Finest. Anyway, I'm sorry you received the brunt of my temporary madness."

I waved off her words. "No worries. As I said, I was just concerned about you." I reached for a black-and-white polka-dot pillbox hat and carefully set it on my head. I couldn't say why, but it was calling out to me.

Kitty reached up and tapped it, tilting it jauntily. "Oh, now, that's darling."

I checked myself out in the mirror. *Cute,* I thought absently, and almost laughed. It was a lot more than cute; it was stylish and fun. I knew I could handle wearing something like this, but the question was, why? What in the world would I do with a four-hundred-dollar polka-dot pillbox hat? Of course, Derek's parents would be here soon, and since they were British, they probably saw lots of fashionable hats everywhere. *Maybe I should get it?* As I contemplated the answer, I said, "I thought you and Bonnie were good friends."

"We were mostly always friends of convenience," Kitty admitted. "Frenemies, I guess you'd call us. But now, forget it. I feel so betrayed. The funny thing is, I knew she would try to steal him away from me. She's done it before. Heck, she's slept with every man in the neighborhood—why not Joey? I guess I never really cared about the others, but with Joey it got personal."

It suddenly hit me. "You loved him."

"I did." She sniffed. "He was easy to love."

"I'm so sorry, Kitty."

"Maybe I would've grown to accept that he was happier being with Bonnie. Maybe we could've been friends again. But then she went and killed him."

Frowning, I took the hat off and placed it back on

the mannequin's head. At least Kitty wasn't screaming the words as she'd done the day before, but it was just as chilling to hear her say it. "You really think she killed him? Why?"

"Why? Because she's crazy." Kitty straightened the little pillbox hat on the mannequin and rearranged a colorful cascade of berets on the table before adding, "And let's not forget the fact that she's done it before."

I was reaching out to touch a silky-looking quilted bag, but that stopped me. "Say . . . what?"

"She killed her husband," she said, her tone matter-of-fact.

"Her husband," I repeated slowly, still not believing what I was hearing. "The one who owned this building?"

"Yes."

The simple, one-word affirmation caused my throat to go dry. She seemed so positive, it was hard not to believe her. "Are you sure about that?"

She gave a reluctant shrug. "No, of course not. But still, I don't doubt it. She's a mean, tough cookie. Believe me."

Okay, since they were "frenemies," I could understand her spreading the usual gossip. But accusing someone of murdering her husband was a little over-the-top. Maybe Kitty wasn't over her "rant" phase as much as she thought she was.

"I guess you know her pretty well," I managed.

"Too well." She emphasized the words.

"Was she ever investigated for the crime?"

She heaved a sigh. "The police looked into it briefly but couldn't find enough evidence. But that doesn't mean she didn't do it."

I knew I was still gaping, still incredulous, but I had to ask. "But . . . exactly what *did* happen?"

With her lips pursed dramatically, she resembled an eight-year-old know-it-all. "Let's just say the poor man died under suspicious circumstances."

"How?" It was probably rude of me to push, but I was dying to find out the details. And also, I really didn't believe she knew anything. "Come on, Kitty. You can't leave me hanging now that you've said this much. Was he stabbed? Shot? Poisoned? Did he die in his sleep? How long ago did it happen?"

"Gosh, it must be five or six years ago by now. Anyway, I have reason to believe she deliberately switched medications on him. One day he was doing fine and a few days later he was dead. It appeared to be a heart attack, but he'd had a complete physical just a few weeks before. So she either poisoned him or fed him some kind of pharmaceutical cocktail that sent him right over the edge."

"Why do you suspect her?"

Kitty stopped fiddling with her hats and turned to face me. "Because she was always talking to me about getting a divorce, but she couldn't because her prenuptial agreement stated that she wouldn't receive any money if she left him."

"That's harsh."

"I thought so, too. But her husband was a sly old dog. And I do mean *old*. He was more than twenty years older than her. And obviously he recognized a gold digger when he saw one. He wasn't going to give her one inch of wiggle room."

"So she could've divorced him, but she cared too

much about the money." I frowned. "But that doesn't mean she killed him."

"Bonnie wasn't exactly subtle about it," Kitty said. "She was always hinting about finding the perfect murder weapon. She would laugh about all the mysteries she liked to read where someone came up with some flawless way to kill someone. And then one day her husband dropped dead. Trust me, it wasn't through natural causes."

"So you suspect she found the perfect weapon."

Her eyes narrowed and she pounded her left fist against her right palm. "I know she did. I just can't prove it."

"He owned this building, right?"

"Right, and several others around town. His death made Bonnie a wealthy woman." She went back to straightening things, lining up the pretty gold chains that dangled on an intricate tree-shaped display. "I have no idea why she hangs around down here when she could live up in Pacific Heights or over in Sea Cliff."

"But this is a beautiful building," I insisted. "And the neighborhood is pretty awesome, don't you think?"

"I don't think Bonnie thinks so. She's always wanted *more*. But I agree with you. I love it here." She turned in a circle. "I love my shop and I love my apartment. Did you know I have a view of the bay from my front room? I'll never leave—unless I'm forced out."

"Would Bonnie force you to move?"

"I hope not." Nervous now, she fiddled with another stack of hats. "Although, after yesterday's little rant, I suppose I wouldn't blame her. I'm trying to keep a low profile today. I haven't dared to venture out of the store. I don't want to see her just yet."

I smiled, trying to keep it light. "That was no little rant, by the way."

She pressed her fingers against her closed eyes. "It was major, wasn't it?"

"Sorry, but yeah, I'd say so." My smile softened. "And as you mentioned, it probably didn't help that you accused her of murder in front of the homicide detective assigned to the case."

"So you're saying it was a little over-the-top?" She snorted a laugh. "Oh man, I really blew it." Leaning against a gold vanity table, she held up her fist in protest. "Okay, if I get a chance to apologize, I will. But that doesn't mean I don't believe she's guilty. I do. She is." With a sigh, she added, "I guess I might've burned a bridge or two there."

"Maybe, but you know, Bonnie wasn't in the best place yesterday, either. Maybe she's forgotten most of it." I didn't really believe that, but there was no point in rubbing it in. "Still, an apology couldn't hurt." I tried to keep a smile on my face. I was so glad to see her remain calm during our conversation. Where was the screaming, ranting harridan of the day before?

"That's good advice. I'll try to be nice."

I hoped so. With Joey's death, it felt as though the Courtyard was already changing rapidly. I didn't want to lose Kitty, too.

"How long ago did Bonnie get involved with Joey?" I asked.

"About four months ago." She strolled around the shop, tidying things as she went. "Maybe she didn't realize how much I loved him. I mean, if you saw Joey and me together, we were always having fun. That's all it looked like, just fun and games. We were happy and we acted like kids together. The thing is, Bonnie can't stand it when someone besides her is happy. She gets jealous at the drop of a hat." Kitty glanced around the shop. "Pardon the pun."

I smiled and tried on another scarf, checked myself out in the mirror, and set it back on the brass bar.

"Anyway," she continued, "Joey was actually with me the night Bonnie made her move. She knocked on my door one evening and begged Joey to come check out some problem she said they were having with the plumbing in Joey's shop."

"Plumbing problems."

"Yeah. Pretty lame, right? But naturally, since it was his shop, he ran off to help her. And he never returned."

I shook my head. "That's not right."

She sniffed again and her mouth worked as she fought to keep more tears at bay. "No, it's not."

"You poor thing." Yes, I was pandering, but so what? I was getting Kitty to talk, and besides, the trick Bonnie pulled to lure Joey away was really not nice.

Of course, Bonnie didn't exactly *kidnap* Joey. He didn't have to stay with her. He should've gone back to Kitty's place, but I had a feeling Kitty wouldn't want to hear me ragging on Joey. Still, if what she said was true, Joey was starting to sound like a bit of a slut.

I mentally bit my tongue for thinking ill of the dead.

Kitty shook her finger in the air. "And I know the only reason why Bonnie went after him was because she was jealous of me. She had to steal him away. She's just psycho that way."

Kitty thought for a moment and then reconsidered her statement. "Okay, that's probably not the only reason she stole him away from me. I mean, you've met Joey, right? He's awesome. An Italian god among men. Tall, strong, sexy, sweet. And, Lord have mercy, he was an animal in bed—let me tell you."

Please don't, I wanted to say, but I just nodded without speaking.

"He made a girl feel like she was the queen of the world."

"Wow. That sounds pretty special."

"I know, right? And now he's gone. I still can't believe it." She blinked and a single tear escaped. She sniffed long and hard, then gazed around the shop, and I wondered if she was going to break down and sob. But after a few seconds, she seemed to remember I was still there.

"Oh, Brooklyn," she said with a sigh. "Let's find you a hat."

I smiled at the obvious pivot and bided my time over the next ten minutes as I tried on almost every hat in her store.

Finally, she scanned a row of casual hats assembled along one wall. She picked out a dignified yet casual straw hat and placed it carefully on my head. Fluffing my hair so that it curled around my shoulders, she tilted her head to study me. "I think that's the one for you."

I turned to stare at myself in the mirror—and fell in love. Kitty was right. It was simply darling, made of thinly woven straw, with a malleable four-inch brim slightly upturned at the edge. The band around the crown was a two-inch-wide white-and-navy-striped grosgrain ribbon. I could see myself wearing it everywhere. To the beach, to a party, to a summer wedding, walking in the vineyards. Everywhere.

I sighed as I turned this way and that. It was love at first sight, but still . . . did I really need a straw hat, no matter how adorable it was?

"It suits you perfectly," she whispered.

I smiled at her. "Is it Gaga-licious?"

"Absolutely. It's spectacular."

I laughed. "Okay, now you're just lying."

"I'm not." Kitty tipped her head to one side to study me. "It was made for you."

"Unfortunately, I completely agree." I took one more look in the mirror and nodded. "I'll take it."

She laughed and shot her fist up in the air in victory. "Yay! Now you have another decision to make." Then she walked over to the wall of hatboxes. "Would you like to go wild or sensible?"

"I've already gone sensible with the hat. Let's go for wild on the hatbox."

"That's the spirit."

As we stood at the cash register, I asked, "I keep hearing rumors of property developers looking to buy the Courtyard. Do you think Bonnie would ever sell the building?"

"She can't," Kitty said as she entered information into the computer.

"Why not?"

She glanced up. "According to her late husband's will, Bonnie can't sell unless every single shop owner agrees to sell. I think her husband did it deliberately because he really loved this place and didn't trust Bonnie not to pull the rug out from under his favorite tenants. So, thanks to that clause in the will, this place will never be sold unless we're all in agreement. No matter what Bonnie wants."

I wondered if the other tenants really felt the same way. I also wondered what would happen once the dust had settled on Joey's murder. I hoped they would all stick together. And what if Bonnie came back around to Kitty in need of a friend? Would Kitty acquiesce? She seemed adamant about never being friends with Bonnie again, but girlfriends sometimes worked these things out.

We chitchatted about the places I might wear my new hat until the sale was finalized. Then, strangely enough, I walked out of Kitty's shop feeling a little happier that I had a new hat and was carrying it in a flashy new shocking pink hatbox. And how weird was that? I didn't need a new hat. I never wore hats, except in winter when I needed something for warmth.

Kitty was right, though, about the hat. And she was right about the hatbox. Carrying it really did make me feel stylish and frivolous and fun. I had the oddest urge to start whistling. I felt happy and plucky. And that was a word I was pretty sure I'd never used about myself before.

Kitty was right about something else, too. High tea with Derek's well-bred English parents was the perfect occasion to wear a hat.

As I crossed the inner courtyard, I knew I'd spent too much time with Kitty, but it was all worth it, I thought. I glanced around, knowing I should've been headed straight to the pie shop, but I detoured into the bookshop first.

"Brooklyn," Eddie cried, greeting me jovially. Then

he noticed what I was carrying. "Ah, I see you've been to visit our Kitty."

I shook my head. "Every time I go in there, I come out with something I never thought I needed."

"I've got the same problem," Eddie said with a shake of his head. After a beat, he added, "That's a joke."

I laughed. "I know. I got it."

"Thank goodness. I didn't want you to think I liked wearing women's hats." He winced. "Not that there's anything wrong with that."

I laughed again, then gazed longingly at the *Alice in Wonderland* tucked away in its protective case. "How's my book today?"

"It's happy and healthy. Thanks. Did you want to take a look at it?"

"No," I said with a smile. "I can be strong for one day. But I might be back tomorrow to check it out."

"We're always here for you."

"Oh, hi there, Brooklyn," Terrence said, walking out of the small storeroom at the back of the shop. "How are you doing?"

"I'm okay. How about you, Terrence?" I decided to push it a little. "That was quite a shock yesterday. Are you doing all right today?"

Eddie frowned. "I guess I missed all the excitement."

"It was a tragedy," Terrence muttered irately. "There was no *excitement*. How callous can you get?"

Eddie glanced at me and rolled his eyes. "I meant no harm, Terrence. Joey was my friend, too."

"Well, you couldn't prove it by me. All you ever did was bitch about him."

Eddie's eyes widened. "I did not."

"Oh, come on. You hated him coming in here." Terrence turned to me. "I can't count the times Eddie grumbled about how Joey's dirty hands were touching all the books. And how he always smelled like shoe wax."

"Well, he did," Eddie said defensively. "And we have very expensive, very old books for sale here that I care about, even if you don't. But look, that doesn't mean I didn't like him. I understand. He was a cobbler. Of course he had dirty hands. But . . . but he cleaned up well."

Terrence scowled. "Bonnie seemed to think so."

"Here we go," Eddie said with a dramatic sigh, which made me think they'd had this discussion a few dozen times in the past.

"Look, let's not get into the whole Bonnie saga," Eddie continued. "Just face it—she likes other men. *Lots* of other men. Get over it."

Terrence's chin jutted out. "She *loved* me."

Eddie shook his head. "You're delusional."

"She gave me a rare gift and it was stolen from—"

"Please stop," Eddie said loudly. "Do yourself and all of us a favor. Don't speak."

I totally agreed with Eddie. I really didn't want to hear what Terrence was about to say next.

"I'd better get going," I said quickly.

Eddie shook his finger at his brother-in-law. "Can you see how you're chasing away our best customers? Will you shut up now?"

Terrence looked grief-stricken. "Brooklyn, are you leaving because of what I said?"

"Of course she is," Eddie said.

"No, not at all," I insisted, then grinned. "I spent too much time trying on hats, so I've got to get going."

Eddie's arms tightened across his chest. "Apologize, Terrence. Give her something."

I started to laugh and waved him off. "Oh, stop. It's okay."

"I'm sorry," Terrence said. "He's right. I'm a dolt. Here's a book for you."

I was still laughing as he handed me the number one bestseller on the market. It had taken me a while, but I'd finally figured out that the beautiful vintage books were Eddie's domain while Terrence loved all the modern thrillers and mysteries. So this book had real meaning for Terrence apparently. Nevertheless, I handed the book back. "Don't be silly, Terrence. I can't take that."

Terrence held up his hands and backed away, refusing to take the book.

"Keep it, Brooklyn," Eddie said. "He's admitting he screwed up, and I don't want you to go away with that being forefront in your mind. So please. Keep the book."

"But I really don't think—"

"You're doing us the favor, kiddo."

"You are both crazy," I said, shaking my head.

Eddie grinned. "Yeah, pretty much."

"You'll like that book," Terrence said. "It's got an awesome doomsday scenario."

I chuckled, thinking maybe Derek would enjoy it. "I love you guys. I'll see you in a day or two."

Eddie brightened. "Hey, when are the in-laws coming?"

"Tomorrow," I said, shoving the book under my arm.

"And thank you for reminding me I've got to go buy a pie."

"Mmm, pie," Terrence said. "Enjoy."

"See you later, Brooklyn," Eddie said.

"Bye, guys." I pushed the door open and walked out. *That was kind of insane,* I thought. But edifying, definitely. Had Terrence just admitted that Bonnie was the one who'd given him the rare *Alice in Wonderland* that was later stolen? Or was he talking more metaphorically, about their *precious love* being stolen? What "rare gift" was he talking about? I was dying to go back and ask, but I was pretty sure that was the last thing they would want to discuss.

Then I forgot all about Terrence and Eddie as the prospect of shopping for pie took over my brain.

Chapter 7

I live in a beautiful city.

Don't get me wrong. San Francisco has plenty of rough edges, but those just add to its charm, infusing the town with an earthy realism, an in-your-face grittiness that is as sharp and crisp as an offshore breeze blustering in from the ocean.

But back to the beautiful parts. The iconic skyline, the parks, the peaks and valleys, the Golden Gate, the bay. And the food. Oh boy, the food. Classic Italian in North Beach. Authentic dim sum in Chinatown. Fresh seafood on Fisherman's Wharf. We had the best coffee. The best sourdough bread.

And now, there was pie.

As of right now, Sweetie Pie bakery was my new favorite place in the city. And why not? The minute I walked into the place, I was cosseted and charmed and fed. Since this was my first visit to the shop, they wouldn't allow me to simply purchase any old pie and walk out. No, they insisted that I taste each of the twelve pies on special today. Each sliver of pie was presented on a clean plate with a new fork, to keep the tasting experience fresh and equitable.

"Like a wine tasting," Colin, the clean-cut young fellow behind the counter, explained. "You want to know exactly what you're getting before you buy."

Their chocolate cream pie was a luscious homage to delicious excess. First of all, it was a huge pie, so the presentation was impressive right off the bat. But then I took a bite and— *Oh, Mommy.* I moaned out loud. The flavors surpassed my greatest expectations. Thick, fluffy piles of whipped cream were generously covered in bittersweet chocolate shavings. The creamy dark chocolate filling was ridiculously decadent, and the crust was a buttery, crumbly feast in and of itself.

What I wanted to do was crawl into a sleeping bag and move into the pie store forever. Since I couldn't, I anticipated walking home in a drugged-out state of bliss.

But before I did so, I would have to make it through eleven more slivers of pie. I enthusiastically took a bite of the next one on the menu, their famous black bottom pie. It was hard to concentrate on conversation with all that sugar coursing through my system, but I gave it my best shot. In between bites, I forced myself to ask Colin questions about Joey's death.

And sadly, as soon as I brought up the subject, asking him what he thought had happened, Colin looked as if he might cry. "I've never known anyone who died before. I mean, my granny, of course. She died last year and it was really rough. But still . . . I've never had, you know, a friend of mine die before."

I swallowed a bite and nodded. My sympathy for him almost ruined my enjoyment of the French apple pie I was munching on. Almost. "I'm sorry about your granny."

"Thanks."

"But I know what you mean about people dying."

"Hearing about Joey—" He blew out a breath. "It was, like, a mind-blowing experience. I had to have a few drinks last night before I went to bed, just to calm down. It scared me, you know?"

"I do. I really do." I realized my plate was clean, so I put my fork down. Apparently, this was his signal to slice me up another piece. I should've stopped him, but I didn't. Because the next piece was their pecan pie with bourbon sauce.

"Here you go." He handed me the thin slice of pie on a clean plate with a new fork.

"Thank you." I took a small bite and shivered. I whispered, "Oh, mercy. That's really good."

"Yeah, we get a lot of requests for that one."

I tried to remember my mission. Something about losing weight and working out for my wedding? Yeah. I'd get right on that the next day. And didn't I have a plan for today? I vaguely recalled making a list and tried to picture what was on that list. All I could remember was *pie*.

"Did you know Joey?" Colin asked.

"Oh." Thank goodness Colin wasn't suffering under the influence of sugar and could recall our ongoing conversation. "Yes, I knew him. He was a great guy."

"He sure was. And a good friend. Damn, I'm gonna miss him."

"Did he have any enemies that you knew of?"

"No, everybody loved him." He wiggled his eyebrows and gave me a wink. "Especially the women."

"I believe it. He was a good-looking guy." I thought about it for a moment. "But, you know, sometimes that can be a curse. Maybe someone was jealous of him."

"He did seem to have a lot of girlfriends." Colin tipped his head to one side and considered it. "But he told me he was just having a good time. None of them was serious, as far as he was concerned."

I shrugged. "Sometimes women take these things more seriously than the guys." I didn't believe that for a minute. I'd known a few pretty obsessive men—like Terrence, for instance. But making it more about women seemed to keep Colin talking.

"You're telling me," he said, as though he could completely relate. "That stuff happens all the time. Still, I can't see anyone wanting to hurt Joey. He was just too nice of a guy."

"Wasn't he dating someone who works around here?" I asked, nibbling on another forkful of my pecan pie.

He grinned. "You mean, wasn't he dating *all* of the women around here? Trust me, the guy was a stud—what can I say?"

I grinned. "Seriously?"

He clicked his teeth and winked at me again. "Yup. Women just really loved him, you know? He was fun to be around and always had a good time."

I was growing tired of the "Joey the stud" part of the conversation and decided to change the subject. "Did Joey have any family or friends who came around much?"

"You're awfully interested in Joey," he said. Had he realized that he might've been talking too much? Was he giving away too much information to a virtual stranger?

"Oh, don't mind me," I said, backing off quickly. I laughed and waved my hand breezily. "I'm just naturally inquisitive. My sisters tell me to mind my own business all the time."

"Yeah, I get that way sometimes, too." Colin nodded sagely. "And hey, nothing like this has ever happened before, so I don't blame you for wondering what went down."

"Well, yeah. And you know, I took my shoes to Joey all the time. He was a great guy. So it's just really sad."

He nodded glumly. "Yeah."

I finished my pecan pie and handed him the plate. "That was fantastic."

"Thanks." He stuck the plate and fork in the dish tub under the counter.

"With all these different pies you guys offer, you must have to get here pretty early in the morning." I tried to strike a casual tone.

"Sure do." He pulled a beautifully encrusted cherry pie out of the glassed-in cabinet and set it on the counter. "The bakers show up about four thirty every morning and I show up an hour later to get the place ready to open up. We start serving at six a.m. every day."

I winced. "Wow, that's an early start. But you probably get used to it."

"I like it. I'm a morning person. I like being up before anyone else." He glanced out the window to the courtyard. "The city's quiet—it's almost like I've got the place to myself."

"You're lucky."

He wiped his big sharp knife clean and carefully plunged it into the pie.

"That looks fantastic," I said, trying to keep the mood casual and pie-oriented.

He grinned. "It's one of our bestsellers."

"I can see why." I took a sip of water and forged ahead with more nosy questions. "So I guess Joey must've been a morning person, too. I heard he was in the Rabbit Hole getting an early-morning smoothie when the accident happened."

Colin took his time, trying to make a precise cut in the pie. "No, he didn't usually show up that early."

"Huh. I wonder what he was doing there at that hour of the morning."

"I don't know." He scooped the perfect sliver out of the pie pan and my stomach groaned at the sight.

"Bonnie's the one that gets here early," he admitted without being prompted. "I always see her around the same time I show up for work. She unlocks the door to the Rabbit Hole and goes in to fix herself a smoothie before Will even shows up."

It was all I could do to keep from quivering with this information, but I kept it cool. "Wow, she must really be an early riser."

"Definitely."

"It's nice that she was there every morning to greet Will."

"Yeah. She's a nice lady."

Thank goodness the cherry pie was the last one on the menu, because I had reached my limit, both in pies and in my ability to squeeze more information out of Colin.

Once I had cleaned my plate, I purchased my chocolate cream pie and headed for home. The first thing I did was slip the pie into the refrigerator. The second thing I did was grab the antacids and a glass of fizzy water. Finally, I lay down on the couch to take a quick nap. I knew I would wake up with a sugar hangover, but what a way to go.

I managed to salvage a few hours later that afternoon to work on my deck of playing cards. Once the deck was done, I would begin work on the matchbox. I sketched out some details on a pad of paper and made a list of supplies I would need to complete the project.

When Derek arrived home a few hours later, I had a full report ready for him. He poured two glasses of wine while I assembled cheese and crackers and olives on a platter, and we chatted about his latest client misbehaving. Derek's high-profile clients paid huge amounts of money to receive the best security, yet despite that, some of them would occasionally try to outwit the very people who were trying to keep them alive. It was profoundly stupid, but what could you do?

We took our wine and snacks into the living room. Derek sat in the big red chair, and I snuggled into the cushions at the end of the couch closest to him. I set the platter on the side table between us. After taking a sip of wine and nibbling on a cracker or two, he smiled. "I can tell you've been dying to tell me something. What happened today?"

And here I thought I was acting so cool and calm. "Colin the pie pusher gave me all sorts of information on the Courtyard comings and goings."

"So the pie pusher was useful in all sorts of ways," he said.

"Yes, especially when it comes to finding the right pie for your father. Sweetie Pies has the most outstanding chocolate cream pie you've ever tasted. Your dad is going to flip."

"That's brilliant," he said. "He'll love it, I'm sure."

"I hope so."

He took another sip of wine. "Now, give me the real scoop. What did you learn from young Colin?"

I ran down the entire conversation, somehow managing to include even greater detail on the pie tasting.

He glanced up at me. "You consumed twelve pieces of pie?"

"They were tiny slivers," I insisted. "But even so, it was too much. I had to gulp down a couple of antacids and take a nap."

He gave me a sympathetic smile. "Are you even hungry for dinner? I thought we might order Thai food."

"Thai sounds good, but only if I can stick to their soup and veggies."

"Excellent idea." He grabbed an olive and popped it into his mouth. After a moment of silence, he said, "So Bonnie was the one who opened up the place each morning."

"Every single day," I said, watching him as I sipped my wine.

His eyes narrowed. "It was a habit of hers."

"Yes," I said, nodding. "And anyone who worked morning hours at the Courtyard would have known that."

He sat back in his chair and crossed his arms over his chest. "So she really could have been the target, and Joey only an accident, poor bastard."

"That's exactly what I thought when Colin told me."

I pictured the crime scene in my head. "All someone would have had to do was wait until they smelled that perfume. As we both know, it enveloped her wherever she went."

"And apparently enveloped whoever she was with," Derek muttered.

"Yes." I frowned. "I told you I smelled her perfume right away. Poor Joey's goose was cooked as soon as he stepped inside the Rabbit Hole. That scent of Bonnie's would have filled the room."

Derek held up his hand. "It's still just a theory, of course."

"Of course." We were both silent, lost in our own thoughts. After a moment, I said, "But there's a chance that our theory of what happened is *exactly* what happened."

"A very good chance."

"I wonder if the police questioned Colin about Bonnie."

"Possibly, but we should probably alert Inspector Lee, just in case."

"I'll call her in the morning and let her know what he told me."

"Good." Derek swirled his wineglass and sniffed the wine before taking another sip. "So now, instead of hunting down Joey's enemies, we might want to turn our attention to Bonnie's enemies."

I stared into my wineglass and frowned. "I have a feeling that's going to be a much longer list."

The next morning I called Inspector Lee to tell her about my conversation with Colin at the pie shop, but my call went to voice mail, so I had to leave her a message. She thanked us for the information and told us she would be in touch. Then Derek drove off to the airport to pick up his mother and father. I was expecting my own parents to arrive at any minute, too. And by popular demand, they were all going to stay here with us. Derek had offered to put his parents up at the Ritz-Carlton, but they'd turned him down. They wanted to be as close as they could get because they rarely saw Derek and had never met me.

My parents had wanted to stay with us, too, and had happily offered to take the smaller guest bedroom. Each of our guest bedrooms had its own bathroom, so I was hoping it would all work out just fine. What could go wrong? Ha! Even I didn't believe me. Don't get me wrong—my parents are wonderful. They're just a little more "out there" than I was willing to bet Derek's parents were. This was going to be either a huge success or a calamity of epic proportions.

But whatever happened, the apartment was ready. Earlier in the week, I'd brought in a small army of house cleaners with mops and sponges and sprays and vacuum cleaners to make sure everything was sparkling clean and pretty for the parents.

Since we'd had the place remodeled recently to blend two apartments together, our new living space was really large. Still, I was starting to get hives just imagining all six of us living under the same roof for the next week.

And me being me, I said a silent prayer that nobody else in the neighborhood would get murdered while Derek's parents were visiting. My parents, on the other hand, wouldn't be shocked. They had already lived through several of these situations with me.

Derek's folks had been flying all night, so I expected them to arrive with a good case of jet lag. It would have been nice if their first day in the city was a relaxing one, I thought. I pictured all of us taking long naps and having quiet conversations.

No such luck.

I was straightening the magazines on the coffee table when the front door suddenly swung open and a man shouted, "The British are coming!"

"Silly! They're already here!" cried a feminine voice.

Lots of laughter erupted as I dashed for the door. But I skidded to an abrupt stop when I saw my mother and another woman—obviously Derek's mum—walking arm in arm, chattering and giggling like old friends.

Derek managed to shoot me a warning glance as he followed the two ladies inside, wheeling several large suitcases and toting two carry-on bags over his shoulder.

Behind Derek, two tall, good-looking men—one of whom was my father—walked into the house, chuckling and murmuring like old college buds. The two of them were wheeling their own luggage, thank goodness.

I smiled at the picture they made. Mom and Dad must have met up with Derek and his folks in the elevator. I assumed the introductions had been made, and now they all seemed to have hit it off like gangbusters. But what had that warning glance from Derek been all about?

"There she is," Derek's mum cried, spying me. "Oh, she's a beauty, Derek."

"Mother," Derek said formally, "this is Brooklyn Wainwright. And, yes, she is beautiful. Brooklyn, darling, my mother, Margaret Stone."

Smiling, I held out my hand. "It's so nice to meet you, Mrs. Stone."

"Oh, it's Meg, dear. I insist." She ignored my outstretched hand and pulled me into her arms in a warm, cushiony hug. After a moment, she held me at arm's length and studied my face. "What a pleasure to finally meet you, Brooklyn. Let me look at you. You are as pretty as a princess."

I couldn't help but grin. She was lovely in her own right, with bright blue eyes, a cheerful smile, and platinum gray hair worn in a stylish short bob. She had an athlete's build, and I wondered if she might have been a runner when she was younger. She was about an inch shorter than me, which put her around five foot seven.

"We're so glad you could come for a visit," I said.

"I wouldn't have missed it for the world." She patted my cheek affectionately. "We'll have a nice long chat soon. I want to hear about all the latest cases you're working on."

Cases? Did she mean bookcases?

"I told you we're not discussing murder cases, Mother," Derek murmured in Meg's ear.

I felt my eyes bug out and was gratified to see Derek rush over to my side in an instant. He quickly directed my attention to his father, John. The man was an older version of Derek, as tall and handsome as his son, with attractive streaks of gray hair along his temples.

"It's wonderful to meet you, Mr. Stone," I said.

"Uh-uh, we'll have none of that." He gave me a brief but heartfelt hug and a kiss on the cheek. "You're to call me John, please. And it's my pleasure to finally meet you, Brooklyn, and welcome you to the family."

His words touched me so deeply, I could feel my eyes begin to water. I was so glad I had that scrumptious pie for this completely lovely man. "That is so sweet. Thank you so much. I'm glad you're able to stay in town for a while. We've planned a full itinerary for you."

"I hope it includes some murderous haunts," Meg whispered to my mom, who nodded eagerly.

"Mother," Derek said mildly. "Brooklyn has nothing to do with murder. She's a bookbinder and an artist."

"Yes, of course, dear." But she winked at me before moving aside so that I could greet my own mother.

"Hi, Mom," I said, hugging her tightly. "It's so good to see you."

"Oh, sweetie, we're going to have the best time," Mom whispered. "Meg is psychic—isn't that wonderful? We're going to throw the tarot and have another purification ceremony."

"Oh dear God," I muttered. My mother had apparently met her soul sister. How was it possible that the two women had just met for the first time? They'd shared a three-minute elevator ride and obviously had already discussed my mother's Wiccan beliefs and Meg's psychic abilities. I couldn't believe it.

On the other hand, if Meg really was psychic, she would've immediately picked up on Mom's witchy ways anyway.

I could feel my left eye beginning to twitch.

A half hour later, after both sets of parents had unpacked and settled into their rooms, we all met back at the kitchen counter for a snack of chips, mango salsa, and guacamole.

"I think I've got the perfect wine to go with all of this," Dad said, and pulled a chilled bottle of viognier from the refrigerator. Dad glanced at Derek. "This should hold up to the salsa."

Derek grinned. "I trust your taste in all things."

"Oh my goodness," Meg said. "Wine before noon— how delightful."

"I think you'll really like this," Dad said. "We've been experimenting with different types and lengths of oak aging. This one came out with a hint of vanilla."

"Sounds wonderful, Dad," I said.

He poured and we all took tastes.

"Oh, I taste the vanilla," Meg said, and took another sip. "And a bit of peach?"

"Yes, that's a dominant flavor of many viogniers."

"It's rather . . . well, creamy, isn't it?" John said.

"That tends to come from the barrel," Dad explained. "Do you like it?"

"Oh, very much." But something across the room had caught John's attention. "And who's this beauty?"

We all turned to see Charlie slinking across the room, only now deciding it was safe to come out to visit.

"This is Charlie," I said, then added, "She's a girl."

John walked over, knelt down, and began to stroke Charlie's furry back until the cat was purring so loudly we could hear her from twenty feet away.

"I think she loves you, Dad," Derek said.

"John is a true cat lover," Meg explained. "We have two at home, Jasper and Ophelia. I love them, too, of course, but they barely give me the time of day. It's John who has a way with animals."

He finally picked up Charlie, carried her over to the kitchen bar, and set her on his lap, where she instantly dozed off.

"She trusts you completely," I murmured.

"She knows I won't hurt her," John said, holding the little creature securely while he continued to pet her.

Dad poured more wine and we caught up on all the latest news, most of which revolved around Derek's and my siblings and their various significant others.

"How is Dalton?" I asked. He was the only one of Derek's brothers I had met, and I was crazy about him. Not as crazy as my sister Savannah was about him, but that was because those two had met and fallen in love at first sight while Dalton was visiting San Francisco last year. I had a feeling they had snuck off to various parts of the world to see each other a few times since then, but Savannah was keeping mum about it.

The conversation was upbeat and copacetic with lots of laughter and smiles—until Derek asked his parents about his brother Dylan.

"Oh, that Dylan." Meg scowled.

"What has he done now?" Derek asked.

She shook her head in dismay. "He wants to get married."

"He's thirty-five years old, Meg," her husband chided lightly. "Old enough to make up his own mind."

"I thought he was old enough, too, until I met *Cruella*." She wiggled her eyebrows to emphasize the epithet.

Mom and I both grinned. Derek turned to give me a look that I could read loud and clear. *Please don't encourage her.*

John sighed dramatically. "Her name is *Camilla*."

"Oh dear," Mom said. "Is there a problem?"

John turned to his wife. "Dearest, the girl's going to be our daughter-in-law. We'd best learn to live with it."

"Which means I'd better hold my tongue. Is that what you're saying?" Behind his back, Meg nodded at me and used hand signals to indicate that we would talk about Cruella later.

Was this a good sign that I had been accepted into the family? I hoped so, although I had to admit I felt sorry for poor Cruella. Still, that wouldn't keep me from sharing some juicy gossip about the woman with my future mother-in-law. I just wasn't that noble.

Derek's expression was calm, but I could see his mind was working overtime.

"Have you met her?" I asked quietly.

"Yes," he murmured, but didn't elaborate.

I couldn't wait to get the full scoop on Camilla.

That afternoon Derek took us all on a tour of the city in the luxury SUV he had rented for the week. We drove along the Embarcadero and through Fisherman's Wharf. We stopped for a quickie Irish coffee at the Buena Vista, then headed for the Golden Gate Bridge. We stood at the bottom of the Filbert Steps and stared up at Coit Tower—and decided that taking that grueling climb through all those amazing tangled gardens and intriguing statuary would be a journey for another day.

We drove through Golden Gate Park and stopped in Haight-Ashbury, where Meg bought souvenir tie-dyed T-shirts for all of her grandchildren. Mom told stories of her days hanging out in the Haight and seemed disappointed that there were no colorful hippies to be seen among the well-heeled urbanites who were pushing baby strollers or shopping and dining at the exclusive boutiques and cafés that lined the Upper Haight.

We rode up to Twin Peaks and down Lombard Street, the "crookedest" street in the world. We took pictures everywhere we went.

Four hours later, we were heading for home, thank goodness. I wasn't sure why I was so exhausted merely from playing tour guide, but I was more than ready for a nap. Probably because of the astronomical level of high energy my mother and Meg were putting out. I'd never seen two women bond as quickly and as joyfully as my mother and Meg Stone had. It was amazing, and a little scary to watch.

They had so much in common, it made me want to laugh. Especially when I remembered how worried I was that Meg would freak out at some of the things Mom said. On the contrary, they seemed remarkably simpatico and delighted to have found each other.

Meanwhile, Dad and John, sitting together in the very back seat, had already covered the subject of best single-malt Scotches on the market and were now completely involved in determining the maximum velocity a car could travel down Lombard Street without going airborne.

As we drove closer to home, I thought the others might be ready to pass out, too, until Meg spoke up from the backseat. "As long as we're driving around the city, Derek, wouldn't it be lovely to have Brooklyn point out some of the places where she had her little adventures?"

Confused, I turned around, and that was when

Mom piped up. "She wants to visit some of the places where you found the bodies, sweetie."

I almost choked on my tongue.

"Mother, I thought we talked about this," Derek intoned while staring into the rearview mirror at his mom.

"Don't blame her, Derek," my mom said. "It was my idea."

I didn't know if she was fibbing or not, but it was clear that our two mothers were in cahoots. I could barely resist burying my head in my hands, but I managed. Turning in my seat, I smiled at our parents. "All right."

"You needn't do this," Derek murmured. "But fair warning—she can be relentless when she gets going."

"It's fine," I whispered. "This way, we'll satisfy her curiosity and she'll get it out of her system."

"One can only hope."

Mom glanced out the window. "Don't you teach your bookbinding classes somewhere around here?"

"Someone died in your class?" Meg said. "How exhilarating!"

"And the television studio is right up the street from there," Mom continued.

"Television studio?" Meg gasped, a grin lighting up her eyes. "Oh my goodness."

I was concerned when I caught her patting her chest. "Are you feeling all right, Meg?"

"I'm as chipper as can be," she said gaily. "Just extremely excited and grateful for this experience."

Derek reached over and squeezed my hand—to give me strength, I figured. But I could see him biting back a smile, too. This had to be the weirdest tour ever. Had I really been worried that the two sets of parents wouldn't get along?

I directed Derek to turn up Fourth Street, and we headed south toward the Bay Area Book Arts Center, or BABA, which had been the scene of a murder several years earlier. Derek played tour guide this time, sharing many details of the case and giving me and my voice a break.

Personally, I found nothing entertaining about murder, but I could understand Meg's interest. Having the separation of time between you and the actual murder probably made it easier to think about, too. And the fact that Derek had been involved in most of the cases meant that she had even more reason to wonder what it was all about. Of course, if she really was psychic, she probably already knew more than I could possibly guess.

From BABA, we drove a few blocks farther south toward Potrero Hill to swing by the local TV station where I had filmed *This Old Attic* last year. Not only had a murderer been lurking on the set, but the host of the show had been tormented by a real-life stalker.

As we finished describing the scene that night in the rain, Meg sighed with pleasure. She and my mother spoke quietly as they looked out at the nondescript studio; then, a few minutes later, they agreed that it was a fine time to head for home.

That night, after a simple dinner of grilled salmon, stir-fried vegetables, and rice, I brought the chocolate cream pie to the table.

"I hope you all have room for dessert," I said, smiling at John. "I've heard you have a fondness for pie."

His eyes lit up. "You'd have heard right."

"Oh, Brooklyn, how sweet of you," Meg said softly.

"We happen to have a wonderful pie shop right across the street, so I couldn't resist."

John kept a keen eye on me as I sliced up the pie and handed out large pieces to everyone. "I've a deep love for all flavors and types of pie," he said. "And Meg bakes a lovely berry pie that she often serves with her homemade vanilla bean ice cream."

"That sounds fabulous," I said.

"It is. But chocolate cream pie is a particular favorite of mine, I must admit."

"Then I hope you enjoy this one."

We all began to eat, and soon after the first bite the happy moans began. Other than that, no one spoke until the last bite was consumed and we all set our forks down.

"Wow," Dad said. "That was a spiritual experience."

John chuckled as he patted his stomach. "I believe I came close to experiencing nirvana."

"I didn't know you had a pie shop in the neighborhood," Mom said. "This is simply amazing."

"It's right across the street," I said. "Sweetie Pies."

"At the Courtyard?"

"Yes."

"We should visit while we're here," Meg said. "We'll have to try another of their pies as well."

"Good idea," Mom said, grinning.

"The Courtyard." Dad frowned. "Didn't I hear something about a break-in there this week?"

Wincing, I exchanged another glance with Derek. These looks back and forth were getting to be a habit of ours, especially when one or more of our parents came up with something we didn't quite know how to deal with.

"There was an incident," Derek said, but didn't elaborate.

Dad frowned. "I thought I heard that someone was badly hurt."

"Oh, that's right," Mom said. "I read about it in the paper. One person was badly hurt in one of the shops, and another person died on the way to the hospital."

"Oh my goodness," Meg whispered. "How awful. Brooklyn, dear, did you know them?"

"Yes, and it was terrible," I murmured, shivering at the memory of Joey buried beneath that pile of ugly twisted steel. "The man who died was a really good person."

"What happened?" John asked, sitting forward in his chair. "Are you comfortable talking about it?"

I truly appreciated him asking the question. I again looked at Derek, who shook his head in surrender. "Might as well tell them, love. They're going to be here all week, so they'll no doubt hear the truth eventually."

I nodded, took in a deep breath, and let it out slowly. After making eye contact with everyone around the table, I finally spoke. "He was murdered."

Chapter 8

The next morning, we all met in the kitchen for a wake-up cup of coffee. I had also made a full pot of tea, the kind with real tea leaves. *Not* tea bags. I knew that much after living with Derek all this time. Still, this was for his mother, so I prayed I'd used an acceptable brand of loose tea. The English were very particular about their favorite beverage.

Everyone had agreed the night before that after a quick cup of coffee or tea here, we would walk across the street and pick up caffe lattes at the Beanery. Then we'd stop in for a savory breakfast pie at Sweetie Pies. And there was talk that, on the way back, some of us would take the opportunity to peek through the windows of the Rabbit Hole, hoping to get a look at the site of my latest "murder magnet" event.

The parents would never use those words, of course. They were much too thoughtful. But I knew what they were thinking. And I couldn't blame them, honestly.

Still, I didn't like the feeling that they were tingling with anticipation that I would stumble over another body while they watched.

Don't get me wrong. I was already in love with Derek's folks, and of course I loved my own parents. Nevertheless, I couldn't help feeling a bit like a circus geek, eating live chickens for the avaricious audience.

Okay, that was a really bad analogy. But I did feel like my oddities were about to be put on display for all to see. And for Pete's sake, I had to stop feeling sorry for myself!

As I walked back to the bedroom to change into my street clothes, Derek's mother caught me in the hall. "Brooklyn, dear, if you'd rather not take us across to the shops, I'll understand. I never should've brought it up."

"Of course we'll go to the shops," I insisted. "Don't worry about me. I'm fine."

"No, you're not. And it's my fault." She leaned against the wall and fiddled with the belt to her bathrobe. "I should've been more sensitive to your feelings. I usually am, honestly."

"Of course you are."

"But the minute I met you, I felt I was meeting another kindred spirit. The same is true for your mother. It's like a dream come true." She paused, reached out, and took my hand to give it a squeeze. "I'm not ashamed to admit that I was a bit nervous about meeting you. But the moment we met, I knew that we would be close and that my worries were for nothing. And Derek is so happy. I can't tell you how thrilled I am that you're all going to be part of our family."

I knew exactly what she meant. I'd been on pins and needles about meeting Derek's parents, hoping they would like me. Hoping I'd like them. And it was such a relief now to find that they were such lovely people. "Now you're going to make me cry."

She grabbed me in a fierce hug. "You sweet girl."

Wrapped up in her arms, I smiled. She smelled of some wonderful lavender-scented soap and English breakfast tea.

"Now," she said after letting me go, "let's get real. It should've occurred to me that finding a dead body was not the pleasurable experience it's chalked up to be. If one has any human feeling at all, I imagine you must suffer terribly. I ought to have known it would be difficult for you, but I can be so obtuse sometimes."

I touched her arm. "Please don't say that. It's not true at all."

She chuckled. "I'm afraid it is. And I blame it on all those gritty cop shows I love to watch on the telly. They make death seem so unreal, and the actors can be so blasé, you know."

"I love those shows, too."

"That's my girl." She gave me another quick hug. "All right. I've begged for your forgiveness and you've granted me absolution, and now we can move on. Let's forgo the Courtyard and do something different instead. I can help whip up a hearty breakfast right here, and afterward we can go for a walk in the park. Or stay home and read a good book. Honestly, that's one of my favorite things to do. What do you say?"

I realized I could have listened to her charming accent all day long. And I found it so admirable, the way she could turn on a dime and carry on. "Thank you, Meg. You're right. It's horribly sad and frightening to come upon sudden violent death. I usually don't like to think about it."

"And here I've dredged it up and made you unhappy."

I smiled. "Don't worry about me. I'm pretty resilient."

"Of course you are," she said staunchly.

"But honestly, I really would love to show you the Courtyard shops. And ever since we started talking about it, I've been practically drooling for a breakfast pie."

She closed her eyes for a moment and pressed her hand to her heart in gratitude. "Oh, thank God. I'll admit it was breaking my heart to pass up a savory pasty."

I laughed and felt much better. "Then we'd better get ready to go."

A half hour later, after greeting Colin and placing our orders, we found a table and lingered in the pie shop with our coffee drinks and breakfast pies—or pasties, as John and Meg called them. We chatted about all the things they wanted to see and do while they were in town, and we all offered suggestions.

Derek and I had already made up an extensive itinerary of all our favorite places, but since we would be together for a whole week, there would be plenty of times when one or more of us would simply want to go for a walk in the park or relax and read a book, just as Meg had suggested earlier. Besides, I had always hated having every hour accounted for in an "activity journal" of some kind, no matter where I was traveling.

After an hour in the pie shop, we split up to go explore

the other Courtyard shops. On my recommendation, Mom and Meg went to check out Kitty's hat shop, and the three men walked around to the back of the building by the parking lot to see how well the graffiti had been painted over. Definitely a guy thing.

I, naturally, headed for the bookshop. We had all agreed to meet there in twenty minutes anyway, but I wanted to get a head start.

The store had been open only a few minutes and no one was inside except Terrence and Eddie, who were busy at the front counter. I was about to greet them when I heard Terrence grumble, "I'm so sick of this."

"You're sick of it?" Eddie countered. "How do you think I feel?"

"I don't care how you feel. It's not all about you every minute of the day, you know. God, you disgust me sometimes!"

"If you don't like it, then just sell the damn shop to me."

"No way."

I slinked back behind a bookshelf and viewed the brothers through a row of cookbooks.

"Then be quiet," Eddie said, sounding fairly mild mannered in the middle of what sounded like a rip-roaring argument. "Look, just face it. You've always been jealous of me—not that I blame you. But you need to work it out. Talk to a therapist. Go find a girlfriend. But get over it."

"I had a girlfriend and you poisoned her mind."

Eddie laughed. "Do you know how pathetic you sound? Bonnie was never your girlfriend, Terrence. We've both known her for years and we've always seen her flitting from one man to the next. She's like a hummingbird flying from flower to flower. She never stops moving."

"She loved me," Terrence whispered, a note of desperation in his voice. "She gave me the book."

"Oh, right," Eddie said, his voice dripping with sarcasm. "The book. Of course she gave you the book. And then she stole it back—that's how much she really loved you. Get a clue, Terrence. You're starting to lose it for real."

"She did not steal it." Terrence bared his teeth, almost snarling at his brother-in-law. "I know it was *you*."

"We've been down this road before. Why would I steal your book?"

"To make me crazy," he muttered.

"Too late for that, bro. You're already crazy." Eddie paced the length of the counter. "Look, Bonnie gave me a book, too. It's a beauty, as you well know. But so what? She's got a thing for guys and books. For all I know, she stole your book from you and gave it to Joey."

"I've already considered that," he muttered.

Eddie ignored his comment and continued. "Why can't you just give it up with Bonnie? I know you've seen her with every other guy in the neighborhood. Including me."

"You don't understand." Terrence moaned.

"I guess I don't. I don't understand why you couldn't just have a good time while it lasted instead of flipping out on her. It's been months, and to this very day, every time she walks by, you have a complete meltdown. You know she's just taunting you, right?"

"If she is, it's your fault."

"Oh yeah, because I poisoned her mind." Eddie scratched his head, clearly bemused. "You know that's ridiculous, right? The truth is, you scared her off, Terrence. You became so obsessed that she couldn't take it anymore."

"So do you really think she gave my book to Joey? That's what I think."

Eddie spun around and faced him. "I have no idea. All I know is that I didn't steal it. Frankly, I have my doubts that she ever actually gave you a book."

"She gave me a book," Terrence said through gritted teeth. "Because she loves me. And you can't stand it."

"Here we go again," Eddie muttered. Then he laughed. "You're delusional. I'll just leave it at that. Otherwise, we'll go round and round again, and my head will start spinning, and then I'll have to go vomit."

He had his back turned, as though completely ignoring Terrence. And sadly, Terrence couldn't stand it.

"That's sickening," Terrence said. Then he came closer, narrowing in on Eddie. "You're just as delusional as I am. That stupid book of yours is a fake and you know it."

From my vantage point, I could see Eddie's ears turning red. "You know that's not true."

Terrence gave a casual shrug, happy to have scored a point. "Maybe it is; maybe it isn't."

Eddie threw up his hands. "You don't know anything about books!"

"I do too."

"No, you don't. You've never even tried to learn. My book isn't a fake. It's a first edition and it's— Forget it.

You don't even care. I don't know why you want to keep working here."

"Maybe just to bug you."

"Well, it's working. But I'm not going to argue with you anymore. I'm sick and tired of it."

"Well, I'm sick and tired of you, too."

"Then why don't you leave?" Eddie implored. "Quit the business. Sell me your half and go."

"You'd love that, wouldn't you?"

Suddenly, Furbie the cat brushed up against me and I almost screamed out loud. Instead, I managed to take a few deep breaths, then hunched down and scratched his soft ears, silently begging him to keep my presence a secret. Because this conversation was really illuminating. Of course, now I was beginning to wonder how I would cover up my being here. At some point, I'd have to go back to the door and make a big production out of entering. Either that, or let the brothers know that I'd been listening in on what was clearly a private conversation. Not something I wanted to do.

"Yes!" Eddie cried. "I've told you a hundred times I wish you'd sell and leave. You don't love this place like I do. You don't even like books! Okay, maybe you like the new ones, but you've even admitted that the smell of old books makes you crazy. But you won't give it up, ever. You'll stay for the sheer joy of driving me mad. I think it makes you happy."

"It's definitely a nice side benefit, but what would really make me happy is if I could sell this stupid place right out from under you."

"You can't," Eddie sneered. "Unless you forgot our agreement."

"If only I could," Terrence muttered.

"Another reason you'll never leave is because you'd have to say good-bye to your beloved Bonnie. And you'll never do that, either, because that would be the *smart* thing to do. And you are not smart, Terrence."

I'd heard enough, and it was breaking my heart. While their backs were turned, I gave Furbie one last scratch and slipped out the door, where I took in some deep breaths of fresh air.

One thing was for sure. I no longer wondered why their wives had left them. Admittedly, most of the time the brothers-in-law were delightful and funny, but they each had a mean streak that could turn vicious when they decided to let loose on each other. I'd never really seen it in action personally before today, but now that I had, I was really depressed by the whole thing.

I leaned against the outer wall and stared up at the trees, taking in the vivid green leaves and blue sky. It was a crisp, cold spring morning, and I was glad our families were visiting when the weather was so beautiful.

After another long moment, my head began to clear. And that was when I started to replay Eddie and Terrence's words.

How was it possible that Eddie's copy of *Alice in Wonderland* was a fake? I'd held it in my hands and studied it. And another thing: If Bonnie had given Terrence the same book, was she also the one who'd stolen it back? Terrence had admitted that he had considered that possibility. And if so, had Bonnie given the book to Joey? Had Terrence ever mentioned the book to Joey?

Probably not. Knowing Joey's good nature, I would bet he would've been happy to hand the book back to Terrence.

I froze on the spot as another thought occurred to me. Was Terrence the one who'd vandalized Joey's shoe repair shop looking for the book?

Just as quickly, I shook my head. I couldn't picture Terrence tearing through Joey's shop, causing all the damage I'd seen the other day. He was much too passive-aggressive to do something so actively destructive.

I was missing something, so I mentally spun back around and went through all my questions again. Why did Terrence call Eddie's copy of *Alice in Wonderland* a fake? Did he know what he was talking about? Eddie's angry reaction made me wonder. But how could it be? I had examined the *Alice* more than a dozen times already, from cover to cover. It was the real deal. Wasn't it?

But you haven't really examined it, I whispered to myself. *Have you?*

I almost groaned out loud. No, I hadn't examined it the way I would have liked to, with my own high-powered instruments in my own workshop. I'd only taken cursory looks at it with Eddie watching me like a hawk every second. Why did he have to be so possessive of the book? He knew I had expertise with books. Was he afraid I would discover that it was really a fake?

And suddenly it began to sink in.

Oh God. *Was Joey's murder all about a book, after all?* I quickly brushed the thought aside since the only way a book could have been a catalyst for murder was if Eddie or Terrence had killed Joey. And I refused to believe that either of them could have done something so evil.

"Who are you talking to, sweetie?"

I jolted. My mother and Meg were standing a foot

away, and I hadn't even noticed them approach. "Mom. Meg. Hi. I didn't see you. Um, yeah, funny thing, I was just talking to myself, um, trying to remember what ingredients go into spaghetti carbonara."

Wow, that was as good a lie as I'd come up with in a long time.

"Nice try, punkin'," Mom said, using my hated childhood nickname. Just because I used to obsess over pumpkin pie, my cruel family had never let me forget it.

"First of all," Mom continued, "seriously, spaghetti carbonara? Honey, you don't cook. And second of all, you're the worst liar in the family. Now, what gives?"

"It's nothing, Mom." I waved her concern away. "I was just blathering to myself."

Over her shoulder, I saw Derek and our dads walking toward me. Derek took one look at me and began to run. "What is it? What happened?"

I blinked. "How can you tell something happened?"

"You look stricken." He grabbed me in a tight hug.

I whispered in his ear, "I just overheard Terrence and Eddie yelling at each other. It got pretty bitter."

"They argued in front of you?"

I winced. "They didn't know I was listening."

"Are you sure?"

I lowered my voice even more. "I think so, but we have to talk."

He nodded. "You heard something important."

"Maybe." Had I? There were so many things running through my mind, I couldn't be sure. But once I had a chance to lay it all out for Derek and we could talk it over, I knew things would start to clear up.

Our parents were growing curious, so Derek and I

broke it up. To his father, I said, "How's the graffiti looking?"

"Not a trace of it anywhere," John said. "I was quite impressed."

"The city pays for it, too," I said. "Isn't that smart?"

"Brilliant," he said, and scowled. "I wish they'd do that in our part of the world."

"You have graffiti in Oxford?"

"Oh, it's an awful blight," Meg griped.

"They deface our beautiful bridges and riverfront properties," John explained. "And the Canal and River Trust can barely afford the manpower to clean it up. So if your property is defaced, forget getting help. It's up to the individual owners to paint over it."

"Which means that a lot of the mess goes unchecked," Meg added.

"That's a shame," I said, thinking of all the beautiful ancient buildings in Oxford and throughout England. "What they've found here in San Francisco and other cities is that if you leave a wall disfigured, it draws gang members or other taggers to the scene. So it's worth the cost to paint over it as soon as possible."

John shook his head, disgusted by the idea of people defacing property. "It's indefensible."

We stood in silence for a moment, mulling over the sorry state of our cities.

"Well, enough of all that," Meg said firmly. "Let's go buy some books."

"Good idea, Meg," Mom said cheerfully.

John held out his arm for me to link mine around. "Derek was already kind enough to pick up some of my favorite authors for me, but I'd still like to take a look at their stock."

I smiled. "I think you'll find their mix of old and new intriguing."

This time when I entered, I made a big show of scraping my feet and chattering to Mom and Meg about all the wonderful goodies they sold there. I called out greetings to Eddie and Terrence and introduced everyone. The brothers were on their best behavior, as helpful as could be, but I could see them straining around the edges.

I wondered if the wedge between them had always been there, or if Bonnie had driven it a little deeper with her shenanigans. I wouldn't have put it past her to play one brother against the other to get what she wanted. It was such a junior high school thing to do. And besides being a stupid way to behave in general, Bonnie was their landlady, for goodness' sake. Rather than divide and conquer, wouldn't it be smarter to keep her tenants happy so that they worked harder to make more money, some of which went into her pockets?

But then, not everyone subscribed to that happy-little-worker theory of mine.

We spent an hour in the bookshop and ended up buying lots of books and book-related goodies; then we headed back home. That afternoon was a designated down day. Jet lag had caught up with Meg and John, so we planned to spend the day around the house, reading and chatting, maybe taking a walk, and then ordering pizza and salad from Pietro's for an early dinner.

It sounded like heaven to me.

But before we could relax, I needed to get Derek aside and tell him everything I'd heard in the bookshop earlier. I finally came up with a plan.

"Derek, would you mind helping me bring some files upstairs? I picked them up from the Covington last week, and they're still in the trunk of my car."

"Of course, love," he said.

"I can help," my dad offered.

"That's okay, Jim," Derek said. "You relax and we'll be right back."

Derek grabbed my hand and we raced out of the apartment before anyone else could try to join us.

"I feel so silly sneaking around on my parents," I said as we dashed into the elevator and pressed the basement button.

Derek chuckled. "I have no doubt my mother has already guessed that we're faking this trip downstairs just to get away from them."

"Of course she guessed, because she's psychic." I glared at him. "And why did you never tell me that?"

He flashed me a pitying look. "Because if my mother really is psychic, she's the worst psychic that's ever lived."

I grinned. "Oh, but she's adorable."

"Yes, she is. Just don't let her read your palm. I can't be held responsible for the nonsense she'll come up with." His smile was loving and indulgent. "She's always believed herself to have powers, and really it does no harm and makes her happy. The rest of us go along because we love her."

"I already love her, too. And thanks for the warning." I sighed. "But here I've been freaking out about our mothers meeting each other, thinking yours would take one look at my New Age wacko mom and go running for the hills."

His lips curved in a sheepish grin. "Ah. Little did you know that my own mystical mum would put yours to shame."

Playfully, I smacked his shoulder. "You could've let me know beforehand."

"And miss your reaction?" he countered. "Not for the world."

I could understand that, since I'd have done the same. "Well, I'd say they're pretty evenly matched."

He rolled his eyes. "I can't wait for the pagan spell-casting throwdown."

Still chuckling, I wrapped my arms around him, and we rode down to the basement holding on to each other. Once the elevator came to a shaky halt, I glanced up at him. "I need to tell you what Eddie and Terrence said."

"Let's step into my office." He took my hand and we walked into the basement garage. It was dimly lit and chilly, but I felt perfectly safe because our new building security system had been extended to the garage. Not to mention that I had my very own security expert at my side.

"So I take it there are no files in the trunk of your car," Derek said.

"No." I frowned. "Hmm. It's going to be tricky getting back into the apartment. I should've thought of a better excuse."

"We'll think of something before we go back upstairs." Derek pulled his key from his pocket and shut off his car alarm so we could lean companionably against his Bentley. "Tell me what the brothers said."

I related the entire conversation to him and then asked him what he thought.

"Darling," he began, then hesitated, shaking his head.

"I'm very glad you weren't seen. I have a feeling Eddie and Terrence would not want some of that information overheard by anyone."

I thought about it. "I don't know if they even realized what they were actually revealing. Most of it sounded like the same stuff they've rehashed before, except for those few glaring moments when they divulged some real secrets."

"I wonder why Terrence doesn't sell his half of the business to Eddie," Derek mused. "He's clearly not happy."

"Not happy at all," I agreed, and felt a little depressed just talking about it. "I have a feeling Eddie is right that Terrence holds on to his half of the business simply for spite. I wish they would split up, though. I hated overhearing all that nasty bickering."

"I don't blame you. Well, let's see. I count two smoking guns in among the words you heard." He held up his fingers. "One, Eddie's book may be fake. And two, Terrence might've been the one who ransacked Joey's shop, looking for the book he claims is his."

"And three," I added, "apparently both men received their books from Bonnie."

"Ah, yes. A definite possibility."

"For their good behavior," I said dryly.

"I'm sure." He frowned at me. "Does Bonnie have a stash of *Alice in Wonderland* books hidden in her apartment?"

"I have no idea, but I would love to find out."

"That might be one of our objectives. But first, we have to get our hands on the two books belonging to Eddie and Terrence."

"If there really are two," I said.

"What's your gut feeling?"

I breathed in and out, thinking about it. "I believe there are two books. Terrence wouldn't have gone to so much trouble trying to track down his book if he never really had one in the first place."

"That's assuming he's the one who trashed Joey's shop."

"Yes."

"Which brings us to another key question."

"What's that?"

Derek's expression was darkly serious. "If Terrence is the one who tore apart Joey's shoe shop, is he also the one who killed him?"

We managed to slink back into the apartment without raising the suspicions of our parents. Derek and the two dads went up to the rooftop patio to check out the view and smoke cigars. I spent a few happy hours showing Meg and Mom my handmade deck of playing cards and explaining how easy it was to make paper. Naturally, they wanted to experiment with the process.

"You are a genius," Meg declared after she pulled her first piece of paper away from the mesh screen. "This is fantastic."

"Oh, Meg, that's so pretty," Mom gushed.

We had torn off a corner of a purple advertising flyer and added it to the blender, giving Meg's paper a lavender hue.

Meg set the damp piece on my worktable and clapped her hands together. "Let's see yours, Becky."

Mom carefully peeled the paper off the screen and held it in her hand. "It's shiny."

"Those are the glitters."

"I added a few extra sprinkles," Mom said, setting the piece down next to Meg's. "I love it. I love all the uneven bits of herbs and grass and flowers. It looks so professional. Why don't we do this all the time?"

"You can," I said, chuckling. "Now that you know how to do it, you can make paper at home anytime you want."

"I'm going to," she said. "Really, I love it."

I carried the blender over to my workshop sink and began to wash it out. "If you're serious, I'll give you the name of a Web site where you can order the wooden frames and other materials."

Meg held up her lavender paper. "I'd like to make cards like this for invitations and thank-you notes. My friends will be so impressed."

"Ooh, and gift tags," Mom said brightly.

Meg grinned. "That's a super idea."

"And it's so simple," Mom said.

Meg's eyes widened and she grabbed my arm. "You shouldn't show anyone else how to do this, Brooklyn. If people learn to make their own paper, nobody will buy yours."

I smiled. "Since I don't earn my living making paper, I'm okay with that."

"Still," she said, glancing around as though checking to make sure we weren't being spied upon. "This should be one of those secret arts that only wizards and elves know about."

"And us," Mom said, laughing.

Meg gave her a conspiratorial nod. "Us, of course."

Mom and Meg sat at my worktable chatting about their favorite types of casting stones and which of their chakras were out of alignment while I cleaned up from the papermaking party. Derek walked in as I was pouring the tub water down my workshop sink.

"My dad and I are going to walk up to Pietro's to pick up dinner," he said.

I glanced at him. "What's my father up to?"

"He's setting up a wine tasting for us." Derek's eyes gleamed. "It looks fantastic."

"I can't wait," Mom said.

Derek smiled. "Jim said this would give Dad and me a chance to talk."

"Isn't that lovely?" Meg said.

"Yes, it is." Derek gave both his mom and mine a kiss on the cheek, and then kissed me. With a wink, he said, "Keep these two out of trouble."

"You're asking a lot," I muttered as I wiped the tub dry with a dishcloth.

"We heard that," Mom protested.

Chuckling, I gave Derek another kiss. "Better hurry back."

"Will do," Derek said, and ducked out of the room.

Less than an hour later, Derek and John returned with two large pizzas, one veggie and one with lots of meat, plus three salads and plenty of garlic toast.

Because we need more bread products, I thought. If I made it through this week without gaining twenty pounds, I would consider my mission a success.

While Derek and his dad were gone, Mom and Meg set the dining room table for dinner. Dad commandeered the kitchen counter for his wine tasting. I counted six bottles of beautiful red wines of various vintages and appellations. Since my family was part of a commune that owned the Dharma vineyard and winery in Sonoma, I had no doubt that every wine we tasted tonight would be world-class.

We put the pizzas and garlic toast into the oven to keep warm and placed the salads in the fridge. We were all set to begin the tasting when Derek called me into his office to look at something.

"What is it?" I asked.

"Close the door," he said quietly, and leaned one hip against his desk.

I took one look at his face and did as he asked. "What's wrong? What happened?"

"When Dad and I were walking back from Pietro's, I happened to look up and noticed Terrence sneaking out of Joey's back door."

"You mean the door to Joey's shop?"

"No." He paused, frowning. "I mean the one to his apartment."

"Are you kidding? You saw him upstairs?"

"I saw him coming down the stairs," he clarified. "I know which apartment is Joey's because it's directly upstairs from the shoe repair shop. And you've seen how each apartment on that side of the building has a set of stairs leading from the kitchen down to the side alley?"

"Yes. They have a nice big laundry room in the basement that everyone uses." I could picture the stairs on that side of the Courtyard, just as Derek had described them. Each apartment had a good-sized covered landing outside its kitchen door, where some people had a small barbecue grill and some others kept a vegetable garden. A set of wooden stairs descended from each of the landings and a sturdy wooden fence ran along the alley, essentially providing a private back entryway for the occupants of the Courtyard apartments.

"So what was Terrence doing in Joey's apartment?" I wondered.

"Good question." Derek folded his arms across his chest. "Brooklyn, he was carrying something, and I would swear it was a book. For what it's worth, it looked about the size of Eddie's copy of *Alice in Wonderland*. He had it wrapped in some sort of cloth. Perhaps a T-shirt or a towel."

I took a deep breath and exhaled slowly, trying to keep from jumping to conclusions. But I wasn't really jumping. Circumstances had pretty much leaped up and grabbed hold of both of us. I could see that Derek was thinking along the same lines, and for just a second I told myself I was a lucky woman, having a man who understood me so well. A man who enjoyed us being a real team.

Then my mind went back to the matter at hand. Under the circumstances, I had to fight to keep calm, but I gave it a shot. "That's a real stretch."

"Of course it is. But given Terrence's disturbing reaction to everything Eddie was saying earlier in the day, it wouldn't be out of the realm of possibility."

"I guess not."

"Suppose Eddie put a bug in Terrence's ear about the possibility of Joey having his book." Still frowning, Derek lined out a scenario that made way too much sense to ignore. "And it gnawed on him all day. He waited until it was getting dark, then worked up the nerve to break into Joey's apartment to try to find it."

"And you just happened to be across the street where you could see him when he came strolling down the stairs. That's just too much. Will anybody believe us?"

"The timing was right," he theorized. "It was dusk

and that side of the building gets dark sooner than the other side. He decided to take the chance."

"Wow." I shook my head, still a little dazed by the news. "So what do we do now?"

"*We* don't do anything," he said briskly. "I might go over and have a look around later, but you're to stay here and entertain our parents."

I smiled. "Are you telling me what to do?"

He laughed. "I suppose I am. So let me rephrase it. Will you *please* stay here with our parents?"

I shook my head. "Not much of an improvement. And here I was just thinking how nice it was that we both enjoy being a *team*."

"We are a team, love. And I wouldn't change a thing." He reached for my arm and pulled me close. "I don't want you hurt. Someone went to a lot of trouble to kill Joey, and then they were desperate enough to hurt Rabbit. I don't want you in the sights of some desperate killer."

He didn't add the word *again*. But it was implied. I gazed up at him. "I could say the same for you."

"I appreciate that," he said, stroking my hair. "But until you achieve the rank of sixth-degree black belt and start carrying a gun, I would beg you to stay home and out of harm's way."

I sighed. "Now you're just showing off. But that's okay. I'll stay home. But only because our parents will ask too many questions."

"Thank God for small favors," he murmured.

"But look—we need to figure out what we're doing. We have to go back to the beginning and ask ourselves, why was Joey murdered?"

Derek held up his hand. "Alternately, we should ask

ourselves another question. Why was Bonnie being targeted?"

"Right. That's the more likely scenario." I thought about it for a moment. "I wonder who stands to inherit the Courtyard."

"Good question. Was it Rabbit? Is that why he was assaulted?"

There was a sudden knock on the door, surprising us both.

Derek frowned. "Come in."

His mother stood at the door. "Can't you two discuss all of this murder-and-assault business over a glass of wine?"

"You heard us?" I blurted. We'd been talking so quietly. Maybe she really was psychic.

Derek looked poleaxed. "Mother, how could you hear what we were talking about?"

"So naive," she murmured, shaking her head. "Derek, I'm the mother of five boys. I can hear mischief through solid steel. And, unlike Superman, even lead doesn't stop me." Smiling, she held up one of our crystal drinking glasses and pressed it against the door. "Especially when I have one of these."

Chapter 9

We joined the others gathered around the dining room table. Everyone was ready to enjoy the wine tasting, but Derek and I were still shaking our heads at his mother's blatant eavesdropping on our conversation. The question on our minds was, could she really have heard us through the door? I made a mental note to experiment with that crystal-glass theory after they'd all gone to bed.

And I have to say, I was sort of enjoying the fact that it wasn't *my* mother being all snoopy and outrageous for a change. Derek was probably less amused, but still, we took it all with good humor, of course.

And frankly, I couldn't blame Meg for wanting to know what was going on. The two of us had been pretty secretive all afternoon.

Dad began to pour small amounts into each of our wineglasses as he described the first bottle. "This is our newest cabernet. It's made from grapes that grow on Summit Ridge."

"Is that on your property?" Meg asked.

"Yes. It's a hilly area to the south of the winery building. If you decide you'd like to drive out there for a day, we'll take a tour of the entire property."

"I'm up for that," John declared.

"Oh, me as well. I've heard so much about Dharma through Derek. John and I would both love to see it." Meg took a sip. "This is quite nice."

"It's relatively young, but well blended and slightly fruity with hints of blackberry jam and cherries."

She frowned. "Why do I smell roses?"

"That's very good, Meg," Dad exclaimed, bringing a happy blush to her cheeks. "We planted red roses at the edge of the cabernet vine rows a few years ago. Their roots have started to seep into the terroir and are adding a new dimension to the fullness of the grapes."

Meg took another sip and swished it around in her mouth as Dad had suggested. Swallowing, she closed her eyes to savor the flavor, then set her glass down. "That taste was even better."

"It keeps opening up. The more it's exposed to air, the more the flavors will grow. That's why we swirl our glasses."

"I didn't realize," she said.

"It helps get the oxygen in there," Dad said, grinning.

"I don't think I've ever tasted such a luscious wine." Meg took another sip. "Well, that settles it—I'm converted. I used to be a Bordeaux girl, but I'm switching teams. I'm all about the cabernet now."

"There's no need to switch," Dad explained. "Many

Bordeaux wines are based on the cabernet sauvignon grape, among others. You can play for both teams."

She chuckled. "Thank you, Jim. I love learning something new. And you've relieved my mind that I can still drink Bordeaux without feeling guilty." Picking up her glass, she gave it a swirl, then shifted toward me and Derek. "Now, children, I would like to discuss what I overheard."

"All right, Mother," Derek said pleasantly, biting back a smile as he sipped his wine. "Go right ahead."

"Right-o," she said. "Now, you said you saw the man leaving the dead fellow's apartment carrying what looked like a book."

"I suppose he could've been carrying anything." Derek shook his head, a little frustrated. "Perhaps my mind convinced my eyes that it was a book."

Taken aback, I said, "No. That's not even worth debating. You are a master at this. Your eyes see everything spot-on. If you saw him carrying a book, then it was a book. And that's that."

He smiled warmly and reached over to squeeze my hand. "All right, then. Thank you, darling. Duly chastened."

I happened to glance at Meg and saw her eyes filled with tears. "Are you all right, Meg?"

"Oh, Brooklyn, that was so sweet," she said, dabbing her eyes with a tissue. "My one hope was that all my sons would one day find true love, but it's lovely to see it happening before my very eyes."

John wrapped his arm around his wife's waist and gave her a squeeze. "She can be a sentimental old thing sometimes."

She slapped his chest lightly. "I'm not that old."

I chuckled; then we all settled in for a quiet moment while we sipped our wine.

Finally I brought the topic back to the issue at hand. "I'm not sure why we're even questioning whether Terrence was carrying a book or not. Of course he was. Finding that book would've been his sole reason for going into Joey's apartment."

John spoke up. "Given what Derek and I saw on our trip back with the pizza, Terrence indeed found the book."

"Did you see it, too, John?"

"My eyes aren't quite as sharp as Derek's," he admitted with a grin. "I did see the man jogging down the stairs, but I couldn't tell you what he was holding."

"No worries, Dad," Derek murmured.

"I should've brought my binoculars," he said, chuckling.

"Next time we'll do that," Meg said. "Ooh. Perhaps we might buy a pair while we're here."

John merely patted her hand, but Meg and my mother exchanged a knowing glance.

I slowly swirled my wineglass. "Terrence has been completely obsessed with that book for the past six months."

"Right," Derek said, nodding. "So if he thought Joey had the book, I believe he would take the chance and break in."

I held up my hand. "To be fair, we don't know for certain that he actually broke in. Maybe when he was ransacking the shoe repair shop, he found Joey's keys."

"That's a good thought, Brooklyn," Meg said.

"*If* he was indeed ransacking Joey's shop," Derek stressed.

"So now what?" Mom wondered aloud.

I glanced at Derek. "Do you think we should call Inspector Lee?"

"And spoil all our fun?" Meg said, then noticed her husband's deep frown. "I'm just teasing the children, dear."

"Wish I could believe that, darling," John said warily.

"We probably should give her a call," Derek reasoned. "Maybe tomorrow, after we've worked out a few of the kinks in our story."

I rubbed my hands together. "I'd love to have her confiscate Eddie's book so I could tell if it's the real deal."

"But so far there's no honest reason to take it," Derek said, "other than you having an interest in looking at the book."

"And verifying whether it's a fake or not," I added a little defensively.

"But still, love, what does that have to do with Jocy's death?"

"I'll think of a reason," I muttered.

Dad drew our attention as he poured a small amount from the second bottle of wine into his glass. Swirling it, he stared at the glass, measuring the wine's legs and checking the color. Then he sniffed it and grinned. "Oh, this is going to be good."

"I'll have a touch of that," John said, holding up his glass.

"Me, too," Meg said.

"This is another one of our cabernets," Dad said. "A few years older than the first. Let me know what you think."

"That is spectacular," John said, after taking a minute sip. He swirled the dark liquid around in his glass and leaned in to take a big sniff. "Marvelous nose."

"We're pretty excited about this one," Dad said. "It's got a bosomy richness and a jammy consistency that is unsurpassed in a lot of the cabs out this year."

"My goodness—that sounds rather thrilling, doesn't it?" Meg said, taking a hearty swig.

"Jim talks like that around the house all the time," Mom said, giggling.

"Aw, give me a break, Becky," Dad said.

Was he blushing? I flashed Derek a look and rolled my eyes. What was going on with our parents? Maybe we should have switched all four of them to coffee instead. *Make that decaf,* I thought, then said, "How about if we get back to our situation across the street?"

"Oh, apologies," Meg said, fluttering her hands. "Yes, back to the case at hand. Derek, I think you should sneak into his apartment and find that book. Becky and I would be happy to create a distraction."

"Oh, what fun!" Mom cried. "Count me in."

My eyes widened and I started to protest. "But—"

"That shouldn't be necessary," Derek rushed to say. "But I appreciate your enthusiasm."

"We'll be standing by," Mom said, giving a snappy salute.

Late that night, after tossing and turning for a few hours, I sat up in bed. I wanted to blame the sausage pizza for my inability to sleep soundly, but it was my own fault for having had a third piece. And dividing up the rest of the leftover chocolate cream pie hadn't helped one bit, either.

I slipped quietly out of bed, not wanting to wake up Derek, and wandered out to the living room. All was peaceful after a rollicking evening of laughs and pizza and wine. I loved this space in the quiet of the night, with moonlight filtering in through the big factory windows on either side of the room.

The building had once been a corset factory, back in the 1800s, and when converting the large spaces into loft apartments, the developers had retained the original brick walls and industrial-glass windows.

I walked into my workshop, just to check that everything was in order there, too. At the far end of the room, I stared out the window at the Courtyard building across the street. It looked so pretty in the moonlight, so tranquil. You would never know that a murder and an assault—and a break-in, too—had occurred there in the last few days. If I leaned all the way to the right, I could look down the street and over a few buildings and see the bay in the distance. It looked calm on the surface and black as pitch without any sunlight shimmering down.

"You couldn't sleep?"

I turned and saw Derek standing in the dimly lit archway leading from the workshop to the living room.

"I'm sorry if I woke you."

"You didn't. I woke up on my own and found you were gone." He joined me at the window, and we gazed out in silence for a moment.

"This is such an odd case," I murmured. "There aren't that many suspects, but I still can't figure it out. Who was really the target? What was the killer's motivation? If Joey was the intended victim, we could look at the two women he was cheating on, or Terrence, who's proven to be insanely jealous of anyone dating Bonnie."

"But with Bonnie as the intended victim, everything changes," Derek said.

"Exactly. I can't think of anyone who had a strong enough motivation to kill her. Kitty, maybe. She said she hated her now, but they were friends once."

"She was screaming some pretty awful things the other day," Derek reminded me.

"I know. But even though she was raging mad at the time, I don't think she has the nerve or the guts to carry it out."

"Terrence is in love with Bonnie," Derek mused.

"And she dumped him. For some people, that would be enough to turn them murderous."

"And yet he's still obsessed with her."

"I know. It's weird. When I hear him talk about her, it's with such deference and hope. There's no way he could have turned around and tried to kill her."

"Eddie?"

I chuckled. "The only reason Eddie would have done it would be to shut Terrence up."

Derek winked. "I've heard of worse motivations."

I sighed. "I just don't see it."

"There could be someone we haven't even thought of."

"Like who?"

"Like a property developer?"

"We talked about this with Inspector Lee," I said. "And I asked Kitty about it, too. She said there are absolutely no developers sniffing around." I frowned. "I'm not sure how she would know that."

"Maybe it's just wishful thinking on her part."

"It could be," I admitted. "But she did say that Bonnie can't sell the building without every tenant's approval, so I can't see why Bonnie would encourage a property developer when nothing will come of it."

"But what about all the vandalism? Is there another reason for someone to do all that damage other than trying to get people to move out?"

"I don't know. Inspector Lee insists there's no gang activity in this area. So maybe it's just a jerky kid who's got nothing better to do."

"Maybe." He didn't sound convinced.

I leaned my head against his chest. "The good news is that, with all this talking, I'm getting sleepy."

"Let's get back to bed, then."

I was about to turn when something caught my eye. "Oh."

Derek straightened. "What is it?"

"I thought I saw a— Look, there it is." I pointed to a bobbling stream of light across the street. "There's a light on somewhere."

Derek stared out the window and saw what I was talking about. "Looks like a flashlight."

"Yes." I stared long and hard at the moving light. "It's inside the Courtyard. Wait. It just disappeared."

"No, they moved to the back of the building. I'm going over there."

"Okay, hurry!" I said.

He tore out of the room.

"Be careful, please," I whispered.

But in less than twenty seconds, he was already gone out the front door. It was a good thing he was wearing sweatpants, I thought, because I couldn't handle the image of him running around the city in boxers and not much else.

From the window I saw him jog across the street and slip around the back. Then I couldn't see him at all and my heart began to race. I couldn't stand it. *I should have gone with him.* It would have been easier than waiting. Wondering. Hoping.

I was wide-awake now and sleep was the last thing on my mind, what with Derek out there chasing down marauders.

Why had I let him go out there by himself? *A vicious killer is on the loose and Derek might very well run into him tonight. I should be there, watching his back.* What kind of team was this if I stayed on the sidelines?

"No way," I muttered, and ran to the bedroom. I threw on sweats and sneakers, then took off down the stairs.

Once I was outside on the street, I tried to ignore the feeling that I'd gone mad. But worrying about Derek helped chase those fears away. Not that he wasn't perfectly capable of handling things by himself, but what if he needed backup? *I should be there for him,* I thought. He might not thank me, but I didn't care about that right then.

I dashed across the street and snuck through the archway leading to the inner courtyard. Once I got there, I stuck close to the wall nearest the bookshop, sliding along until I got near the heart of the courtyard. There were dim lights on either side, enough for the tenants to make their way safely across the flagstone patio, but the trees blocked enough of the direct light that I felt safely hidden from anyone glancing out a window. I couldn't see or hear another soul and wondered where Derek was hiding.

Suddenly there was a crash in the parking lot, followed by scrambling feet.

"Derek!" I raced across the courtyard and out through the other archway that led to the parking lot. At the edge of the lot I stopped in my tracks. A stepladder lay collapsed against the building and a few cans of spray paint rolled around on the ground. The graffiti vandal had struck again.

But where was Derek?

I stood there for a few minutes, scared to death to find him hurt somewhere nearby, but afraid to venture too far from the building in case he returned. Just as I was about to step back into the courtyard to look around, Derek came jogging up the side street. He ran over as soon as he saw me.

"Brooklyn, what are you doing here? You could've been hurt or mugged at the very least. You promised to stay home."

"I didn't exactly promise, but let's not split hairs." I wrapped my arms around him and held on tightly. "Are you all right?"

"I'm fine," he said, clearly irritated with himself—and maybe a little bit with me, too. But he grabbed onto me just as firmly as I held him. I gave it a long minute before I felt okay letting him go.

He scowled as he raked his fingers through his hair in disgust. "Bloody plonker got away from me. I scared him off and he went running. I chased him, but he was more familiar with the streets and alleys around here than I am. I lost him down by Mission Creek."

I wasn't sure what shocked me more: Derek's sliding

into British slang or the fact that he had lost his prey. "Were you down by the houseboats?"

"They're on the other side of the creek, but yes."

Mission Creek Marina was a sleepy little stretch of water extending inland from China Basin, and a few dozen houseboats were moored along its shore. The creek was surrounded by high-tech start-up companies, a Caltrain station, and the massive UCSF campus, yet it felt like its own little world. A world that time had forgotten. It was another oddly fascinating San Francisco neighborhood that few outsiders knew about, despite its proximity to the Giants' stadium.

"Did you get a good look at him?" I asked.

"No. He was wearing a ski mask and a nondescript black jacket. And he was fast."

"Fast, or desperate," I said.

"Possibly both."

I nodded. "Let's go home."

"In just a minute," he said. "First I want to check one thing." He led the way around the building to the stairs leading up to Joey's back door.

"I want to see if the lock has been damaged."

I gazed up the stairs and frowned. "It's awfully dark over here."

"So it's a good thing I brought this along." He reached into his pocket and pulled out a high-powered mini-flashlight.

"You are awesome," I whispered.

He chuckled. "Come on."

We began climbing quickly, but slowed down when it became clear that we were making too much noise. The old wooden stairs creaked and groaned with every step, and we didn't want to wake up everyone in the building.

At the kitchen door, Derek shined the light on the lock.

"It looks undamaged," I whispered.

He knelt down to get a better look, then shook his head. "You're right. It's clean. Terrence must've had a key to the door."

"And I wonder where he got that."

We descended the stairs and made it around to the back parking lot before we spoke again.

I frowned as I thought of the different scenarios. "It's possible that Terrence had the key all along. Joey might've given him a key to his place when he went on vacation or just in case there was an emergency. You know, the way I have a key to Vinnie and Suzie's place, just in case."

"Yes, I considered that, too," Derek murmured. "Darling, take off your hoodie, will you?"

"What for? It's cold out here."

"I would use my shirt but I'm afraid it's sweaty and I don't want to compromise any fingerprints or other evidence we might pick up from these items." He indicated the spray cans the vandal had left on the ground.

"Oh, good idea." I tore off my hoodie and used it to gather up the cans.

"I'll drive these over to police headquarters in the morning." Derek stared at the stepladder for a moment, then shrugged and pulled off his T-shirt. "Guess I'll have to take a chance with my sweaty shirt after all." He wrapped it around the side of the stepladder and picked it up, and we walked back home together.

"If Terrence already had a key," I said, "then maybe someone else ransacked Joey's shop."

"Maybe, but Terrence still might've done it if he thought Joey was keeping the book in his shop."

I yawned. "There are too many options to think about tonight. We need to get some sleep."

As I punched the button for the elevator, Derek gritted his teeth. "It appears we have another good reason to call Inspector Lee tomorrow after all."

On the phone the next morning, Inspector Lee listened quietly as I told her what Colin the pie man had said about Bonnie being an early riser. She even thanked me for the information, which made me think that Colin might not have been as forthcoming with the police as he was with me. Then Derek mentioned the graffiti evidence, and the inspector agreed to meet us at the Courtyard at eleven o'clock that morning, which gave us plenty of time to eat breakfast before she arrived. I walked over with Derek and our parents to the Beanery, and after picking up a caffe latte, I left them at the door to Sweetie Pies. They went inside and I didn't. That place was getting to be a dangerous habit, so I'd already decided to take my latte and stop in at the bookshop instead. But as I was about to walk away, I noticed Bonnie sitting at a table at the edge of the room, talking to a good-looking man wearing a suit and tie. I didn't recognize him and my curiosity was burning me up inside, so I strolled inside and over to the counter and waited until Colin was free. In a quiet voice, I asked, "Do you know who Bonnie's sitting with?"

"Yeah, she's been in here with him before. She introduced him a few weeks ago. Jared? Jason? Somebody."

"Does he live around here?"

"I don't think so." He squinted as he tried to think. "He said he works for some company, something . . . with a tree name, I think. Cypress? Ponderosa?" He shrugged with regret. "I can't remember. You want me to introduce you?"

"No, that's okay. You know me, just being nosy."

He grinned. "No worries."

"Thanks, Colin." I walked out and headed quickly for the bookshop. Before Inspector Lee confiscated Eddie's copy of *Alice in Wonderland*, I was hoping to get another look at it—as if I hadn't already seen it enough times. But this time I would be looking with new eyes. I wasn't sure what I would find, but I'd seen enough fraudulent books in my day to know what to look for.

Usually the fraud was accomplished by adding a fake title page to the book. This was the page that included the publication date, so by aging the book a few years, you could increase the price by thousands of dollars. This bogus page could be inserted and glued in a very subtle way, or sewn in with the other pages, something that was rarely noticed by your average book fan. An experienced collector could sometimes tell the difference, but since most book sales were done over the Internet these days, the fraud wasn't always caught until money had already changed hands.

The other giveaway was the paper itself. It was difficult to match the exact paper for a book created over two hundred years ago. Book counterfeiters were clever, though, and sometimes would take a very thin piece of rice paper or something comparable and glue it right onto one of the blank pages at the front of the book instead of trying to match the paper itself. The thin page would be printed with all of the counterfeit information required to raise the price.

And then sometimes the original date was simply smudged out and a new date carefully inked in.

Again, a skilled collector or buyer would be able to tell the difference.

"Good morning," I said cheerily as I walked into the shop.

"Hello, Brooklyn," Eddie said.

Terrence waved. "Hey, Brooklyn."

"Eddie, I was wondering if I could look at your *Alice* again."

He raised an eyebrow. "I'm not going to sell it to you."

We both chuckled and I said, "I'm not going to ask. Well, not today, anyway."

Still smiling, he unlocked the Plexiglas case and handed the book to me.

"Still so beautiful," I murmured.

"It's a pleasure to see you enjoy our books," Eddie said, his voice measured.

"Thank you for the opportunity." I leaned over the book and breathed in its scent. The rich fragrances of leather and vellum were intoxicating. To me they represented rare, ageless beauty.

I took a cursory look at the endpapers where they met the leather turnover. Nothing suspicious there. Turning to the title page, I stared at the gutter where the pages were sewn together. Depending on how the book was made, the pages might be sewn so tightly that the gutter was virtually invisible—unless you were willing to break the spine.

I wasn't.

Again, nothing about the title page looked suspicious. I noted once again that the book was in amazing condition. Clean white pages with almost no foxing anywhere. That in itself could've been a warning sign for some aged books, but in the case of this *Alice*, it was simply an indication that the book had been stored under excellent conditions.

I could see no issues of fraud with this book, so I still wasn't sure what Terrence had been talking about during the argument I'd overheard. I should've handed the book back to Eddie right then, but I couldn't help myself. I began to turn the pages, feeling the thickness of the paper and studying the beautiful font style of the book. I took another moment to gaze at some of my favorite illustrations, particularly the drawing of Alice trying to play croquet with a flamingo as the mallet, and the look on her face while attending the Mad Hatter's tea party. The young girl appeared very close to losing her temper. I couldn't blame her. Those creatures were quite insane!

Finally I closed the book and handed it back to Eddie. "Thank you."

"You bet, kiddo. Anytime."

Not to be ignored, Terrence piped up. "I have a book just like that one."

I smiled tolerantly. "I know, Terrence. But it got stolen, right?"

He frowned. "Yes. That's right."

"I always hate hearing about a lost book," I said with sympathy. "Good luck finding it."

He was still frowning when I waved good-bye.

I ran into Inspector Lee and Bonnie in the parking lot

behind the Courtyard. I was dying to tell the inspector how Derek had chased away the graffiti artist the night before, but for some reason I didn't want to mention it in front of Bonnie. I would just have to wait another half hour until our official eleven o'clock meeting to tell all.

"At this rate, the city's going to start charging me," Bonnie was saying as she scowled at the graffiti on the wall.

"I'm sure they won't," I said. "They want to get rid of the graffiti as much as you do."

"I hope so. Still, it's a little depressing." She gazed at the black scribblings that marred half of the wall. "Why do they keep targeting us?"

"Do you have any enemies?" Inspector Lee asked.

"I didn't think so, but now I'm not sure." She chuckled contritely. "I suppose I might've annoyed a few of the fellows I used to date, but that's not enough reason to try and destroy my livelihood, is it?"

"You never know," Lee said ominously.

"Are there any developers interested in the building?" I asked, pleased that I could finally ask Bonnie directly the question that I'd asked practically everyone else around here. She looked taken aback, maybe because she figured it was none of my business. But when had that ever stopped me?

"All the time," she admitted. "But I discourage them. I can't sell the place without permission from every tenant here. That's how my husband set up the will. But I wouldn't want to sell it anyway."

"You wouldn't want to sell the Courtyard?" I said, remembering Kitty's words about Bonnie hating to be tied to the building. "But you could make a lot of money."

"I don't care," she insisted. "I love it here."

Even though I questioned the truth of her statement, I felt a rush of relief. "I'm so glad to hear it, because I love it, too."

"The whole neighborhood loves it," Bonnie said, shrugging.

"It's a cool old building," Inspector Lee said.

"I know, right? And if I sold it, the buyer would tear it down in a heartbeat and put up condos," she said, annoyed. "And believe me, I would have plenty of enemies then."

I shook my head at the thought. "I would hate to see it torn down."

"Everyone would," Bonnie said with a blasé wave of her hand. "This building is a landmark."

Bonnie seemed to have run out of interest in the conversation, making me wonder again if she was really serious about loving the building. Kitty had tried to convince me otherwise, but maybe I wasn't being fair. She probably had places to go, people to see.

"Thanks again for your time, Ms. Carson," Inspector Lee said, handing her a business card. "Call me if you remember anything else."

"I will. Thanks. See you, Brooklyn."

I lifted my hand in a wave. "See you later, Bonnie."

We watched her walk away toward the alley; then Inspector Lee and I walked to the archway leading into the courtyard. Before we got there, I stopped her. "I need to tell you something."

She turned and frowned at me. "You withholding evidence again?"

"No, I promise." I glanced around and saw a car pull into the parking lot. "There are too many people around here. Do you mind if we walk around the building?"

"This better be good, Brooklyn."

I knew she was half kidding, so I ignored the comment and led the way. I waited to speak until we were on the opposite side of the building from the alley, where there was very little traffic of either the human or the automobile variety. Just trees and a walkway. And cold. This side of the building was a natural wind tunnel. Maybe I should've chosen a warmer place to talk, but since I wanted to get through this conversation quickly, I wasn't about to move elsewhere. I zipped my jacket up to my neck to keep the chill out.

"I just heard this yesterday from one of the shopkeepers, so I haven't been keeping it from you." I turned to check again that we were alone. "I'm not sure what you can do about it."

"Tell me what it is and I'll figure it out."

I lowered my voice. "Kitty from the hat shop thinks that Bonnie killed her husband."

"What?"

I held up both hands. "I know it's bizarre. And now I'm a little surprised she didn't mention it when you first interviewed her, seeing as how she was screaming and yelling about Bonnie killing Joey. Anyway, I thought it was just sour grapes coming from Kitty because Bonnie stole Joey away from her. But I thought I'd better mention it to you anyway."

She frowned. "Kitty. She's the dark-haired woman."

"That's her. I know she was crazed at the time, but she's calmed down since then."

"Calmed down," Lee repeated wryly. "And yet she's still accusing the woman of murder."

"Yeah." I shook my head and pushed my hair out of my face when a sharp, cold blast of wind slapped it across my eyes. "I don't know what to think. But I swear, when I talked to her she seemed perfectly calm and sure of herself. She said the police investigated the man's death but nothing was ever proved."

Inspector Lee shrugged. "It happens."

"I know. I guess Bonnie's husband was older. Maybe he died of a heart attack? I can't say for sure."

"I'll check it out. Good job, Brooklyn."

"Thanks."

"So now I've got to talk to Kitty again." She pulled out her notebook and jotted down a few sentences as a reminder. "You're keeping me busy."

"Sorry about that." Ready to escape the wind tunnel, I led the way out to the front sidewalk, where her car was parked. "There's one other thing."

"Oh boy. What is with you?"

I shook my head, took a deep breath, and plunged forward. "I know you're going to think I'm crazy, but there's this book. I think it might be connected to Joey's death."

"Why would I think you're crazy?"

"Because." I gave her a look of concern. "It's about a *book*."

She chuckled. "I was just kidding around. You're definitely crazy if you think you'll convince me that this crime has anything to do with a book."

"Just hear me out."

"Take your best shot." She folded her arms across her chest tightly. "I can't wait to hear this."

"Just the two people I was looking for."

We both turned and watched Derek approach. I smiled with relief. "And you're just the person I was hoping would walk by."

He gave me a quick kiss and then nodded his head at Janice. "Inspector, good morning."

"Hello, Commander."

I glanced around, but he was alone. "Where are our parental units?"

"They're enjoying their late breakfast at Sweetie Pies."

"Good. That gives us a few minutes to talk."

"How is that place, by the way?" Janice asked.

My eyes widened. "Sweetie Pies? Oh my God, it's the best pie you've ever tasted. They have savory pies, too. Amazing."

"They really are fantastic," Derek chimed in.

"Good to know," she said. "Since I've got to go grill the guy who runs the place anyway, maybe I'll pick something up for my mom."

"She will love whatever you get."

"Okay, thanks for the recommendation," she said.

I said a silent prayer for Colin the pie man. Inspector Lee could be a formidable interrogator.

"I hate to interrupt your conversation," Derek said. "But I wanted to remind you that I'm holding some evidence for you." He went into more detail about his run-in the night before with the graffiti vandal and the two of them arranged to meet later so Derek could hand off the paint cans and stepladder.

"Now, about this book," Lee said, focusing in on me again.

"I was just going to tell her about Terrence's book when you joined us." I gazed up at Derek, silently pleading for his help. My hero stepped right in and began to explain the situation. It was a little frustrating, knowing

Janice would take the news better coming from him than from me. But I chalked it up to books. The plain fact was that I was an expert in books, and with every investigation we'd ever been involved in, a *book* was the central motivation for murder. The police often pooh-poohed it, insisting that just because someone coveted a book didn't mean they had a reason to kill. But the police were usually wrong.

I wasn't thrilled about it, but whether or not the police believed it, people were more than happy to kill for a first edition, a rare manuscript—heck, probably even a comic book if it was the right one.

Derek went through the whole story, explaining Terrence's obsession with the book that Bonnie had given him. "It's been months now and he won't let it go," Derek said. "We think that at some point yesterday morning in a conversation with Eddie, it occurred to Terrence that Joey might have the book. We think he was driven to break into the man's apartment to look for it."

"And we think he might have found it," I said.

Lee glared at me. "You *think*?"

"To be honest, Inspector, I can't say for certain," Derek clarified. "I was standing across the street about fifty feet away. But I saw him exit Joey's place carrying what looked like a book similar in size to the one Eddie has on display in the bookshop."

"I'm the one who overheard the argument Terrence was having with Eddie yesterday morning," I said. "It was alarming to see how angry he was. So I think Derek is right. Terrence absolutely had to break into Joey's apartment to find the book." I winced as I added, "He's become a little unhinged."

"We also think he might be the one who ransacked Joey's shoe repair shop," Derek said. "He could've been looking for the book or, at the very least, Joey's apartment keys."

Inspector Lee didn't look happy. No surprise there. "This is a real stretch, you guys."

My shoulders slumped, but I picked myself up. "I know it is. And believe me, I hate that Joey's murder might be all about this book. But I would love to try and find out for sure."

"Yeah, I know." She was obviously taking pity on me because I was clearly upset about this turn of events. "Look, let me give it a day or two and then I'll question the guy, but I can't promise anything."

"No problem," Derek said.

"One more thing?" I said quickly as she was turning to walk away.

"Oh, for God's sake, Brooklyn," she said. "What's left?"

I shot a glance at Derek for strength, then said, "I'm wondering if you could confiscate the book that's on display in the bookshop. I'd like to examine it to make sure it's not a fake."

"What would that prove?"

My throat had gone dry and I had to swallow carefully. "Eddie's book might've been switched for the one Terrence was looking for. I won't know until I can see it up close. It's the *Alice in Wonderland* inside the Plexiglas case at the front counter. Could you do that for me, please?"

She tilted her head to study me. "For *you*?"

I almost choked on my tongue. "Uh—no! I mean, not

for *me*. It's for the cause of justice. Truth. The American way. You know. All that stuff."

She laughed. "Sorry, but you're just too easy to tease, Brooklyn. Truth and justice, my butt."

I smiled and shrugged. "It was worth a shot."

"Yeah, I can appreciate that. Look, I know you believe it's all about a book, but let me do some actual investigating first, okay?"

"Of course." A heavy sigh of relief escaped my lungs.

"Thank you, Inspector," Derek said, and gave me a one-arm hug. I leaned into him. I was exhausted from just trying to convince her. It felt like I'd slogged through mud to get to this point and I still didn't know if she would agree to obtain the *Alice* book for me.

"Oh, I keep forgetting to ask you," I said. "But have you heard how Will Rabbit is doing?"

"As a matter of fact, I stopped by there this morning," Lee said. "He's responding well to stimulus, but he's still in a coma. The doctors seem to think it's just a matter of time before he wakes up."

I glanced up at Derek, who looked as worried as I felt. "I really hope he comes out of it soon."

"You and me both," she said. "Well, I've got to shake down the pie man."

"Good luck," Derek said, flashing a grin.

"And if you do decide to confiscate that book," I said, eternally hopeful, "please call me. I'll be working at home, but I'll meet you wherever you want to meet."

"I'll think about it," she said cheerfully, and walked away.

Chapter 10

I felt so much calmer sitting in my workshop than I'd felt talking to Inspector Lee a few minutes earlier. I really enjoyed her company and wanted us to be great friends and go shopping and hang out, but she tested me at every step. And that wasn't necessarily a bad thing. It was just the nature of our relationship, and I was up to the challenge. Besides, to be fair, I no doubt caused *her* some indigestion, too. After all, how many friends did she have who kept discovering bodies? Because what was friendship all about anyway?

Mom and Meg were off exploring the neighborhood and Dad and John had taken a walk down to the Giants' stadium, so I had a few hours to get some work done.

Before I gathered up any of the supplies I would need in order to create my matchbook box, I grabbed my sketchbook and began to draw out exactly what I wanted to make. Sometimes it helped to have a concept rather than diving in blind. I'd done plenty of blind diving, too, but I knew what I wanted this time around and I intended to make it look fantastic.

I hadn't done a matchbook box in a while, so I figured it wouldn't be as easy as constructing one of the clamshell boxes I regularly built for special projects.

But the earthiness of the handmade playing cards called for something different and artsy.

I envisioned the gallery display with the box partially opened and the cards inside easily seen. Maybe two or three could be scattered around the box. My accordion book would pop up from its special place on top of the box.

I began sketching out some ideas of what the final pieces would look like. There would be a box to hold the playing cards, and that box would slide into an open-ended case. The case would contain an additional cut-out space on top to hold the small accordion book made from handmade paper.

The accordion book would be small, about two by three inches in size, and extend out to fifty-three pages, making it quite thick. I decided I'd better start with the accordion book and go backward from there so that I wouldn't accidentally make the box too small.

With an accordion book of fifty-three pages, there was no way I could make one continuous piece of handmade paper and fold it accordion-style. I could always build a new wooden frame, but in this case it would mean making a frame that was 106 inches long. That was over eight feet long. And that was crazy.

I would have to make numerous twelve-inch pieces and glue them together to build a 106-inch accordion book. The gluing process would be critical. I didn't want anyone viewing the piece to be able to see where the glue had been applied.

To cover the box, I wanted to use part paper and part morocco leather. I had a beautiful piece of black goatskin that was soft and pliable. It would be gorgeous as a highlight to the pale pink handmade paper. The paper would have to be thinner and more easily manipulated than the thick paper I'd created for the playing cards.

"You have your work cut out for you," I muttered. But that was just the way I liked it.

After spreading my pages of drawings across the worktable, I happened to glance up at the clock and realized that an hour had passed. This was just one reason why I loved my work. I could zone out and leave the worries of the world behind me.

The security phone rang just then, bringing all those worries back. I ran to the kitchen to answer it and was pleased to see Inspector Lee standing there. "Guess what I've got for you."

"You got it? You got the book?"

She laughed. "Let me in, Brooklyn."

"Yes, definitely. Come in." I pressed the button to release the door and she disappeared from the screen. A few minutes later, I was waiting at the door of my apartment as she got out of the elevator and walked my way.

"Thank you so much for doing this," I said.

"You're the one doing all the work."

I grinned. "Well, then, you're welcome."

"Funny." She followed me into the workshop and watched as I pulled a clean white cloth from the drawer and spread it on the table. I set the book down on the cloth and walked over to my desk, where I found my strongest magnifying glass and set it down next to the book.

"So what's with this book?" she asked.

"I don't know," I admitted. "I just know that Bonnie gave one book to Eddie and another one to Terrence. And then somehow Terrence's book disappeared and Joey ended up with a book. But whose book belongs to whom? That is the question."

She spread her hands out on the worktable. "Why don't you just ask Bonnie?"

I smiled ruefully. "I guess that would make sense, but I don't trust her to tell me the truth."

"Because of what Kitty said? About her killing her husband? We don't have any proof of that. It's just a rumor at this point."

"I know." I wasn't so unfair, I hoped, to judge someone on another person's opinion. "It's not just that. I mean, of course we don't even know if it's true. But now that you mention it, I'm not sure I trust Kitty, either."

"I don't blame you." Inspector Lee sighed a little. "I guess I'll pay them each a visit again."

"You'd probably get an honest answer. Maybe." I shrugged because I really didn't know anymore. "But here's the thing. Bonnie is super aggressive around men. Nothing wrong with that, I guess. But she really bugs Derek. He avoids her like a nest of wasps. And I seriously believe she pulled a fast one on Terrence." I stopped and thought about it. "And now I'm wondering if she also pulled a fast one on Eddie."

"So you're saying you're not comfortable talking to her."

"Unfortunately, I'm not." I chuckled and added, "Even though it makes me sound like a wimp."

"Hey, nobody wants to hang around a wasps' nest." She shuddered dramatically.

I chuckled. "Thanks for that."

"No worries. I'd better get going. Thanks for the work you're putting in on this."

"No problem." I walked with her to the door. "Hey, since I'm sort of helping you out here, do you want to designate me as a civilian police consultant or something?"

She snorted a laugh. "No. But thanks for your support."

I grinned. "Just checking."

"Yeah. Good try, though." She pulled the door open, then turned. "So you think you'll be finished with the book sometime tomorrow?"

"I'll make sure I'm done by noon."

"Okay. I'll swing by and pick it up around then."

I walked with her out to the elevator. "Look, I'm sure Eddie gave you a hard time about taking the book, so thanks again."

"Hey, it's always fun intimidating the public," she said, stepping into the elevator.

"Glad I could help with that," I said, laughing again.

Twenty minutes later, Derek walked in and set a book down on my worktable. I took a quick look and then did a double take. "Are you kidding?"

He grinned. "Nope."

"But how?" I picked up the book and pressed it to my heart. "Where did you find it?"

"I slipped into Terrence's apartment while he was

diverted. The book was sitting on top of his bedroom dresser, buried under a stack of magazines and unopened mail. I was a bit surprised, but there it was."

"That's amazing." I stared at the cover and checked the spine. *Alice's Adventures in Wonderland.* "I just knew he took it from Joey. When I was looking at Eddie's book earlier today, Terrence did his usual routine, except instead of saying he 'used to have a book like this,' he said, 'I have a book like that.'"

"Ah, he gave himself away. Subtle, but telling." He rubbed my shoulders. "Good job, love."

"Thanks." I gazed up at him, smiling. "But why would he throw a stack of magazines on top of a priceless book if it's so important to him?"

"I have no idea. His entire apartment is quite messy. More proof that he's a bit of an oddball?"

"Maybe. I'm just amazed and impressed that you found the book at all. You are a master cat burglar." I slowly replayed what he had just said. "Wait. How did you divert him?"

Meg and Mom walked in just then, looking flushed and happy.

"Oh, that was such fun," Meg said as she unwrapped her wool scarf from around her neck. "Thank you, Derek."

"You were a natural, Meg," Mom said, laughing. "You should've seen her, Brooklyn. She had both of those men at her beck and call. I was so proud of you."

Meg batted her eyelashes demurely and we all laughed. "Thank you, Becky. But you're no slouch yourself. I thought your line to Eddie about there being so many handsome men in this city was perfect. He was practically preening like a cat in front of you."

I glanced from Derek to the moms, almost afraid to ask. "What did you do?"

"It was Derek's idea," Mom said, grinning. "He needed us to create a diversion for a few minutes and we were happy to provide that service."

I stared at Derek, slightly appalled that he'd enlisted our mothers, but too pleased about the book to give him any real grief. Well, not too much anyway. "You could've been caught. I should've been with you to watch the door."

"Believe it or not, love, I'd broken into my share of buildings long before I had such lovely backup to call on." He gave me a quick hug. "I took a chance, you see. And our mothers were right there in the pinch. It worked out quite well. I was in and out of his apartment in less than two minutes."

I had to admit, it had been a great plan. Our moms had gotten the excitement they'd been craving and the chance to be a part of "the case." And Derek had gotten the book. So really, I was in no position to complain.

"He's really careless, isn't he?" I turned the book over and stared at the back cover. "I'm stunned that he didn't have this locked up."

"So am I, frankly," Derek said. "But grateful as well."

I shook my head. "After all his whining about losing the book, he doesn't even keep it safe. I mean, it worked in our favor, but it just doesn't make sense."

Derek leaned against my worktable. "I suppose he thought it was safe enough behind the locked door of his apartment."

"He thought wrong," I murmured. "He'll have a cow

when he discovers it missing, but we'll get it back to him soon enough."

Mom pulled the band off her windblown ponytail and fluffed her hair back. "We're happy to go back tomorrow and divert him again if you need to return the book."

"Yes, we'd be delighted to help," Meg agreed.

Mom grabbed her hand. "Wasn't that exciting?"

"I feel like we're starring in a caper," Meg exclaimed, squeezing Mom's hand. "It's like Audrey Hepburn and Cary Grant in that fabulous movie."

"I love that movie." Mom linked arms with her and the two of them strolled back to the living room. "We should watch it. Have some wine and popcorn and chillax."

I glanced at Derek, who was holding one hand over his eyes.

"Don't look away." I laughed. "It's too late. You must reap what you have sown."

He bent down, rested his forehead against mine. "And now you're quoting the Bible? Excellent. I don't feel guilty at all."

I heard Mom and Meg's trilling laughter, and it made me smile. "It's okay. You really made their day."

"I know." He straightened, shook his head, and began to chuckle. "They'll feast on this one for years to come."

I spent the rest of the afternoon in my workshop studying the two books. My initial excitement was tamped down by my need to work fast and compare the two books side by side.

I had to admit I had been shocked earlier, but also

a little impressed, to hear that Derek had snuck into Terrence's apartment in broad daylight while the man was working downstairs at the bookshop. And I still couldn't believe that the book had just been sitting on top of a dresser. Terrence hadn't gone to any trouble to hide it, and why would he? He couldn't have known that a master spy would be sneaking around his apartment at two o'clock on a sunny afternoon.

The first thing I noticed without even opening the two books was that Terrence's *Alice* was quite a bit shabbier than Eddie's, especially around the corners and along the spine. The headband was frayed. The gilding on the spine was faded and the leather in spots was rubbed. But the more I studied it, the less all that seemed to matter.

When I opened the book to check out the endpapers, I almost fainted at the sight of a bookplate with Bonnie's name pasted on the front inside cover.

"What is wrong with her?" I muttered. She had managed to diminish the book's value by at least five percent. *And she's a book person,* I thought. There was no excuse for it.

I stared at the bookplate, which was a common-looking square showing a unicorn and a stack of books and a place to write one's name. Among serious collectors, a pasted-in bookplate with the owner's name on it was considered defacing an otherwise fine book.

Finally, I shrugged. Just because someone owned a bookshop and sold books didn't mean they knew anything about the care and repair of fine bindings.

Bonnie did seem to have an affinity for certain books and authors, though, which was nice. She obviously had collected at least two excellent copies of *Alice in*

Wonderland over the years, and maybe some other titles, too. But other than making them look pretty on a shelf, she had no knowledge of the most basic tenets of book conservation. She wouldn't even be considered a hobbyist, since most of the people I knew who called themselves book hobbyists knew enough to keep bookplates out of their books. The serious hobbyist took pride in his books, stored them in clear archival covers, and tried to follow the rules handed down by the best book conservationists in the country.

The only good thing about Bonnie's bookplate was that it confirmed that she had owned the book and had apparently passed it on to Terrence. The question was, how did the book get from Terrence to Joey? Did Bonnie steal it back from Terrence? Did Joey?

I looked up as another possibility occurred. "Did *Eddie* steal it?"

I couldn't think of a reason Eddie would have done that, except to torment his poor brother-in-law. Unless he was in cahoots with Bonnie, playing tricks behind Terrence's back, I couldn't picture Eddie as the bad guy. I knew Eddie and Terrence were argumentative, but Eddie had never seemed that vindictive.

Well, until the other morning, when both of them had said some pretty awful things to each other.

I picked up my magnifying glass and carefully paged through Terrence's book. On page 134, I found a fingerprint and made a note to show it to Derek. He might be able to use his fingerprinting kit to discover whose it was. Without ruining the paper, I hoped.

Besides being in better condition on the outside, Eddie's book was, overall, more vibrant than Terrence's. The illustrations were brighter and the print was crisper in Eddie's copy. Terrence's copy seemed a little world-weary, if I could attach such a characteristic to an inanimate object.

I wasn't trying to attribute the differences in the books to their individual personalities, but I couldn't help it. The fact was that Eddie was a little brighter than Terrence, with a better sense of humor. Terrence was a bit stodgy and stubborn and, yes, frayed around the edges. He worried more and didn't seem to enjoy life as much as Eddie did.

Their books seemed to reflect those character traits. But I absolutely refused to believe that Bonnie had actually considered those qualities when she'd handed out the books. She just wasn't that insightful.

Despite those variances between the books, the paper in both volumes was an equally lovely thick vellum and the covers were both finely bound in quality scarlet red morocco leather. I already knew that Eddie's book had been bound by the renowned bookbinder to Queen Mary, George Bayntun, while Terrence's copy had been bound by the arguably even more famous company Sangorski and Sutcliffe. The binders' names were stamped in tiny letters on the inner flyleaf page of each book.

I was pleased to see that with Terrence's copy, the bindery had included the original cloth book covers in the rebinding. These days, unlike in Victorian times, a book in its original binding was often considered more valuable than if that same book had been rebound in leather. The exception was when an important bookbinder—such as Sangorski and Sutcliffe—had done the work.

I closed both books and stared for a long time at the covers. It was amazing how similar they were, and I wondered again about Bonnie. Why did she collect such expensive books only to give them away for sexual favors? The thought made me feel a little queasy.

I was about to quit for the day when I realized that I hadn't compared the title pages. I hadn't even considered it important since I thought they would be exactly the same. I turned to the page in Terrence's book and gasped.

"No way," I whispered, picking my chin off the floor. I repeated it louder. "No way!"

I shook my head and closed my eyes for a long moment. "You are a dingbat." Why hadn't I checked this sooner? I had been so sure that the books were the same that I hadn't even bothered.

"No wonder the illustrations in Terrence's book are dull," I muttered, turning to those pages and comparing them with Eddie's.

Terrence's book had been published in 1865.

My vision spun and I had to blink a few times to be sure. Yes, it was true. Terrence's book was one of the lost first editions. The ones that Lewis Carroll had famously sent back to the publisher when he'd found that the illustrations of John Tenniel's delicate pencil work had been poorly reproduced. The printer had retraced Tenniel's work onto new woodblocks and then engraved those onto electrotype plates, using them as masters. The second attempt was more successful and those new books were then published as first editions.

But some of the original versions had filtered out to the public. It was thought that there were possibly two dozen of the original versions left in the world, maybe fewer. So whereas Eddie's book might have been worth thirty thousand dollars at auction, Terrence's book could have been worth anywhere from several hundred thousand to two million dollars.

Which meant that Terrence's book was beyond rare and infinitely more valuable.

"I don't understand," Meg said. "Lewis Carroll sent the books back?"

Over a glass of wine, I had explained the difference between the two books to Derek and our parents. "Yes, Lewis Carroll sent them back. You see, John Tenniel was a famous illustrator in Victorian England. He was most renowned for his political cartoons, but he had agreed to illustrate *Alice in Wonderland*, and Lewis Carroll wanted the very best-quality books out on the market.

"Tenniel and Carroll—whose real name was Charles Dodgson, by the way—immediately recognized that the work had been badly reproduced, so Lewis Carroll shipped everything back to the publisher and asked that the books be destroyed and new ones reprinted. Apparently, though, he had already distributed several dozen books to family and friends before the problem was realized."

Meg frowned. "So the fact that there are so few copies of the first book makes it much rarer and substantially more valuable than virtually the exact same book that is prettier and cleaner and newer by a few measly months."

I smiled. "Yes. Terrence's copy is a true first edition. Eddie's is considered a first edition, *second issue*. It makes all the difference in the world."

"It's fascinating, isn't it?" Meg said, clutching Mom's hand.

"It's a mystery and a miracle," Mom murmured.

Meg nodded. "Well said, Becky."

The following day, Inspector Lee came by to pick up Eddie's book about noon to return it to him. Derek and I had debated whether to tell her about Terrence's book, and we ended up spilling the beans. I mentioned how much money the book was worth at auction, and she blinked, then shook her head in disbelief. After a quick rant, she insisted that we stop talking because she really didn't want to hear how we had obtained something so off-the-charts rare and valuable. She probably had a sneaking suspicion, but now her biggest concern was in keeping the extremely valuable book safe. I offered to tuck it away in my home safe, and she agreed. The alternative was to leave it in the trunk of her car all day while she drove down to Santa Cruz to spend the day with friends. She wasn't sure what she would tell Terrence. Perhaps she would let him sit and stew for a day or two. But she did assure us that she and Derek and I would be having another conversation very soon. At that time, she would explain the limits of our participation in her criminal investigations from now on. After she left, I breathed freely for the first time since she'd arrived. And Derek admitted we were lucky she hadn't carted us off to jail right then and there.

An hour later, Derek and I took the parents to high tea at the Garden Court in the Palace Hotel. There were plenty of lovely places to have tea in San Francisco, but the Garden Court was at the top of the list. The massive open space was famous for its spectacular stained-glass dome ceiling. Sparkling crystal chandeliers hung from the ceiling and thick Italian marble columns lined the room. It was a fun way to treat Derek's parents to a bit of San Francisco opulence and I was determined to forget about all of the scary, bad things that were happening in our neighborhood and enjoy myself. The tea service was wonderfully fancy, with savory tea sandwiches followed by dessert scones, delicate pastries, and pots of tea, of course.

I wore my new hat and both Mom and Meg went wild over it. Derek loved it, too. I considered that a grand slam and silently thanked Kitty for her insistence that I buy it.

I also wore my serviceable burgundy pumps and praised all the gods of heaven that Inspector Lee had rescued them from an uncertain future in Joey's shoe repair shop. Meg had won my gratitude when she complimented me on my shoes the first time I wore them, but now I wondered if she might have been having doubts about my fashion sense, since I was wearing them for the third time this week. I couldn't worry too much, though, because my shoes were just so comfortable. Still, I tucked my feet under the tablecloth and tried to concentrate on my pretty new hat instead of my boring old shoes.

While we dined, Mom and Meg chatted about different pagan rituals they'd witnessed. They shared their guidelines on tarot card readings and their personal choice of familiars. Sure enough, Mom regaled Meg with stories of her astral travels with her spirit guide, Ramlar X, and Meg shared her numerous psychic encounters. I was completely fascinated, watching them interact as though they'd known each other all their lives. Strangely enough, I enjoyed their camaraderie way too much to be weirded out by the subject matter of their conversation. It was just amazing to see them laugh and share their secrets with each other. Their relationship boded well for future family gatherings.

And meanwhile, we demolished every bit of food on the table.

"Oh, wasn't this outstanding?" Meg said, leaning back in her chair. "Everything was so yummy. Excellent choice, kids."

Mom sighed and patted her stomach. "I couldn't get enough of those curried chicken sandwiches. I may regret it later, but right now I'm suffused with joy."

"Suffused with joy," Dad murmured. "Good one, Becky. I personally was suffused with those puffy round purple things."

"Those were outstanding," John agreed. "But the mini napoleons were my favorites."

I smiled, happy that everyone was enjoying themselves.

"Brooklyn, dear," Meg said, pulling a small bag out from under the table. "I've brought you a gift from home and I think this is the perfect time to give it to you."

I was taken aback. "You didn't have to do that."

"But I wanted to," she said, then winked. "I think it will prove beyond a shadow of a doubt that my psychic abilities are strong."

I was sure I looked gobsmacked. I'd picked up that word from Derek. British slang fit the occasion so perfectly sometimes. "But . . . but I never had any doubt about your abilities."

She laughed. "Oh, you're a sweetheart." She handed me a wrapped package that was shaped suspiciously like a book. "Here you are. I hope you'll be pleased."

I stared at the gift. "This is so nice of you. Thank you."

"You haven't opened it yet."

"Then I'd better get to it." I carefully unwrapped the ribbon and pulled the paper off. And stared at the book Meg had chosen for me.

"Oh, Meg, how thoughtful," Mom murmured.

"I think it suits her," she whispered. "It's a sweet old book. Not a first edition or anything fancy, of course, but wonderful."

"Alice Through the Looking-Glass," I said. It was a vintage copy of the book, and it appeared to be in very good condition. It didn't look like a terribly pricey purchase, thank goodness, but the red cloth cover was still bright and smooth and the pages were straight and clean. "You couldn't have given me a more perfect gift."

Pushing my chair back, I walked over and gave her a wholehearted hug. "Thank you so much."

"I'm so glad you like it."

"I love it."

"You really are psychic, Meg," my mom declared. "I never doubted it for a minute. I had a feeling about it from the first minute we met."

"As did I, Becky," Meg said. "As did I."

"I sometimes get a tingling in my left shoulder blade," Mom said. "That's when I know I'm in the presence of something mystical."

"Isn't that fascinating?" Meg leaned closer. "My little toe begins to twinge."

And they were off on another spiritual tangent.

Watching them, I had to admit that Meg bringing me this particular book, a continuation of the *Alice in Wonderland* story, did strike me as more than coincidental. So whether or not Derek was willing to believe in his mom's abilities, I was ready to give her the benefit of the doubt.

Derek reached over and squeezed my hand. "That is a lovely gift."

"Isn't it?" I gazed at the book. "I'm blown away." And I wondered what the chances were that she'd just happened to pick that very book, out of every other book in the small shop on Oxford High Street.

"I'm going to run across the street to check on Terrence," I announced after we'd been home a few minutes. "Now that Eddie has his book back, I want to make sure Terrence's head hasn't exploded over his missing book."

"I just have to make a quick phone call," Derek said, "and then I'll follow you over there."

"I hope so."

"I'd love to go with you," Meg said. Smiling at my mother, she added, "Becky, care to take a walk?"

"I think I'm going to take a short nap. You and Brooklyn go along and enjoy yourselves."

My mother never took naps, so I was pretty sure she just wanted Meg and me to have a few minutes together. And I loved her for being so thoughtful.

"What fun," Meg said, linking her arm through mine. "I'm still so stuffed from tea, but while we're out, we might think about picking up a little something for dinner later."

"We could get something light, like bowls of soup

from the Thai restaurant," I said. "Although I'm not hungry at all yet."

"I'm not, either, but soup sounds delicious," Meg said. "Or it will, I hope, once I've digested my tea."

We walked out to the sidewalk and waited for the traffic to clear. As we stood on the curb and chatted, I noticed Bonnie across the street talking to a man. The same man she'd been with at Sweetie Pies the morning before. Their conversation appeared flirtatious, but maybe that was just my imagination, given my knowledge of Bonnie. The man finally walked away, and Bonnie moved closer in our direction, standing on the opposite side of the street from us. I waved at her until she saw me and gave a weak wave back.

"Let's go," I said to Meg. "Do you see that woman walking our way? She's the one who owns the building."

"Ah," she said. "The infamous Bonnie, then. The one who gives books out to men who satisfy her."

I laughed. "That's about the size of it."

We'd almost made it across one lane when I suddenly heard a car engine revving up. I turned and saw a small black foreign car come screeching toward Bonnie at the other end of the crosswalk.

I screamed, "Bonnie! Move!"

But she was staring at her phone and didn't notice, so I yelled at Meg to get back on the sidewalk and raced across the street. I shoved Bonnie back toward the curb just as the car streaked by us.

She fell backward on her butt and I went down, too. I could feel the tender skin on my leg and knew I'd scraped myself up, but at least I was alive. So was Bonnie.

The black car raced away, its tires squealing as it spun around the corner and disappeared.

Meg dashed over and quickly ran her hands up and down my body, checking for breaks. "Are you hurt? Oh my God—that car could've killed you both."

"What the hell?" Bonnie muttered, a little dazed. "Why did you push me?"

I just gaped at her for a second. Really? Was she that oblivious? "You were going to get run over by that car. I shouted for you to move but you didn't hear me. Didn't you see it?"

She squinted, and I wondered if she'd hit her head on the pavement. "I heard something. Screeching brakes? Something." She shook her head and took a few deep breaths.

I stood and held my hand out. "Here, let me help you." I pulled her up and we all walked a few feet over to the sidewalk.

"I've never seen anything so awful," Meg cried. "He almost ran you down." She helped brush dirt and bits of blacktop off of Bonnie's pants.

Bonnie looked dismayed. "I guess I owe you one."

"That's okay," I said. "I'm just glad you weren't hurt too badly."

"I think my butt will be black-and-blue for a while, but I'll survive."

"That was horrible," Meg cried. "That person didn't even watch where he was going."

I scowled. "On the contrary, I think he knew exactly where he was going."

Bonnie stared at me. "What do you mean? You think it was deliberate?"

I watched her to judge her reaction. "Yes, I think they saw you coming, aimed the car, and sped up to hit you."

She looked completely confused and a bit worried. "But . . . why?"

I just stared at her for a moment until I finally saw a spark of awareness in her eyes.

"You really think someone's trying to kill me?" Bonnie looked around as if half expecting some killer to jump out at her. I couldn't really blame her.

"Who was that man you were with?" I asked, no longer caring if I was being nosy or not.

"Who?" She blinked again. "Oh, Stan. We just met. He's . . . um, he's a developer with Sequoia. No big deal. Wanted to know if I would sell the building. I said no and that's the end of it."

Sequoia, I thought. That was the "tree" name Colin had been trying to think of. Sequoia was only one of the biggest property development firms in the city. What was Bonnie doing with that guy? And why was she lying, saying that she'd just met him? I'd seen her with him before today. But I couldn't confront her on that issue just now, so I pivoted to another subject. "Where were you going just now?"

"To pick up a pizza, if it's any of your business."

I ignored that. "Did you call in an order?"

"Yeah. I order from Pete a lot. He's the best. Always gives me extra sausage."

I was doing some fast thinking. "Who else knew you were having pizza tonight?"

She thought for a minute, then winced. "Just about everyone in the building. In case you haven't noticed, I'm not exactly a shrinking violet. I tend to broadcast whatever I'm doing, so when I decided to have pizza for dinner, I guess I made sure everyone knew about it." She shrugged. "That's just me."

"I understand." And she was right. Bonnie wasn't the most circumspect person in the world. "So who did you tell?"

"So let's see." She frowned as she tried to remember. "I mentioned it to Colin while Dr. Wan—he's our acupuncturist—was ordering an apple pie. And I told Eddie and Terrence while I was in the bookshop. Oh, wait. Kitty was there, too, with one of her customers, showing her some fashion book or something. And the Beanery baristas knew about it because I stopped in there for a shot of espresso a little while ago."

I pinched my lips together in frustration. "So basically it could've been anyone."

"Basically?" Bonnie sighed. "Yeah."

I pulled out my phone and called Inspector Lee. Our new friendship was about to be tested again.

Chapter 11

Bonnie took the attempt on her life in stride, insisting that she still needed to pick up her pizza. She had no intention of hiding out in her apartment as Inspector Lee had suggested she do. I couldn't blame her. After all, she had no idea who she was hiding *from*, or how long she'd have to do it, so why not continue to live life? Part of me admired her spirit. But still, there was a killer on the loose and she appeared to be his number one target.

I called Derek to fill him in while Meg gave Inspector Lee a helpful description of the car. All I'd noticed was the fact that it was black, with those annoying blacked-out windows that made it impossible to identify the driver. But Meg had recognized the car's logo, and Inspector Lee was grateful for the information. Hopefully, someone in the neighborhood would recognize the vehicle and we would be in luck.

Inspector Lee walked off with Bonnie. Meg and I turned to face each other.

"Well, that was terrifying," she said.

I couldn't argue with that. I could still feel the *whoosh* of air made as the car had raced past me. "I'm so sorry. Do you want to go home?"

"Don't you want to visit the bookstore?" she asked.

"Yes, but just for a minute. And I want Derek to come with us. He should be here any minute."

"All rightie." She strolled around the inner courtyard, staring up at the trees. "This is such a lovely spot."

The British really were unflappable. I smiled to myself, realizing that not only was Meg my future mother-in-law, but she was also becoming a friend.

"It is," I said. "I really like it. I hope Bonnie never sells this building."

"That would be a shame," she said, then brightened as she looked beyond me. "Here comes Derek."

He hurried forward, giving each of us a quick once-over as he approached. "Are you both all right?"

"I'm fit as a Finn," Meg said, giving him a light pat on the forearm. "But Brooklyn could've been killed. She was very brave, rushing out to save Bonnie as she did, but I've never been so frightened in my life."

"I'm fine," I said, quickly waving away Meg's statement. "Everything's fine. Bonnie's got a few bumps and bruises, but she's all right."

Derek frowned. "Bonnie?"

Meg took Derek's arm. "Brooklyn saved that woman's life. She's being quite modest, but honestly, she was positively heroic. Didn't hesitate in the slightest."

He frowned and looked from his mother to me and back again. "What happened exactly?"

Meg spoke up before I had a chance. "A car tried to run Bonnie down in the street. Brooklyn rushed forward and pushed her out of the way just in the nick of time. And we think it was deliberate."

Derek took hold of my shoulders and stared into my eyes. "Are you sure you're all right?"

"I'm fine. I have a little scrape on my leg, but it'll heal."

He yanked me into his arms and squeezed me close to him. He didn't say a word, but I knew what he was thinking. I would've been doing the same thing if it had happened to him. This love business was wonderful, but the terror that could come along with it was staggering.

I eased back and gazed up at him. "We're just going to stop off at the bookshop to make sure everything's okay with Terrence. I'm still a little concerned that he might be ready to blow a gasket."

"I have that same concern," he said. "Let's go."

The three of us crossed the courtyard and entered through the cheerfully soothing pale blue door of the shop. Once inside, I calmed down a little. Bookstores did that to me. Even with all the wrangling between Eddie and Terrence, a bookshop was still an oasis of happy books and goodies. The smell of books alone was enough to soothe away any remaining frazzled edges. I only hoped they wouldn't refrazzle.

And didn't I sound like Little Miss Sunshine all of a sudden? I tended to get that way after surviving sudden attacks from motor vehicles.

"Good afternoon, Eddie," Meg said, approaching the front counter.

"Well, hello there, Miss Meg," Eddie said.

"We're just checking up on you boys. Everything hunky-dory in here?"

"Yes, ma'am," Eddie said, grinning. "Everything's right as rain."

Eddie sounded like a schoolboy with a crush on his pretty teacher. Who knew? Meg was proving to be an accomplished flirt and I couldn't have been prouder. I stood back to enjoy the moment.

"We're just going to do a little browsing," she said, "and we'll let you know if we need any help."

"I'm here for you anytime."

Meg looked at Derek and me. "I just want to look at the cards. I'd like to send a few home to the children."

"All right, Mum," Derek said. "We'll browse along with you."

He kept a firm hold on my hand, apparently afraid to let me go for fear I'd run off and put my life in danger again. I was grateful for his closeness. I didn't care for being threatened any more than he did.

At that moment, Terrence stormed into the store and shouted, "You won't get away with it this time."

I heard Meg suck in a breath. "Good heavens."

Terrence didn't even look our way, just stomped along toward Eddie. He must have just discovered that his book was missing, because he was furious. He obviously blamed his partner.

"I'm going to kill you," he cried, and came at Eddie's neck with his hands outstretched. Was he going to strangle him? He clearly didn't realize there were witnesses standing there horrified, watching him.

"Derek," I said.

"I'll take care of it." He moved quickly to the front counter, but Eddie was already defending himself. He was stronger and more muscular than Terrence, but he was no better a fighter than his brother-in-law. I'd once thought Terrence was built like a boxer, but apparently he'd never been in a real fight before.

Derek stood away from the fray to watch them for a moment. It had descended into a slapping match, and even then they kept missing their marks. Honestly, it looked like a comedy fight. Or one between third-graders who hadn't really figured out how to have a fist-fight.

"I can't believe you took it again!" Terrence screeched. "I'm sick of dealing with you and your treachery. I want you to die!"

"And I'm sick of you attacking me all the time." Eddie smacked him upside the head, hard. "For once and for all, I didn't take your freaking stupid book!"

Terrence tried to slap him again, and finally Derek was fed up. He stepped around the counter and easily grabbed hold of both their shirts, yanking them apart. "That's enough of this clown show."

I was pretty disgusted myself. What a couple of nincompoops they were! With all the books in their store, you'd think they would have read a few and gained some brain cells.

They were both struggling to loosen Derek's grip, and I had a sudden moment of remorse. After all, we were the ones who had stolen Terrence's book. But at least we had told the police what we'd done, and we would bring his book back eventually. And yet, I knew in my heart that those two would never give up their horrible bickering.

"Are you going to stop fighting?" Derek asked mildly.

"I'm not the one who's fighting," Eddie insisted. "He's insane."

I believed him. Terrence looked dazed and unsure of where he was. And then, all of a sudden, I saw him focus in on Meg. I sidled closer to her, just in case.

But he simply nodded at her and said, "Hello, Miss Meg."

She took a deep breath and said, "Hello, Terrence."

"It's nice to see you today."

"And you as well," she said, her clear English accent a little wobbly—from stress, no doubt. "And don't you look handsome in your fishing shirt?"

He glanced down at his shirt. "Thank you, ma'am."

Okay, now it was getting weird. Meg seemed to have a hypnotic hold on them both. Maybe it was the accent. But the last thing I would've noticed was Terrence's short-sleeved shirt with fishermen holding fishing poles all over it.

I had to hand it to Meg—she really could defuse a situation. A moment later, Derek, a frustrated expression on his face, let the men go and walked out from behind the counter.

"Hey," someone said from the doorway. "Hi, everybody."

"Rabbit!" I had to catch my breath from the shock. "What a welcome surprise."

Terrence blinked and said, "Is it really you?"

"It's me," he said. "Colin just brought me home."

I wondered if he'd seen any of the commotion that had just occurred. And I watched carefully as the two brothers reacted to Rabbit's sudden appearance. If one of them had tried to kill Rabbit, wouldn't he be afraid that Rabbit could identify him? But all I could read on their faces was pure elation that their friend had returned.

"Hey, man," Eddie said, rushing over to give him a hug. "I'm glad you're back."

"Thanks. I can't tell you how happy I am to be here." He wore a bandage around his head and he was walking slowly, but he looked fantastic. He looked alive.

Terrence joined his brother-in-law and gave Rabbit a careful hug. It was clear that the younger man was still a little unsteady on his feet.

When the brothers stepped back, I moved in. "It's so good to see you."

"Thanks, Brooklyn. Hey, Derek."

He walked up and shook Rabbit's hand. "Will, welcome back. What a wonderful surprise."

The door swung open and Bonnie ran in, sobbing. She wrapped her arms around her nephew's waist and clung to him. "I can't believe it. I heard you were back. Oh my God—I'm so happy to see you!"

"I'm okay, Aunt Bonnie," he said, grinning as he hugged her back.

She sniffled and laughed at the same time. "What a relief."

"For me, too. I'm ready to get back to work."

Everyone cheered. I noticed Furbie stretching and winding his way around Rabbit's ankles. So it was unanimous. The whole world loved Will Rabbit—

except for the person who had bashed him over the head the other day. Whoever that was.

Bonnie clutched his arm. "The Rabbit Hole is ready for you, too, honey."

We introduced Rabbit to Meg and explained how Will fit into the picture of the Rabbit Hole incident.

When the excitement died down, I turned to Rabbit and asked quietly, "Do you recall what happened to you?"

"All I remember is waking up in the hospital with a really bad headache. The doctors think I'll get my memory back eventually, but I'm not so sure." He gave a carefree shrug. "Anyway, I'm just really glad to see everyone. Hope you'll all stop by the Rabbit Hole and say hi when you have time."

"We'll be there," Eddie said, and Terrence nodded eagerly.

"We wouldn't miss it for the world," Derek said.

Rather than being worn-out by all of the food we'd consumed at high tea followed by our near miss with a speeding car, Meg was energized and insisted on taking charge of making a light evening meal for everyone.

"We're having naughty appetizers for dinner," she announced as we walked into the Rabbit Hole, and proceeded to pick up a dozen different items before heading over to our local butcher shop two blocks away. Mom and I helped in the kitchen, and the three of us barely got through the prep work, we were laughing so hard. Derek poured wine for everyone, and Dad and John set the table. It was a perfect division of labor, and once the appetizer platters were placed on the table, we all sat down to eat.

"This looks good," Dad said, reaching for a deep-fried jalapeño popper. "What's it called?"

"That's Hot Stuff in a Blanket," Meg replied. "Be careful. They have a kick to them."

"And this?" Derek asked as he held up a savory chunk of sausage wrapped in puff pastry. He took a bite. "Mmm, delicious."

"That's a Spicy Surprise," Meg said with a straight face. "Brooklyn made them."

"Marvelous, darling," he said with a grin.

Meg's Perky Breast Nibbles were a big hit, too. She had sliced up chicken breasts and marinated them, then threaded the pieces onto bamboo skewers and roasted them for a few minutes. She served them with a sweet, tart sauce that was both delicious and easy to make.

Meg chuckled at all the yummy noises heard around the table. "Back home the girls and I serve naughty appetizers whenever we get together to play cribbage. The Perky Breasts are always a favorite."

"They're a favorite of mine, certainly," Dad said, munching happily.

"So you play cribbage with your friends?" Mom asked, intrigued.

"Oh, it's great fun. There are six of us girls, and we pair up and play one-on-one. Cribbage is best played with two people, you see."

"I played it once or twice years ago," I said. "You keep score using a board, right?"

"Yes, you move the little pegs to keep score."

"What fun," Mom said.

"As a matter of fact," Meg continued, "that's where the idea for our appetizers came from. You see, back in the old days, the original game of cribbage was known as *Noddy*." She spelled the word. "We would serve each other our *Noddy* appetizers, and well, they evolved into 'naughty' appetizers."

Mom laughed. "Oh, Meg, that's wonderful."

Also on the "naughty" menu were Doughy Thighs, made by shredding cooked, marinated chicken thighs, popping the meat into savory biscuit dough, and baking; Cheesy Balls (a smaller, bite-sized version of the classic cheese ball); Naked Skins, which were crispy baked potato skins "dressed" in sour cream, bacon bits, and grated cheese; and Meg's personal favorite, Hot Buttered Rump Bites, made by sautéing marinated chunks of rare rump roast in butter, then using toothpicks to skewer each piece with a small hunk of cheese and a homemade crouton. Meg also prepared a plate of raw vegetables served with something she called "Skinny Dip."

Once we got past our initial giggling at all the silly names Meg had come up with, we turned to the more serious subject of the Courtyard situation. Now that Rabbit was back and had freely admitted that his memory wasn't back yet but might return eventually, I wondered if he would be attacked again. Had he seen his assailant that morning when Joey was killed? Was he safe back home at the Courtyard?

"I'm worried about Rabbit," I said after discarding another toothpick.

"I don't blame you, dear," Meg said. "And I'm also worried that Terrence will snap again when we aren't around."

"Do you think he might hurt Eddie?" Mom asked.

Derek spoke up. "Both of those men are too incompetent to really hurt each other. But he could land a lucky punch. Terrence is mainly a danger because he's clearly unbalanced. God forbid he had a more dangerous weapon at his disposal."

I glanced around the table and settled on Derek. "We have to get that book back to him, just to calm him down. But I must confess I don't want to."

"Why not?" Mom asked. "He seems like a nice enough man when he's not going berserk."

I smiled at her characterization. "I know it's silly, but I'm concerned that he doesn't know anything about the book's value. I don't trust him to keep it in good condition."

"Perhaps you could teach him," Meg suggested.

I frowned. "I don't really want to tell him how much it's worth. I'm afraid he would rub it in Eddie's nose and start a real battle that would end in bloodshed."

"That would be awful," John said thoughtfully.

Derek waited for everyone else to comment before he finally spoke. "I believe I have a plan."

Much later that night, Derek and I snuck across the street, and thanks to Derek's exemplary cat burglar skills and the special tools he used for such occasions, we were able to break into the bookshop. I found Eddie's key where he always kept it, in the drawer behind the front counter, and quickly opened the Plexiglas case that held Eddie's copy of *Alice in Wonderland*. Lifting the book from the case, I handed it to Derek.

He passed me the other book and I set it down carefully inside the case, replacing the one that had been there. I locked the case and slipped the key back into the drawer.

Quietly, we left the bookshop and hovered in the shadows for a moment. Derek stared up at the second- and third-floor windows. It was after two o'clock in the morning and no lights could be seen in any of the apartments above the shops. I was pretty sure everyone in the building was fast asleep.

"Wait here," Derek whispered into my ear. "I'll be back in less than two minutes."

"I'm going to start counting," I said. "Be careful."

In barely ninety seconds he was back, and I could breathe again. "Let's go home," he said.

After we gathered around the kitchen coffeepot the next morning, John was the first to ask the question. "You switched the books?"

"We did." I took a sip of coffee to help wake up. It had been a long night. "Last night before we left, I used a leather polish to make Terrence's book appear shinier than it had before. I'm hoping that Eddie won't notice the difference for a few days until I can figure out exactly how to handle this situation."

"If it gets sticky, Inspector Lee might be able to help us out," Derek said.

"I hope so."

Derek's plan had been brilliant. To protect Terrence's extremely valuable book, we had decided to sneak it into the Plexiglas case, where it would be safe from Terrence's sloppy habits. We assumed Eddie's book would be perfectly fine on Terrence's dresser, buried under magazines, for a few days. And Terrence would be happy—if he even figured out that the book was there. But we really needed to resolve this situation as quickly as we could. We planned to call

Inspector Lee a little later to let her know what we'd done. Despite my insistence that we'd done the right thing to protect the book, I wasn't looking forward to making that call.

Derek leaned against the kitchen counter, sipping coffee. "While we're on the phone with Inspector Lee, we might ask her to talk to Bonnie. I believe she would be considered the rightful owner of the more valuable book. If she took it from Terrence to give to Joey, she might not want Terrence to have it anymore. In which case, he shouldn't have it."

"I suppose I agree with you," I said. "Although she did give it away, and that was just dumb."

Derek smiled. "Dumb or not, she should be consulted."

I grumbled, but finally nodded in agreement.

"Derek's right," Meg chimed in. "Talk to Bonnie. At the very least, she might be able to clear up this muddle. Maybe she would consider donating the book to a good cause."

"The Covington Library," I said brightly.

Mom nodded eagerly. "That would be ideal."

"I'll ask Inspector Lee to mention that possibility when she talks to Bonnie."

"You don't like that woman, do you?" John guessed.

I glanced at Derek. "Believe it or not, I'm getting to like Bonnie a little better on a superficial level, but I still don't trust her." I paused to get my thoughts straight. "The truth is, I don't understand her. I've known other women who've come on all sexy and dynamic like she does, but they're usually more honest about themselves."

"I know exactly what you mean, Brooklyn," Meg

said, blowing on her teacup to cool the hot liquid. "I only spent a few minutes with her, but I don't trust her, either. Let Inspector Lee handle it."

I gave her a grateful smile. "Thank you, Meg. I think I will."

Our parents drove off to explore Chinatown while Derek and I had our long-awaited conversation with Inspector Lee. We sat around our dining room table and served coffee and sweet rolls in an attempt to soften her up. She took the news of our switching books with better humor than I had anticipated. We admitted that we'd essentially broken the law, but she had to agree that it was probably the best place the two books could have been for the moment. So that part of the conversation ended well.

Then we asked her about talking to Bonnie about the books. The good news was that she agreed it would be best if she took care of talking to Bonnie instead of us. The bad news was that she gave us a boatload of grief for thinking for even one minute that we should have been the ones to investigate Bonnie's connection to the pilfered book.

So much for softening her up.

"How many times do I have to say it? That's for the cops to look into, not you guys." Despite the critical words, her tone was actually milder than I would've expected. But then, Derek was there, and that made a difference. She was generally deferential to him, and although I didn't always approve of that, at the moment I appreciated it.

She took off to find Bonnie, leaving us with the admonition to wait until she got back to do anything or go anywhere. So we waited. Barely a half hour later, she returned with a bunch of strange new information.

"Are you kidding?" I said. "She says she didn't realize that Terrence had been obsessing over his missing book? It's been going on for six months."

"She insisted she had no idea."

I glanced at Derek, who was frowning, too. "I don't buy that," I said. "She is always flirting with both Eddie and Terrence. And she knows everything that goes on at the Courtyard at all times. She would have heard about their little war from someone, wouldn't she?"

Derek nodded. "A woman like that knows the effect she's having on men like them. I'm certain she considered them putty in her hands. Terrence, anyway. Eddie's a bit savvier about things like that."

Inspector Lee shrugged. "I can only go by what she says, even if I don't believe her."

"So what does she want to do with the books?" I asked, then stopped. "If she has any right to them. She did give them away, after all."

Inspector Lee hesitated, biting her lip as she thought about something else. "Stop me if you think I'm wrong, but I had the weirdest feeling while talking to her that she might have stolen the books."

I was speechless. I think my mouth gaped open and my eyes might have spun around in my head. "You think Bonnie stole the books?"

"It's worth considering. Look, she says she doesn't care who keeps them. She just doesn't want them back. Who thinks that way about something worth so much money?"

I leaned forward, my elbows on the table. "I can't believe that. She doesn't want them back?"

"You heard me right. Look, I'm not one to jump to conclusions, but the woman doesn't strike me as the most trustworthy person in town. So I was just thinking, maybe there's a reason she gave those books away. If she knows they're stolen, for instance. It could happen."

"Holy moly," I muttered.

She held up her hand in caution. "And the only reason I'm letting you in on this little theory of mine is because you could probably hunt down the information faster than any of my people could. You know where to look to track down the— What do you call it? When you're trying to find out where the book came from?"

"Provenance?"

"Yeah, that's it."

She was right. I'd had plenty of experience researching the provenance of different books. It was an important step in establishing a book's true value. Sometimes the fact that a book had been owned by a famous person was more important to its value than the actual character and design of the book itself. And there were a number of ways to prove the history of ownership of a rare book: annotated diaries that discussed the book, a purchase receipt, unusual markings within the pages of the book. Even signed bookplates, despite my derision of them, were helpful in authenticating a book's ownership history.

Which made me wonder why Bonnie had stuck a bookplate in the priceless copy she'd given to Terrence. Maybe she wanted to make it clear that she was the

rightful owner. Or maybe she wanted to purposely de-
value the book to throw off someone who might have
been investigating the book's true ownership. Or was
there something else printed *under* the bookplate?
Like the real owner's name, for instance?

"It'll be my pleasure," I said, grinning. But then I
sobered. "Can we get the books back from the guys?"

Her sigh was deep and mournful. "I figured you
would push that card."

"I'm sorry," I said. "But it's essential to have the
books in front of me when I'm researching this kind of
information. Otherwise, I'm sort of lost."

"Yeah, I get that." She reached into her tote bag,
pulled out both *Alice in Wonderland* copies, and set
them on the table. "So I already took care of it."

I laughed. "How did you manage that?"

She shrugged. "I'm a cop. I told them the books
were evidence in the murder case and they'd get them
back when we were finished with them."

"Which is the truth," Derek said.

But I'd heard the glee in her voice. "You've really
got a hidden mean streak, don't you?"

She gave me a lopsided grin. "It's how I roll."

"I like it."

Chapter 12

That afternoon I got as far as I could researching both books—which wasn't very far. At times like this, I was grateful for one piece of advice my mentor, Abraham, had given me many years ago: Never throw away an antiquarian book dealer's catalog. Considering all the book auctions and book fairs I had attended in the last twenty years or so, I had amassed a collection of at least a few thousand catalogs by now. I had also inherited all of Abraham's catalogs after he died, and they were all contained in a floor-to-ceiling bookshelf in my workshop. I began looking through them one by one. It was a tedious job but necessary.

I also sent an email with photographs of the books to the two binderies—both still in existence in England—inquiring as to when each book was rebound and requesting information on the original owner of the book. Then I called a friend from my bookbinding chat group to ask his opinion on provenance in general and bookplates specifically.

Finally, I had to remove Bonnie's bookplate. There were differing opinions on this, and some friends insisted that you should simply leave the bookplate there because it rarely takes that much away from the value of the book. Others actually liked to see a bookplate in an old book because it added a certain charm and gave some sense of history to the book. But in the case of Bonnie's bookplate, I couldn't wait to get rid of it. Especially in a book like this that was so incredibly rare.

There were various ways of removing a bookplate, but in all cases, you also had to deal with removing the glue that held it on the page. In the past, depending on the type of paper involved, I had found success by applying a damp sponge to the plate until it was soaked through, including the glue. Within a minute, I could remove the bookplate and rub away some of the melted glue. Then I laid a thick piece of paper over the affected area and used a hot iron to dry the paper.

With less valuable books, I had also used the simple technique of applying a wet paper towel to the bookplate and leaving it to soak in for twenty or thirty minutes. I always slipped a piece of waxed paper between the bookplate page and the next one to protect the rest of the book from any excess water damage. Once the paper towel was lifted off, the bookplate came away fairly easily. But again, the remaining glue had to be rubbed off, using another damp paper towel, or carefully scraped off, using a knife. The page would be slightly wrinkled, and I'd found that using a light iron would straighten it out. You could also slip it into a book press for a short period of time to fix it.

There was no way I was going to use either of those techniques with this book. Instead, I decided to go with a light application of steam. I found my old portable steamer and plugged it in. I didn't want it to get hot because the heat might destroy the paper beneath the bookplate.

In barely a minute, the steam had dissolved the glue, and I was able to carefully lift the bookplate off the page. After some very cautious rubbing to remove the excess glue, I discovered that Bonnie had indeed been covering up something. Someone had written the initials "JC" on the page. Frankly, it was even more infuriating to see the book marred by those two initials because the bookplate could be removed but those initials were permanent.

I wanted to scream, but I managed to control myself as I pressed a thick piece of paper against the page and added several book weights to straighten out the mild wrinkles that had been caused by the steam.

I had no idea who or what "JC" stood for, and I was determined to ask Bonnie herself. I also wanted to know why she had ever thought it was a good idea to put the bookplate there. Was it just a dumb move on her part? Or was it strategic? Even though she had all these rare books, she didn't seem to know enough about taking care of them. And that was something I couldn't forgive her for.

I finally had to quit working and get ready for the evening. I locked both books in my closet safe and dressed warmly. Tonight we were going out to one of our favorite Italian restaurants in North Beach.

While we were en route to the restaurant, I was still mulling over Bonnie's motivation for pasting that dumb bookplate into the 1865 *Alice*. As Derek turned onto Columbus Avenue, I decided that I could do all the research in the world on tracking down the provenance of those two books, but none of it would be as valuable as talking to Bonnie herself and insisting on answers. Where had the books come from? Who had owned them before her? And, for the hundredth time, why in the world had she put that dumb bookplate in there? All I could figure was that Bonnie didn't know as much about books as she'd tried to claim. And since I couldn't come up with another reason, I decided to let it go for now and try to enjoy the evening out with Derek and our parents.

On Thursday, we drove up to the Sonoma wine country to take Meg and John to the town of Dharma, where I had grown up and my parents still lived. I rarely passed up an opportunity to visit Dharma, but I'd almost begged off this time, given the importance of tracking down the provenance of the two *Alice in Wonderland* books. I was also worried about leaving the neighborhood because of concern for Rabbit's safety, but Inspector Lee assured me that the police would be patrolling past the Courtyard shops hourly until this mystery was solved. She promised to call us if anything happened while we were gone.

I sent a quick email to my chat room buddy, and he promised to call when he found the answers to my question. So I kept my phone plugged into the charger all the way up to Dharma, scared to death of missing a phone call if it came in.

We spent the morning touring the town. We stopped in to visit with my sister China, who owned Warped, the popular yarn and knitting shop on the town's main street, Shakespeare Lane—now known as "the Lane," a destination point for visitors from all over the Bay Area. As we strolled farther along the Lane, Mom steered us into one of our local bakeries. Dad, Derek, and John kept walking and agreed to meet us at the town hall a while later.

"Doesn't this look yummy?" Meg said, glancing around the shop.

"I'm so glad you made it," Suzette, the proprietor, said. "I've got everything ready." She and I had gone to high school together, and I gave her a quick hug.

"Um, ready for what?" I asked, unsure of what she meant.

She grinned. "Why don't you all have a seat and I'll bring our sample tray over?"

I frowned at Mom. "What's going on?"

"I thought since Meg won't be around for all of the prewedding decisions, we could have a mini-wedding-cake tasting."

"Oh, Becky," Meg said, sniffling and dabbing her eyes. "That is the sweetest thing."

As a sympathetic crier, I began to sniffle a little myself. But I smiled at Mom. "This is really lovely of you."

"Well, let's eat some cake," Mom said merrily.

"The chocolate cake with the white chocolate ganache was my favorite," Meg said in the car on the way up the hill to my parents' home. "Although the carrot cake was a marvelous surprise."

"I loved the lemon filling in the white cake," Mom said.

"That was a treat," Meg agreed. "And what about that hazelnut almond cake?"

"Oh my goodness," Mom gushed. "With the chocolate mousse filling."

"And the mocha buttercream frosting," Meg added. "I thought I would swoon on the spot."

My mom gasped. "Why not do a five-layer cake using one of those flavors in each layer?"

"Oh, Becky, that is a fantastic idea."

Nobody asked for my opinion, I thought with a chuckle. And that was just fine. The point had been to have a good time with Mom and Meg, and we definitely had done that.

Despite being stuffed with cake, we were headed for my parents' house to have a casual lunch on their terrace. If nothing else, we could take an hour to relax and enjoy the gorgeous view of Mom's apple orchard and the beautiful rolling hills filled with vineyards that could be seen from almost anywhere in town.

But I continued to check my phone for any incoming calls, just in case. I wasn't sure what I was expecting to hear from Inspector Lee. Would Bonnie confess to killing Joey while we were gone? Would Eddie strangle Terrence? Would some sneaky property developer blow up the building, forcing Bonnie to sell the tattered ruins of the beautiful Courtyard shops?

My imagination was working overtime. All I could do was take slow, deep breaths and try to relax.

After a leisurely lunch, we spent a few hours at the Dharma winery, which was run by Dad and my brothers, Austin and Jackson. We toured the new wine cave and tasted some of the latest wines, straight from the barrels. We were all feeling very happy when we finally showed up at Arugula, my sister Savannah's fancy restaurant on the Lane.

Derek, Dad, and John dropped us off and drove away to find parking. Mom, Meg, and I walked into the restaurant just as Savannah was coming out from the kitchen to greet us. She was wearing her chef's coat and her trademark red beret.

"Hello, everybody," she said. "Welcome to Arugula." She turned and held her hand out to Meg. "Mrs. Stone, it's lovely to meet you."

"It's so nice to finally meet you, Savannah," Meg said, giving my sister a light hug. When they parted, Meg noticed Savannah's red beret had tipped back. "Oh my goodness. You're bald."

I turned to look at Meg. "Didn't Dalton mention that?"

"No," she murmured, still staring at Savannah's smooth head. "I suppose he wanted it to be a surprise."

Mom laughed. "That's quite a surprise. But I think the hairless look works for Savannah."

"Oh, it definitely does." She reached out and squeezed Mom's arm. "What beautiful children you have, Becky."

Beaming, Mom patted her hand. "Thank you, Meg. And I'll say the same to you. Your boys are handsome as sin."

"And devilish to boot," she said, laughing.

I was watching Savannah as they spoke. I had to admit it was still a shocker for me to see Savannah's shaved head instead of the mop of curly hair she'd grown up with. But, as Mom said, the look worked for her with her peaches-and-cream skin and petite facial features.

She had first shaved her head a few years earlier after a close girlfriend had announced she had cancer. The friend had been in remission now for five years, I was happy to say. But meanwhile, Savannah had discovered a new look that totally worked for her.

My sister was completely self-assured in both her business and her personal life, and yet she just smiled silently as the two mothers chatted. She was clearly unsure of what to say to Meg. This was Dalton's mother, after all.

To distract Savannah, I grabbed her in a hug and asked, "What's on the menu tonight, sis?"

"We've added a bunch of new things and it's all fantastic tonight," she said, managing to shake herself out of her momentary stupor. "But let me wait and tell everyone at once."

"Savannah, your restaurant is charming," Meg said, glancing around. "I love all the blond wood. It's so soothing. And I read those reviews out front. You are a superstar."

"Oh, thank you, Mrs. Stone. I'm very lucky. We seem to be doing well," she said, downplaying her status. But it was true. Arugula had climbed to the top of the lists of all the major reviewers. For a restaurant that featured gourmet vegetarian cuisine, that was practically unheard-of.

"Isn't that wonderful?" Meg said, then reached out and touched Savannah's shoulder. "But, Savannah, there will be no more Mrs. Stone tonight. You are to call me Meg."

Savannah's smile was radiant. "Thank you, Meg. Now, why don't I get you all a glass of wine to start while we wait for the others to arrive?"

"What a perfect idea," Meg said cheerfully. "We simply haven't had enough wine today."

As the bartender handed out glasses of pinot noir, Derek and our fathers walked in.

Shortly after that, my best friend, Robin, arrived with her husband, my brother Austin.

But the biggest surprise of my night was when Robson Benedict showed up. Robson, or Guru Bob as we kids used to call him, was the leader of my parents' commune, where we had all been raised. When the commune had started over twenty-five years ago, he had encouraged his followers to grow grapes for wine. The rest was history as the town of Dharma flourished and grew as strong and healthy as those grapevines to become one of the most visited spots in all of wine country.

I greeted Guru Bob with a big hug. I felt particularly close to him after I'd recently helped him clear up an ugly incident that had marred his family history and troubled him for many years.

Just as we were sitting down at our table, my cell phone rang. It was Inspector Lee. I jumped up so quickly, I almost upset the entire table.

"I'm so sorry," I said. "I've got to take this call."

"We've been waiting to hear back from the police," Derek explained to everyone, and followed me outside to the back parking lot. I pressed the speakerphone so we could both listen.

"Just a couple of things," she said. "I wanted to let you know that we didn't find any fingerprints on the stepladder or the paint cans."

"Oh, bummer," I said. If we could've figured out who was doing the graffiti, it might've connected us to Joey's killer.

"It was a long shot at best," Derek reasoned, but I could tell he was disappointed, especially after he'd gone chasing after the guy in the middle of the night.

"Hey, it was worth a try," Inspector Lee said. "And another thing you both might want to know: The car that your mom described, the one that tried to run down Bonnie and you, Brooklyn—we're pretty sure it belongs to Bonnie."

"Someone used her own car to try to kill her?" Derek frowned. "That's awfully cold."

"Yeah. We checked for fingerprints but only found Bonnie's. The driver must've been wearing gloves."

I shook my head. "We can't get a break."

"Sorry about that," Inspector Lee said. "So any progress on the provenance?"

"I'm still doing the research, and I have some leads, but I think my best bet is going to be to confront Bonnie and simply ask her where she got the books."

"If you want me to be there when you do that, let me know."

I smiled. "I would love it if you were there."

"No problem. I can be as scary as you want me to be."

"I know. That's one of your best traits."

She laughed, thank goodness. Then, after confirming that all was quiet at the Courtyard, we ended the call. I checked my emails and found several. My chat group friend had sent some info on bookplates, but it was nothing I hadn't heard before. Both binderies had responded with lovely messages regarding my request for information about the rebound books. Their messages were similar: It would takes weeks for them to hunt down their old records, but they were willing to do so if I could possibly forward a payment in the range of one to three hundred dollars to cover their expenses. While that was perfectly reasonable, I decided not to make a decision until I spoke with Bonnie. If Inspector Lee's formidable presence could convince her to tell me what I wanted to know, I wouldn't have to go any further in my provenance research. I slipped my phone into my purse, and we went back inside, determined to forget about everything but enjoying this time with our family.

Dinner was fantastic, as always. For appetizers, I started with the heirloom tomato and burrata salad. Meg had Savannah's signature pear and watercress salad served with a feathery-light blue cheese from Point Reyes and a golden balsamic dressing. Derek had the pupusas—deep-fried dumplings stuffed with summer squash, onions, serrano chilies, and smoked cheddar—served with a wonderful pickled herb and avocado salsa.

For my main course, I had linguini with chanterelle mushrooms, slow-roasted Juliet tomatoes, savoy spinach, green onions, herb butter, and gobs of grated Grana Padano, a fabulous Italian cheese. Meg decided to try the grilled cauliflower steak after seeing it on the menu and giggling about it. Needless to say, it was a big hit—crunchy and perfectly herb-rubbed on the outside while tender on the inside, and served with a fantastic wild mushroom risotto.

Everyone at the table ordered something different and we all shared bites, which was my favorite part of family meals.

I confess to being a meat eater, and I love a good rare steak. But I could eat Savannah's exquisite vegetarian meals for the rest of my life and be happy. The only downside was the sad fact that I hadn't inherited one ounce of her cooking ability. That just seemed so wrong.

At one point during the meal, Meg left the table. I watched her weave her way through the room to the kitchen and disappear behind the door. She was gone for almost ten minutes, and I wondered if she was chatting with Savannah—who would have had to be frazzled with Dalton's mother standing there, watching her work. But then Meg walked back to the table wearing a smug look on her face, and I knew I would be crawling the walls until I could ask Savannah what they had talked about.

But with a warm glow enveloping me, thanks to my good friends and family, along with a second glass of wine, I completely forgot to ask Savannah what had gone on between her and Meg.

For the moment anyway.

We spent most of Friday morning checking up on our friends at the Courtyard. Terrence and Eddie were both in pretty good moods, considering all the squabbling they'd been doing lately. Rabbit was in his element back at the Rabbit Hole, and he was giving away free mini-smoothies to one and all to celebrate his return. Sadly, he still couldn't remember what had happened to him, although he was upbeat about his memory returning eventually. He didn't seem to connect his memory returning with the fact that Joey's killer would be revealed and he would be in even more danger than before.

It felt like the calm before the storm.

That afternoon, despite the feeling of doom in the pit of my stomach, we took the parents to the Ferry Building down by the Embarcadero. We must have stopped at every food stall to nibble and shop for all the goodies on display. Grilled oysters, rich cheeses and chunks of thick sourdough bread, chocolates, tiny fruit tarts, thin slices of prosciutto and salami, an apricot-preserve tasting, tiny handfuls of homemade granola, spicy olives, mini pizza slices, pâté, and of course a wine tasting were among the many delights we enjoyed. We relaxed outside on the pier, drinking caffe lattes and taking in the spectacular view of the bay. We watched the massive ferryboats pull into their berths and take off again, traveling back and forth to Sausalito, Larkspur, Oakland, and beyond. The weather was perfect—cold and clear—and it was a fun, stress-free day, or it would've been if I hadn't been so worried about Rabbit.

"Ready to get back to the hood?" Derek asked.

I smiled, knowing he was reading my mind again. "Yeah, I'm more than ready."

Back home, while Mom and Meg began to prepare dinner, Derek and I jogged across the street to check on Rabbit. He was surprised but happy to see us and immediately handed us two smoothie samples. "You guys have been coming by a lot lately. You must really love these green zombie smoothies."

I glanced at Derek, who couldn't stomach what he called "healthy green slime."

I was just happy to see Rabbit in a genial mood and thanked him for the smoothies. We left quickly after that and headed for home. "I don't have the heart to tell him his life might be in danger."

Derek scowled. "I don't have the heart to tell him those smoothies are wretched."

I chuckled but quickly sobered. "I just hope the police have warned him to be careful. He seems so cheerful. It's like he doesn't get it."

"We'll have to remain vigilant."

The aroma of Mom's thick, rich spaghetti sauce with Italian sausages permeated the hall as we exited the freight elevator, and I was salivating by the time we made it into the apartment. Meg had whipped up a beautiful salad, and Mom served the sauce over penne.

After the dishes had been cleared, I asked, "Who wants dessert?"

"Sweetie," Mom said, "why don't we have dessert in the living room? Meg wants to read your palm. And then I'm going to work a protection spell on you. Won't that be fun?"

I could feel my eyes widening. In fear? Maybe. If you'd seen my mother work a spell, you would understand. "But . . . why?"

"Because you're under a lot of stress lately with this murder business."

"Listen to your mother, Brooklyn," Meg said, her tone serious. "I wasn't going to say anything because John scoffs at me, but I got a good case of the willies while the two of us were shopping at the hat shop. I felt the same vibrations while in the bookshop the other day, too. I think someone will hurt you if you're not careful."

"And besides," Mom added, "you've been working so hard with your projects and all the books you're researching, I'm afraid you aren't taking good care of yourself."

"Derek takes good care of me."

"But a protection spell couldn't hurt," Derek said.

I flashed him a look that indicated in no uncertain terms that I would have to kill him later. He simply laughed.

"Sounds like fun," Dad said. "I've got a snazzy new dessert wine I'd like to pour for the occasion."

John grinned. "I'm up for that."

"That's sounds super, Dad," I said weakly.

As everyone resettled in the living room, Meg linked her arm through mine. "You needn't worry that I'll delve too deeply into your psyche, Brooklyn dear." She brightened. "I know. We'll do Derek's first."

I turned in time to catch Derek's sudden panicked expression. "No, Mother. I couldn't go ahead of Brooklyn. I'll wait."

"That's very sweet of you, dear," she said.

I grabbed Derek and whispered in his ear, "You are a big chicken."

"Absolutely," he said. "You won't catch me submitting to that kind of torture."

"But it's okay for me?"

"Well, yes." He smiled. "Don't you want my mother to be happy?"

I feigned shock. "You are evil."

"Not usually," he said, laughing. "But in the spirit of self-protection, I do what I have to do."

*   *   *

I had to admit, the palm reading was fun. Meg had kept it light and told me only good things. She was quite good at it. She knew how to read each of the three major lines, and she also delved into the meaning of the shape, color, and texture of my hands, fingers, and thumb, a practice that she called chiromancy. Also, she read both my right and left palms, which I'd never seen done before. Apparently, each hand signified different aspects of my personality, psychology, and destiny.

She was starting to wrap up her reading when I noticed there were tears in her eyes.

"Meg, what's wrong?" I asked. "What do you see?"

"Oh, Brooklyn. I'm just so overwhelmed."

I clutched her hand. "I'm sorry."

"No, no," she said, sniffling and laughing at the same time. "It's wonderful. Everything I see in your hands tells me that you and Derek will have a rich, long, satisfying life together. And I couldn't be happier." She sniffed again and then pulled me close in a hug.

By the time she'd let me go, I was tearing up as well. Because her words were so sweet—and, as had been proven before, I was nothing if not a sympathetic crier.

Afterward, Meg clamored for Mom to cast one of her famous protection spells. I was frankly surprised at how sedate Mom was. This wasn't the usual wild and crazy presentation she was capable of. I wondered why, but wasn't about to complain.

She handed me a large amethyst crystal to hold while she recited these simple words:

Great Goddess of the day and night,
Protect my girl with all your might.

After repeating it three times, she opened her eyes and looked at me. "The crystal orb you hold is filled with positive energy that will block others' negative emotions and thoughts. Keep it with you at all times this week."

"I will," I said. "Thank you, Mom."

She wrapped her own hands around mine and the crystal. "Sweetie, this won't protect you against demons or curses, but it will hold up against bad people and their motivations."

"I'm pretty sure I won't have to deal with demons this week."

She smiled. "Then we're good to go."

I gave her a hug. By the end of the night, I felt safe and happy and cared for by our two moms. And they were happy as well, and that was all that mattered.

Chapter 13

Originally, Derek was going to drive his parents back to the airport by himself, but we had all grown so close to one another by the end of our week that all six of us climbed into the SUV and drove off to San Francisco airport together.

It was a bittersweet departure. We hugged a lot and promised one another we would call to talk at least once a week.

"We'll be back in a few months for the wedding," Meg said, patting my cheek. "You'll hardly have a chance to miss us."

But I was going to miss them very much. I had to blink a few times to chase away the tears that threatened to fall. On the bright side, this would give us a great excuse to visit England more often.

"After the wedding you'll stay on with us in Dharma for a few days," Dad insisted.

"Absolutely," John said. He and Dad gave each other manly hugs, and we all hugged and kissed one more time.

Finally they walked into the terminal. We waved until we couldn't see them anymore. Then Mom and Dad and Derek and I got back into the car and drove home, quietly reminiscing about our fun time together.

Mom and Dad took off for Dharma a little while after that. Derek and I sat down on the couch and just stared at each other.

"What a week," he said.

"My head is still spinning. I want to write down everything we did, but I can't even remember some of it."

"We'll be reliving it for weeks," he said wryly.

I laughed. "Some parts will be more fun to relive than others."

"Like chocolate cream pie and high tea."

"Yes, exactly. And Italian food and Thai food and, oh my God, naughty appetizers and . . . Well, we ate like piggies."

"It was a good time."

I scooted over and rested my head on his shoulder. "I was thinking how wonderful your parents are and how sweet it is that everyone got along so well."

"We couldn't have hoped for a better outcome," he said.

Within minutes, we were both dozing. A fitting end to a whirlwind week of murder, mayhem and in-laws. Just the two of us again. As much as I loved our families, I loved these kinds of moments the most.

* * *

Monday morning, Derek went off to the office and I went into my workshop to continue with my playing card project.

My cell phone rang, and I clicked my Bluetooth into my ear to answer it.

"Hello, sweetie."

"Hi, Mom."

"I just heard from Meg."

That was fast. "How nice. I'm so glad you two hit it off."

"I am, too. She's like the sister I always wanted."

I felt a little tear coming on and sniffed. "I couldn't be happier for you, Mom."

"I know, honey. It's funny, isn't it?"

"It was a shock to see you two together. You really do seem more like sisters."

"I know. I think we'll be running up the phone bill with calls back and forth every week. I just feel like I can tell her anything."

"I'm so happy about that, Mom."

"Me, too. Well, speaking of shocks, you'll never guess who showed up in Dharma this morning."

I frowned. "Who?"

"Dalton Stone."

"Derek's brother? But how—I mean, why?" But suddenly I knew exactly how and why he'd come to be there. Meg must've worked her magic when she'd gone into the kitchen to talk with Savannah. Something must have occurred during the conversation that resulted in Dalton showing up in Dharma three days later.

I said, "I'm going to bet that Meg had something to do with his visit."

"I'm not sure it's a visit," Mom said, sounding a little dazed.

"What do you mean?" I blinked. "Wait. You think he's moving to Dharma?"

"I suppose we'll have to wait and see, but it's looking that way."

"Wow. Meg is carrying around some powerful juju."

"Indeed she is," Mom said, chuckling. "And something else. Remember Camilla?"

I had to think for a minute. "Oh yeah, Dylan's girlfriend. Cruella. We forgot to talk about her."

"Meg told me a little something about her. I'll fill you in later. But guess what. When Meg and John returned home, they found out that Dylan had broken up with Camilla."

"What?" I blinked. "Okay, this is getting spooky."

"I know." She giggled, but quickly sobered. "But that reminds me of the real reason I'm calling. It's because Meg is concerned that something is definitely amiss at both the bookshop and the hat shop. She said she worried about it for the entire flight home."

"Poor thing. I'm sorry to hear she had a bad flight."

"Her flight was fine, but she's not. Frankly, sweetie, I'm worried, too."

"But why, Mom?"

"Well, she just can't shake that feeling of the willies she got while we were shopping."

"Oh, Mom." I remembered Meg talking about the willies before Mom did her protection spell. But really, the willies?

"Don't scoff like John does," Mom said. "Meg thinks that if you're looking for your killer, you'll find him at the hat shop or the bookshop. Or maybe one of those other places at the Courtyard."

I couldn't respond for a few seconds. I kept imagining telling Derek that we should call the police because his mother had gotten a case of the willies. Still, we were talking about the hat shop and the bookshop. *Or one of those other places.* Hmm. Pretty easy guesses, considering what had been going on at the Courtyard all week.

"Okay, Mom. I'll talk to Derek and we'll call the police together."

"Good. Please don't go off by yourself and try to apprehend anyone. I worry."

"I'll be careful."

"I hope so," she said. "And hold on to that crystal."

"I've got it with me. Thanks, Mom. I love you."

We hung up and I shook my head in bewilderment. I pictured Derek and me surrounded by our beloved parents and siblings for many years to come, and I knew that one thing was for certain. Our lives would never be boring.

When Derek returned home that night, I put a bowl of chips and salsa on the table, poured two glasses of wine, and then told him all about my mother's phone call and his own mother's dire warnings. As predicted, he laughed off their concerns.

"I'm hardly willing to convict someone of murder based on my mum's 'willies.'" He shook his head, smiling fondly.

"I had the exact same thought," I said, chuckling as I scooped salsa onto a chip.

But as we got into bed later that night, I had another

weird thought. My mother had had hunches before, and they occasionally turned out to be right. So why wouldn't I trust Derek's mother with those same sorts of feelings?

I mentioned my thoughts to Derek again, and he advised that we stick to old-fashioned investigative work. I knew he was right, but I still wondered. And I tossed and turned all night long.

Tuesday morning, Derek left early, and I ran out to the supermarket to restock the cupboards and refrigerator. When I arrived home, I found the answering machine flashing. I checked the time and saw that the message had come in barely a minute before I got home. I pressed the button and played it back.

"Hey there, Brooklyn. This is Eddie at the bookshop. We received a shipment from an estate sale and there's a book or two you might be interested in."

"Cool," I whispered.

"Come on over," his message continued, "and check it out when you have a minute. I think you'll really— What? No, I'm on the phone. Hey! What's wrong with you? Wait. Terrence! No. Stop. Put it down. No!"

Suddenly, there was a loud bang that sounded very much like a gunshot. And the phone went dead.

"What the—?" I played it back, just to be sure. It was my worst fear come true. Terrence had gone off the deep end.

I called Derek to tell him what had happened. "I'm running over there. Would you please call the police for me?"

"Brooklyn, don't go over there by yourself. I'm on my way. Wait for me."

But I could hear Eddie's voice in my head, and I shuddered involuntarily. "The call came in one minute before I got home. I still might be able to save him."

"Brooklyn, no!"

Meanwhile, Eddie could have been bleeding to death while we argued about it.

"Derek, you know I've got to go. Please call the police?"

"Of course I will and I promise they'll be there shortly. And I'm on my way. Be careful."

"I will. Thanks." I hung up the phone, grabbed my purse, and ran out of the house.

I tore across the street and shoved the bookshop door open. And almost slunk away. All hell had broken loose inside. Kitty was screaming and Bonnie was crying.

Then I saw Eddie sitting near the front counter, tied to a chair. His shoulder was bleeding.

I started to rush toward him, but Kitty's next words stopped me in my tracks.

"Terrence, put down the gun!" she screamed.

"No!" he said, waving a pistol around like a magician with his wand. "I'm sick of everyone telling me what to do."

"Stop yelling, both of you!" Bonnie shouted. She was wielding a baseball bat she must have found behind the front counter and looked absolutely furious.

"Shut up, you cow," Kitty sobbed. "I should've killed you when I had the chance."

"What?" I couldn't help speaking up. What was she talking about? "Should've killed whom?" I asked, glancing from face to face. "When?"

"Oh, now look who's here," Bonnie said, giving me a quick, dismissive glance. "Miss Nosy Pants herself."

"I called her," Eddie grumbled. "Leave her alone."

"Why?" Bonnie demanded. "She's the one who's been interfering in our business, stirring up trouble."

"No, that would be you, Bonnie," Eddie said scornfully. "You're the one who delights in causing chaos wherever you go. You just can't help yourself, can you? You crave attention, and we're all supposed to kiss your feet whenever you walk into the room. It's a sickness, you know."

She frowned. "I can't help it if I'm popular."

Eddie made a groaning sound, flung his head back, and shut his eyes.

I thought I heard him mutter, "Dumb as a post," but I couldn't be sure. For myself, I couldn't say whether she was dumb or not, but she did seem stuck in a junior high school mean-girl time warp.

"But wait." Ignoring them both, I turned to Kitty. "What were you talking about a minute ago? Who did you want to kill?"

Kitty looked exasperated. "Bonnie, of course. Haven't you been paying attention?"

I stared long and hard at her. "Were you driving the car that tried to run her down?"

"What if I was?" she griped. "That didn't give you permission to run over and save her."

"I should've known it was you." Bonnie lifted the bat threateningly and took two steps toward Kitty. "You couldn't even face me like a woman. You had to hide behind the wheel of my own car."

"Put down that bat!" Terrence shouted.

Bonnie whipped around to glare at Terrence, and it was enough of a distraction that Kitty was able to run up behind her and yank the bat out of her hands.

"Now you're not so tough, are you?" Kitty said, swinging the bat around. "Just back off and maybe I won't beat you till you're dead. That's what you deserve."

Bonnie just smirked—while also taking a few steps backward. "You're so full of it. You don't have the guts to hit me. I'm the only one with guts enough to get the job done around here. Give me the bat, Kitty."

"No way."

Terrence scowled. "Yeah, Bonnie. You have guts all right. Enough that you tricked me into killing your own husband."

Bonnie gasped. "Shut up, Terrence."

It was as if I was at a bad play with horrible actors, but the dialogue was so intriguing I couldn't look away.

"Wait," I said slowly. "You killed Bonnie's husband?"

"I did it for Bonnie," Terrence cried. "Jack was sick, and Bonnie asked me to give him his medication. I didn't know it wasn't the right stuff." He gazed longingly at Bonnie. "But I would've done it anyway even if I'd known. I'd do it for you, Bonnie."

"Shut up, Terrence," Bonnie repeated through clenched teeth.

Hearing Terrence's words, Kitty dropped the bat and bounced her shoulders back and forth in a happy little dance. "Ha! Are you talking about her first husband or her second husband?"

I knew my mouth was gaping. Two husbands? This was yet another revelation.

"What happened to your first husband?" I had to

ask. If Bonnie really had killed her second husband, maybe she'd killed the first one, too.

Bonnie glared at me. "We grew apart. What business is it of yours?"

"So he's still alive?"

"Yes. Alive and well and living in Santa Fe, New Mexico." She flashed me a look of disgust. "What's wrong with you? Mind your own beeswax."

"She saved your sorry ass," Kitty said. "You might want to be a little nicer."

Terrence was still staring at Bonnie in shock. He brought the gun around and aimed it at Bonnie. "You had *two* husbands?"

"Put the gun down, Terrence," Bonnie said wearily. "You don't have the nerve to use it anyway."

Terrence's chest puffed up. "I have plenty of nerve. I shot Eddie, didn't I?"

Eddie merely grunted and that worried me. Was he losing too much blood?

"Yeah, you did, you idiot," Bonnie muttered in response.

Terrence did not like being called an idiot and huffed angrily. "I am not an idiot."

His enunciated words dripped with hatred for the woman—and that was when it hit me. "Terrence, did you kill Joey?"

He whipped around to face me, and his mouth gaped. His skin turned pale as the guilt became sickeningly obvious.

Kitty and Bonnie both gasped. Terrence's face was now a shade of green I'd never seen before.

Kitty's eyes widened on Terrence, and then she

whirled around and stared at Bonnie. "He killed Joey? Did you know that?"

Looking aghast, Bonnie kept shaking her head. "I . . . No, I . . . Terrence? You didn't, did you?"

"Oh, don't play the poor little victim," Terrence said viciously. "Your hotshot lover was no saint."

Kitty shrieked and went running straight for Terrence. It didn't occur to him to shoot her. Instead, he held up both his hands to protect his face. Kitty grabbed him by the shoulders and shoved him backward. He fell to the floor and she landed on top of him. The gun went off and Terrence let out a shriek as it flew from his hand.

Everyone screamed and ducked to avoid the wild bullet. Did it hit Kitty? No, she was still smacking Terrence back and forth across his face. I went scooting up and down the aisles, looking for anyone who might be bleeding or moaning. So where had the bullet gone? I just hoped it hadn't killed any books.

I suddenly remembered Furbie and worried that the cat was hiding somewhere, completely traumatized.

Kitty scrambled to grab the gun and then pushed herself up off the floor. Once she was standing, she turned the gun on Terrence and pulled the trigger. The powerful shot threw her whole body backward, and she hit the wall and slid to the floor.

Terrence screamed. Blood began to ooze from his thigh as he moaned in agony and disbelief. "You shot me!"

"What a wimp," Bonnie said, clearly disgusted. "It's barely a flesh wound."

Kitty sat on the floor, stunned that she'd actually shot the gun.

I was close enough to take a chance. I circled around and managed to wrestle the gun from Kitty's hand. Luckily no shots rang out, but I still wouldn't be mentioning any of this to Derek.

"Give it back," Kitty cried. "I want to kill him."

"Nope, sorry." I ran down one of the aisles to get closer to the front door. I just hoped the police and Derek showed up soon.

Bonnie picked up the bat and pointed it at Terrence. "You are so dead."

Kitty stared at Terrence. "I'll kill you first." She was set to run right at him and I was pretty sure she would try to strangle him or something.

"Wait!" Terrence cried.

"Hey, gang."

Everything stopped as if someone had frozen the frame. I whipped around and found Will Rabbit standing right behind me.

"Will," I whispered.

"What's going on?" he asked, frowning as he looked around the room. "Aunt Bonnie, what are you doing with that bat?"

"Will, thank God!" she cried, sounding helpless all of a sudden. She dropped the bat. "They all attacked me, but I managed to fight them off. Can you help tie up Kitty for me?"

"But why?" he asked, incredulous. "What did you do?"

"I didn't do anything," she bellowed. "She tried to kill me!"

"Help me," Terrence cried.

Will held up both hands and took a step back. "All right. Everybody calm down." His gaze panned across the room again. "Terrence, you're bleeding. Eddie? Are you all right?"

"Your aunt shot us both," Terrence said, his voice weak.

"No, I didn't," Bonnie said, insulted. "Terrence shot Eddie and Kitty shot Terrence."

"I'm confused," Rabbit said, scratching his head.

"You're not the only one," I muttered, stroking the amethyst crystal in my pocket. I didn't know if it would protect me or not, but it felt good to have it there.

"Call the police, Will," Eddie said, his voice a whisper.

"I've already taken care of that," I said. "They'll be here any minute."

That was when Bonnie noticed me again. "You again. You're always making trouble. Will, tie her up."

"Don't be ridiculous," I said, raising the gun in her direction. I shivered and put the gun down. I never would have pointed a gun at anyone, but Bonnie was just so annoying. I looked around the room at this odd group.

"Kitty," I said. "You tried to kill Bonnie and almost got me, too. Why?"

"Because I hate her. She stole Joey from me and then he died. It's her fault."

"It wasn't my fault he died," Bonnie argued. "Terrence killed him."

"Maybe I did," Terrence said, sounding more defensive by the minute. "But it was an accident."

"Oh, yeah." Bonnie snorted. "How was that an accident?"

"Because I meant to kill *you*," Terrence said with an indignant sniff.

Bonnie gasped. "What did I ever do to you?"

Despite the shock, everyone in the room guffawed. Even Rabbit snickered. I couldn't believe my ears.

"You are a horrible person, Bonnie," Terrence said quietly. "You destroy people. You destroyed me. So I realized what I had to do. I knew your routine by heart. Every morning you go into Rabbit's juice bar before it opens to make yourself a raspberry smoothie with a shot of protein powder."

Bonnie's face revealed a crack in her armor as she heard Terrence recite her schedule so precisely. "How do you know all that?"

He ignored her question and continued. "I'd helped Rabbit reorganize the store in the past, so I knew what I had to do. I got in there earlier and was waiting behind the shelf when I heard someone walk inside." He glared at her. "I smelled your perfume."

"But it wasn't me."

"No, but your perfume had rubbed off on Joey. I couldn't see him, but I smelled him and thought it was you. So I pushed that damn shelf over and killed him. And I wish it had been you."

Bonnie looked freaked-out, and I couldn't blame her. "That's just sick, Terrence."

Terrence didn't blink, just kept talking. "What was sick was realizing that Joey was enveloped in your scent. As far as I'm concerned, you're the one who killed Joey. You lured him into your bed and you caused him to die."

"No," Bonnie cried. "You did that. Your mind is warped. It's twisted."

"Did you hit me, Terrence?" Rabbit asked quietly.

The room grew quiet again. For the first time since

he began talking, Terrence reacted. His face grew pale and he turned slowly. "I—I'm sorry, Will. I didn't mean it. You surprised me. I was expecting to make a clean escape."

Rabbit nodded. "Just got in your way, did I?"

"Nice going, Terrence," Eddie murmured.

Terrence looked completely horrified and dumbfounded, but finally managed to find his voice. "It . . . it was all Bonnie's fault."

Bonnie stomped her foot. "I gave you all places to live and work to do." She pointed at Terrence. "You never would've had your little bookshop if I hadn't decided to hand it over to you."

"Hold it, lady," Eddie balked softly. "Thanks to us, that shop is making ten times more money than you ever made in twelve years working there."

Ignoring him, Bonnie turned to Kitty. "And you. That hat shop was nothing until I brought in a decorator to spruce it up."

Kitty let loose a harsh laugh. "I had to pay for the guy, and he wasn't cheap, so don't act like you were doing me any favors."

Bonnie kept talking as if Kitty hadn't said a word. "I could've sold this building a thousand times over, but I didn't."

"But you're trying to, aren't you, Bonnie?" I said. "You've been meeting with the same property developer for a while now. Are you cooking something up with Stan from Sequoia that your tenants don't know about?"

"Aunt Bonnie, no!" Rabbit said.

Kitty snorted. "Of course she is. She hired crooks to vandalize the place, spraying graffiti everywhere, trying to scare us off. So don't pretend you're doing anything out of the kindness of your heart, Bonnie. You can't wait to dump this place."

Bonnie frowned. "That might be true, but I never paid anyone to vandalize the place."

"Then who was doing the graffiti?"

She glanced around at the faces in the room. "I don't know. Terrence?"

"It wasn't me," he groused. "I wish I'd thought of it, though. Anything to get out of this place."

I happened to catch Eddie's reaction and saw he was smiling at Terrence's words. And that was when something clicked and I recalled that Eddie was a runner. I should've known. "Eddie, are you the graffiti artist?"

He gave a light shrug, actually looking proud of himself. "Figured if I could scare Terrence with some petty vandalism, he might agree to let me buy him out."

"You!" Bonnie cried. "You defaced my building."

Eddie looked unshaken. "The city cleans it up, so don't go getting on your high horse about it."

"I'm surrounded by traitors!" Bonnie cried.

"Oh, spare me," Kitty muttered. "You're trying to sell the place out from under us, so don't expect any sympathy from me or anyone else."

Now that Terrence no longer had his gun and was unable to hurt me, I took a chance to ask the question that had been burning a hole in my brain for a while now. "Terrence, why did you steal Joey's copy of *Alice in Wonderland*?"

Bonnie's head whipped around. "You stole Joey's book?"

"Why not?" he snapped. "Joey won't be using it anymore."

"But you already had a book." She sounded hurt.

Terrence's eyes turned fiery, and I could imagine blood-soaked daggers shooting in Bonnie's direction. "No, I don't, because someone stole my book from me."

Bonnie gulped. "It wasn't me."

Was she just lying again? I was confused.

"Fine. It doesn't matter who took it," he said.

Yes, it does! I thought, but kept my mouth shut. I would get to the bottom of this somehow.

"That book was mine to give to whomever I chose," Bonnie said righteously.

"Too bad. It's mine now. And believe me, I'm not happy about it."

"Why not?" I asked.

"Because Joey ruined it," he said. "The book Bonnie gave me was as clean as could be and I kept it that way. But Joey must've rubbed it in the dirt or something, because when I finally took it back, the pages were dull and the leather was faded." He shook his head in disgust. "Some people shouldn't own nice things."

"Wait a minute," I said. "What do you mean, your book was originally *clean*?"

"Clean," he insisted loudly. "My book had a shiny leather cover and the pages were straight and bright. No frayed edges." He sniffed. "I would never treat a book so badly."

I gazed around the room, completely baffled by this latest bit of information. If Terrence was telling the truth, then it meant that he had never been given the priceless 1865 version of *Alice*.

"Bonnie, did you give Terrence a clean, shiny copy of *Alice in Wonderland*?"

She shrugged. "I don't remember."

I actually believed her. But then where was Terrence's "shiny" copy? And did that mean that Bonnie had been holding on to *three* rare copies of *Alice in Wonderland*?

This screwy enigma was becoming curiouser and curiouser.

I hesitated to ask, but I was the one holding the gun, so I was willing to use it to get answers. Not that I would shoot anyone, but my curiosity was even stronger than my need for caution. "Bonnie, do you happen to collect copies of *Alice in Wonderland*?"

"My husband did." She grunted in disgust. "What a twit he was. His first wife's name was Alice—can you believe it? So that's why he collected copies of *Alice in Wonderland*."

"Huh," Kitty said. "Never knew that."

"At least he was rich," Terrence muttered.

"I hated that woman," Bonnie continued. "And I hated those books. So I figured, why not give them away to my dates?"

My eyebrows shot up at her use of the word "dates," but that was none of my business. Interestingly, Inspector Lee's theory that Bonnie had stolen the books wasn't true. They had been hers to give to whomever she wanted. More than ever, I had to find out why. "So you gave one book to Joey? And one to Eddie? And Terrence? Anyone else?"

"A few men you don't need to know about. And who cares, anyway? I wanted to get rid of those dumb books and I did."

But I *did* need to know. And something Terrence had said was tickling the edge of my mind. "Your husband's name was Jack, right?"

"Yeah, so what?"

So his name was Jack Carson. JC. "Did he write his initials in his books?"

"Yeah, and as soon as he died, I put my own book-plates in there to cover it all up." She sounded so proud of herself, I wanted to smack her.

"Didn't you use to own this bookshop?" I asked.

"Yes."

"Were you aware of the value of those books?"

She shrugged. "I knew they were worth something, but I didn't pay for them, so why should I care?"

My stunned expression must've given me away. She shook her finger at me and said, "Don't you dare judge me. Just because I couldn't give a hoot about a bunch of stupid books? I have better things to do with my time than worry about some dumb book about a girl falling down a rabbit hole."

I wanted to scream. I was surrounded by book idiots! Suddenly, I could completely relate to young Alice on trial, facing the Queen of Hearts in the courtroom. *You're nothing but a pack of cards!*

But I kept my mouth closed, knowing that if I mentioned that the book might be worth up to two million dollars, it might give one of those knuckleheads an excuse to actually kill someone.

I heard a soft *meow* and glanced down to see Furbie snuggling up against Will Rabbit's foot. Despite the danger surrounding me, I breathed a short sigh of relief that the cat was safe. So far.

"Will, honey," Bonnie said sweetly. "You know I wouldn't ask if it wasn't important. Could you please grab some of that rope on the counter and tie up Kitty?

She tried to kill Terrence with this gun. I don't want her sneaking out of here."

"Sorry, Auntie. I'm not going to tie anyone up."

"Good man, Will," Eddie said.

Terrence spun around. "You shut up, you vandal."

"If only it had driven you out of here," Eddie said, his energy beginning to flag, "it would've been so worth it."

"Oh, yeah?"

I ignored their bickering as something else occurred to me. "Terrence, did you ransack Joey's shop?"

Abruptly, he stared down at his feet, unable to make eye contact.

Bonnie huffed. "Well, that's just plain mean."

"I saw the two of you together, Bonnie," he said angrily. "You were flaunting it for all the world to see."

"So that's the best you could do?" she said. "Make a mess of his shop?"

"Oh, shut up," Terrence muttered.

She shook her head. "You're pitiful."

Well, she was right about that, at least. I had already figured out that when Terrence had looted the shop, he hadn't yet determined that Bonnie had given Joey the book. No, it had just been out of sheer spite.

Their ridiculous sniping might have continued, but right then the door swung open and Inspector Lee and her partner, Nathan Jaglom, rushed in with their weapons in hand.

Inspector Lee looked at me. "Does anyone have a weapon?"

"Just me." I immediately handed her the gun. Lee cleared the chamber and then shoved it into her belt.

Jaglom rushed over to check Eddie's and Terrence's wounds while two uniformed cops ran in after them to help subdue Bonnie and Kitty.

A moment later Derek followed. He grabbed me in his arms.

"Thank God you're here," I whispered.

"I'm so glad you're safe," he said, holding me so tightly I wasn't sure he would ever let me go. "I was so worried I wouldn't get here in time."

"You were right on time. Thank you."

"Thank God." He gazed down at me and smoothed my hair back from my face. "I swear I'm going to kill you later, but for now I'm pitifully grateful you're not hurt."

"Me, too." I laughed from sheer relief. "And, boy, wait till you hear this story."

As the paramedics worked on Eddie and Terrence, I stood outside with Derek and Inspectors Lee and Jaglom, giving my informal statement. "Basically, Terrence killed Joey and attacked Rabbit, Terrence shot Eddie, Kitty shot Terrence, Kitty tried to run down Bonnie using Bonnie's car, Eddie vandalized the building, Bonnie lied to everyone, and Rabbit was the hero."

Nathan flashed a crooked smile. "We'll get a more detailed report from you later. Right now you probably want to go home and forget all this."

"You're right," I said. "Oh, but it's good to see you, Inspector Jaglom."

"Yeah, good to see you, too, Ms. Wainwright. And you, Commander."

They shook hands and we walked away.

*   *   *

Later, Inspector Lee called to let us know that after being confronted by Kitty and the others, Bonnie had confessed to having killed her husband.

"Wow," I said. "That's a lot worse than lying to her tenants about selling the place."

"Definitely. And I guess my theory that she stole the books herself didn't quite pan out."

"True," I said, dismayed. "Unfortunately, they were hers to dispose of."

"Speaking of which, Bonnie gave us the name of the guy who has the third *Alice* book."

I was delighted. "Can we get it back from him?"

"I knew you'd ask me that," she said. "The guy sold it a couple of weeks ago."

Instantly deflated, I said, "Bummer. Wonder how much he got for it."

"Believe it or not, he was willing to tell me. He sold it for seventy-four thousand dollars. Guy said it was better than winning the lottery."

I blinked a few times, shocked to realize that I'd seen a report of that very book sale online when I first looked up what Terrence's book might be worth. I had little doubt that the book was the very same one that Bonnie had given Terrence and then taken away from him.

Inspector Lee had moved on to another topic. "Do you think if Bonnie had gotten hold of the gun, she would've shot someone?"

I thought about it. "Hard to say. She talks a good game, but I seriously doubt she would've used the gun. It's funny. Both Kitty and Terrence shot someone outright, but I think Bonnie prefers sneakier methods."

"I would've thought she'd be the first to pull the trigger."

"Me, too," I said. "But she used drugs—and Terrence—to kill her own husband. I suspect she's just as big a wimp as she accused the others of being. And a liar, to boot."

"I won't be surprised if she recants her confession," Lee mused. "It's often easier to convince oneself of one's innocence when the act hasn't caused actual bloodshed."

"I suppose." I shook my head in disgust. "But what an awful woman."

"Yeah. Well, thanks for your help, Brooklyn," she said. "You did good, kiddo."

I beamed with pleasure. A compliment from Inspector Lee was hard to come by.

"And don't think I've forgotten we're going shopping," she added. "I'll call you."

Now, why did that sound like a threat? I smiled anyway. "I can't wait."

It was early evening, after a day of insanity. Derek and I were sharing a bottle of wine, about to sit down to dine on leftover pizza and a big healthy salad. Charlie was already curled up on one of the dining table chairs, watching us as we bustled back and forth from the kitchen.

I was pouting a little as I placed a mound of salad on each of our plates. "With Bonnie and Eddie and Terrence and Kitty all going to jail for various amounts of time, who's going to keep the Courtyard going?"

Derek carried the warmed pizza box to the table.

"When I was over there earlier buying lettuce for our salad, I spoke to Will Rabbit. He's certain Bonnie will have to sell the place after all." Derek frowned. "I asked if he would be willing to take on the management of the building, but he doesn't think he can handle that kind of pressure on his own."

"No, he seems awfully fragile after his assault. And then having to watch his aunt being carted off to jail . . . I can't imagine he's doing too well." I set the plates down on the table. "I wish there was something we could do to help. I hate the thought of them having to sell the building."

"Rabbit said that the tenants have already agreed unanimously that they've got to sell the building."

"Oh, dear. So as soon as they find a buyer, it's a done deal."

We sat down to eat. My heart hurt at the thought of the Courtyard being torn down, but I still managed to finish a piece of pizza. After a few minutes of small talk and munching, Derek looked at me with a gleam in his eye. "I've been thinking."

"I always love to hear your thoughts," I said as I sipped my wine.

He smiled. "I've come up with an idea of where you might invest some of your money."

I blinked. "I'd forgotten all about that. I guess Carl the lawyer will be happy to know you've been putting some energy into complying with his request. What did you have in mind?"

"I think we should buy the Courtyard."

My mouth dropped open.

"I believe the tenants would be happy to have you as their landlady."

It took me a full minute to wrap my mind around his startling proposal.

"That way," he continued, "we can guarantee that it will never be torn down. Besides, it's an excellent investment. And just think, you'll own a bookshop."

"We'll own a *pie* shop," I finally managed to whisper.

He laughed. "That, too."

My shock was wearing off and I began clapping my hands in excitement. "Oh my God, Derek. That's the best idea you've ever had."

He stood up, circled over to my side of the table, and reached for my hand to pull me up from my chair. Wrapping his arms around me, he held me close for several long moments, and I reveled in the warmth of his embrace.

"No, darling," he said. "The best idea I've ever had was asking you to marry me."

Recipes

Here are just a few of the recipes for "naughty" appetizers that Brooklyn's future mother-in-law concocted for the family. Enjoy!

HOT BUTTERED RUMP BITES

3 lb. rump roast, cut into half-inch chunks

MARINADE AND DIPPING SAUCE:

1 C beef broth
¼ C red wine
¼ C soy sauce
2 Tbsp Worcestershire sauce
½ C minced onion
¼ C minced parsley
2 cloves minced garlic

vegetable oil for cooking the meat
¼ C butter

CROUTONS:

½ baguette, cut into half-inch chunks
2 Tbsp butter, melted

16 oz. Swiss cheese, cut into ¼-inch chunks

1. Mix together the beef broth through garlic. Set aside half for dipping sauce. Marinate the beef in the other half for at least an hour, or as long as overnight. Heat vegetable oil over medium-high heat in a heavy-bottomed pan. Add rump bites, but avoid overcrowding. You may need to cook them in batches. When all the beef is done, melt the butter in the pan and toss with beef chunks.

2. To make the croutons, toss the bread chunks with butter and bake at 375 degrees F for 8–12 minutes, until golden.

3. Skewer one crouton, one piece of cheese, and one rump bite with a toothpick, with the beef on the end that will rest on the plate. Serve with dipping sauce. This is like a bite-sized French dip sandwich.

SKINNY DIP

16 oz. nonfat plain Greek yogurt
2 Tbsp minced fresh dill
2 Tbsp minced chives

¼ C minced red bell pepper
1 tsp garlic salt
¼ tsp Tabasco

Mix together. Best if flavors are allowed to meld for at least an hour. Serve with fresh vegetables.

PERKY BREAST NIBBLES

2 lb. boneless, skinless chicken breasts

MARINADE:

¼ C fresh lemon juice
½ C olive oil
3 cloves minced garlic

DIP:

*1 C mayonnaise
juice and zest of ½ lemon
1 Tbsp maple syrup*

1. Slice the chicken breasts lengthwise into half-inch slices and thread onto bamboo skewers that have been soaked in water. Mix together the marinade ingredients and pour over the chicken breasts. Marinate for one hour.

2. Mix together the dip ingredients.

3. Preheat the oven to 425 degrees F. Discard marinade. Roast the chicken skewers for 5 minutes, then flip and roast for another 5–8 minutes, until cooked through. Serve with dip.

DIRTY CUCUMBER SANDWICHES

8 oz. cream cheese, softened
2 Tbsp mayonnaise
1 packet of Italian salad dressing mix
¼ C minced fresh dill
¼ C minced green onions
1 loaf cocktail rye bread
1 cucumber, peeled and thinly sliced

Mix together the cream cheese, mayonnaise, salad dressing mix, dill, and onions. Spread on two pieces of rye. Put 2 or 3 cucumber slices between the pieces of bread.

CHEESY BALLS

8 oz. cream cheese, softened
1 C shredded cheddar
½ C grated Parmesan
1 tsp Worcestershire sauce
1 Tbsp hot sauce (Frank's is Brooklyn's favorite)
1 tsp garlic powder
1 tsp paprika
kosher salt
freshly ground black pepper
⅓ C chopped chives
⅓ C finely chopped walnuts or pecans
4–5 slices bacon, cooked and chopped
several carrots cut into thin but sturdy sticks

1. Mix together cheeses, Worcestershire sauce, hot sauce, garlic powder, and paprika and season to taste with salt and pepper. Form into 15–18 small balls and chill at least one hour.

2. Stir together chives, nuts, and bacon.

3. Roll chilled balls in chive mixture and insert a thin carrot stick in each ball. (Pretzel sticks can be substituted for carrot sticks, but be careful not to break them while inserting into cheese balls.)

4. Serve immediately or cover in plastic wrap and chill until ready to serve. (Best if brought back to room temperature 15 minutes before serving.)

Read on for an excerpt
from Kate Carlisle's new Bibliophile mystery,

Buried in Books

Available now from Berkley Prime Crime!

"The name is Wainwright," I said to the conference volunteer seated at the registration table before me. "Brooklyn Wainwright."

The young woman gave an absent nod and began to skim the thick row of envelopes standing upright in the box in front of her. Not exactly friendly, but the crowd was huge and the woman was probably feeling overwhelmed. Halfway through the row, she stopped suddenly and stared up at me. "Wait. You're Brooklyn Wainwright? I signed up for your workshop."

"Oh." I smiled. "I hope you'll enjoy it."

"I know it'll be fantastic," she said brightly. "I'm, like, your biggest fan."

"That's so nice. Thanks."

For the fifth year in a row, I had been asked to present the bookbinding workshop for the annual National Librarians Association conference. I was thrilled that the conference was being held in San Francisco this year s

I wouldn't have to lug all of my supplies and equipment halfway across the country.

Sighing inwardly, I admitted that I would've been looking forward to the workshop a lot more if I hadn't botched up my schedule so badly. But nobody here needed to know that.

The volunteer flipped her pink-streaked hair away from her face and continued to stare at me as though I were a rock star. Her former bored interest had turned into wide-eyed excitement. It was fun, but also a little intimidating. She knew me and my work. What if she hated the workshop?

"I saw your pop-up display at the Covington Library," she said. "It was amazing."

"Thank you." I sensed the people in line behind me getting antsy to move things along. I turned and flashed an apologetic smile.

But my new biggest fan didn't seem to notice the impatient crowd. Instead, she leaned forward and whispered loudly, "Everyone says you're going to dish about the murders during the workshop. I'm so psyched!"

"Uh . . . what?"

She nodded eagerly. "Is it true you found a body inside the Covington? What a rush!"

"Umm, no, I . . ." I had no words. The fact was, I *had* found a body inside the Covington. More than once, to be honest. But I wasn't about to discuss the details with a stranger.

She frowned at me, clearly confused by my reticence. Then she began to nod slowly as if she and I were in on a secret together. "Ah, I get it. You're saving the gory details for the workshop. I understand. Don't worry. I ˙an wait."

Snapping back into work mode, she pulled a manila envelope from the stack and handed it to me. "Here you go. This envelope contains your badge and your program book. It's got all the events listed as well as the speakers' bios. And there's a map inside the back cover. This place is huge, so we don't want anyone to get lost." She pointed toward the opposite side of the massive hall. "You can pick up a book bag at the south end of the auditorium."

I peered at her badge to catch her name. "Okay. Thanks, Lucy."

"Enjoy the conference, Brooklyn." She gave me a conspiratorial wink. "See you at the workshop."

"You bet." A little dazed and a touch breathless, I stepped away from the registration table, feeling like I'd just run a sprint.

An enormous woman in pink bumped into me and kept walking, obviously in a hurry to get her conference bag. I hardly noticed.

Was someone spreading the word that I would be talking about murder? Seriously? I didn't even like *thinking* about the bodies I'd stumbled across, let alone using them as filler in my workshop program. It wasn't going to happen. Which meant that no doubt there were going to be some disappointed people—like Lucy, for instance. I sighed and shook my head. The conference just got more complicated.

I'm a bookbinder specializing in rare-book restoration, which means I make my living refurbishing old books. I also enjoy creating handmade books when I'm feeling particularly artistic. Unfortunately, in connection with my work, I happened to have stumbled across more than a few dead bodies over the past two or three years. And yes, the victims were all connected to the various books I had been working on at the time.

But that didn't mean I knew anything about the subject of murder! And I absolutely refused to draw attention to myself because of my weird proclivity for finding dead people. So why would anyone think I would take time out of a bookbinding class to talk about murder?

When it came to any connection between rare books and murder, the only bit of information I was willing to offer was this: If you thought that books weren't worth killing for, you were dead wrong.

I scanned the enormous hall, noting that in the time it had taken me to register, hundreds more people had arrived for the conference. Dozens were waiting in line to register. Some peered around anxiously, trying to get their bearings. Others were gathered in small groups, chatting and laughing and, in the case of the cluster of five women closest to me, shrieking.

I did a quick mental calculation as I studied the diverse crowd. There had to be at least eight hundred people milling around this cavernous space. Probably closer to a thousand. No wonder the noise level was deafening.

The racket didn't bother me. These were my people. Librarians. Book nerds. "And apparently a few murder fans," I muttered to myself.

I headed toward the south end of the convention center, asking myself all the way: Did I really need a book bag?

More importantly, did I really need to be here at all?

It had been months since I'd first agreed to give the

bookbinding workshop. Then somewhere along the way they had also roped me into giving a speech on book conservation. And if that wasn't enough, I had also said yes when they asked if I'd like to donate a raffle prize. I was all for fund-raising for librarians, but I couldn't just give a basket of books or a gift card. No, I had offered to take twenty lucky librarians on a three-hour "Booklover's Tour" of San Francisco. We were renting a bus and everything. Good grief. What had I been thinking?

Of course, all those months ago, I had never dreamed that I would be getting married to Derek Stone this weekend.

My gaze softened and I sighed happily at the thought of marriage to Derek—and almost crashed into a gray-haired man minding his own business, reading the program booklet.

"Sorry," I muttered, and kept walking. It wasn't the first time I'd spaced out and almost injured someone lately. Whenever I thought of Derek and our imminent wedding, I sort of lost consciousness for a few seconds.

I had considered canceling my conference events this week, but after talking it over with Derek, we decided that it would be a good idea for me to keep to my original conference schedule. Because amazingly, every last detail of the wedding was taken care of. And Derek had pointed out that attending the conference would—hopefully—distract me from any prewedding jitters I might have been susceptible to. He had a good argument there, seeing as how I was more than a little overwhelmed by the fact that his entire family—including his parents, four brothers and their spouses and children, and various aunts and uncles—would be arriving from England any minute now.

My entire family and my friends would be arriving as well, but I wasn't worried about them. We had all grown up in Sonoma and knew San Francisco intimately. And my parents and brothers and sisters were more than willing to show Derek's family around town while I was busy at the conference. Derek insisted that his family would take my occasional absences in stride. They were all looking forward to exploring the best parts of San Francisco and the wine country. They didn't need me to play tour guide.

It had all sounded good in theory. But now that I was here, I began to wonder if there wasn't something I should've been doing to prepare for the wedding. I checked my watch. Would it be wrong to leave after I'd just arrived?

Not just wrong but stupid, I silently lectured myself as I made my way through the crowd toward the book bag counter. Attending this conference would be great for my business and my career, I reminded myself. I would make new contacts, possibly acquire some new clients, and reacquaint myself with old friends.

So I was here to stay. At least for a few hours. As I wound my way through the crowd, I grinned as I looked around and realized that despite my neurotic compulsion to check all of my wedding lists on an hourly basis, I was happy to be here. I always enjoyed this conference, and I was grateful to the organization for all the good things I'd received by being a part of it. Besides, being among all these librarians always made me feel nostalgic for my postgraduate years. Those were good times.

Even though I'd never planned to work as a librarian, I knew that starting out with a degree in Library Science was one of the best routes to a career as a bookbinder. Consequently, everyone I'd known in school had been working feverishly toward their Master of Library Science degrees back then. I had to admit it was daunting to be surrounded by all of those highly intelligent, compulsively organized, overwhelmingly detail-oriented people. I coped by wearing T-shirts that said things like: *Did you wash your hands today?* and *Do you spell* anal retentive *with a hyphen?*

Instead of the quick laugh I always expected when I showed up wearing one of my dumb T-shirts, my gifted friends would actually spend an hour or two discussing whatever statements I was displaying.

God, I missed them!

I finally snagged my book bag and was headed for the coffee kiosk when I heard someone call my name.

"Brooklyn?"

I whirled around and stared at the red-haired woman standing a few feet away. "Yes?"

She laughed and ruffled her short hair self-consciously. "I know it's been years and I've changed a few things, but I don't look that different, do I?"

I blinked. "Oh my God. Heather? Heather Babcock?"

"Yes!" She squealed and grabbed me in a crushing hug. "I was so afraid I wouldn't find you!"

"I was just thinking about you," I said. Absolute truth. She had been one of my favorite people back in the day. "I didn't realize you were coming. Why didn't you call me?"

"I didn't know I was coming until two days ago, and then it was like a whirlwind, trying to get ready for the trip."

"Wow. What a stunner. A good one," I added quickly, grinning to hide the fact that I was in complete shock. Heather had been one of my college roommates and a best pal from the good old days. She was always so beautiful, but today she looked . . . haggard. "Gosh, it's been . . . how many years?"

"Ten, maybe? You look fantastic."

"So do you."

"Yeah, right." She chuckled ruefully. "I do own mirrors. Let's not get carried away."

"Don't be silly. You're beautiful," I insisted but quickly changed the subject. "Do you have time for a cup of coffee?"

"Of course."

I bought two caffe lattes and two biscotti, and we found a small table in the far corner. Within seconds we were talking and laughing like the old friends we were, as if ten long years hadn't passed since we'd last seen each other.

Heather and I, along with our best friend, Sara Martin, had been roommates back in Library School. We had clicked from the get-go and become so inseparable that our classmates took to calling us the Three Musketeers. Sadly, though, one week before graduation, Sara and Heather had a major falling-out when Heather found out that her boyfriend, Roderick, had been cheating on her—with *Sara*.

Heather was inconsolable, especially when Sara and

Rod ran off and got married. About a year later, I heard through the grapevine that Sara had caught Rod cheating on her. This was not a big surprise to anyone since Rod was adorable, but very shallow and prone to believing his own hyped-up PR. But in the end, Sara forgave him, and they were still together, as far as I knew.

Heather and I avoided the dreaded subject of Sara and Roderick. Instead, Heather talked about her fulfilling job at the local library in her small town, and I told her all about my adventures in bookbinding and my upcoming wedding to Derek. After thirty minutes of chatting and catching up, we both sat back and smiled.

"It's really good to see you," I said wistfully.

"You, too." Heather's smile turned enigmatic. "So, are we ever going to mention the big, fat, bitchy elephant in the room?"

I reached over and grabbed her hand. "I didn't want to ask."

She raised an eyebrow. "But you're dying to know."

"Sorry," I said, wincing. "But yeah, I would love to know if you've had any news or run-ins with . . ."

Heather inhaled quickly, as if she were about to take some horrible-tasting medicine. "No. I haven't seen Sara in ten years. But I have a friend who has a friend who knows her, so I hear things."

I frowned. "Do you think she'll be coming to the conference?"

"I sure hope not," Heather said. Her jaw tightened, and her eyes narrowed in unrepressed fury. "Because I swear, if I ever see Sara Martin again, I'll kill her."

Ready to find
your next great read?

Let us help.

Visit prh.com/nextread

Penguin
Random
House